THREE INTO TWO WON'T GO

THREE INTO TWO WON'T GO

Andrea Newman

Doubleday & Company, Inc., Garden City, N.Y.

1968

All of the characters in this book
are fictitious, and any resemblance
to actual persons, living or dead,
is purely coincidental.

49,549

THREE INTO TWO WON'T GO

1

The girl was standing by the roadside. Dressed as a conventional hitch-hiker, she wore a shirt and jeans and was equipped with a rucksack which could be strapped to her back or laid, as now, at her feet. She had a short coat slung over one arm. Her hair was long and dark and hung limply over her shoulders because there was no breeze to lift it.

This much he took in automatically. What first struck him as odd was her attitude. She was not sitting down exhausted to attract sympathy nor walking on bravely to arouse admiration. And she was not, even as the car drew nearer, using the hitch-hiker's thumb. Instead she leaned against the mileage post, partially obscuring it, so that he appeared nearer to his destination than he really was, one leg straight the other bent, one arm on her hip the other by her side. He had seen the pose before, now that he considered the matter, in his wife's magazines. It was the awkward, self-conscious, elegant posture of a model.

He debated with himself about stopping. He had a night to spare; the trip had gone well; he had earned a break. But he was not sure he was in the mood: he had slept badly the night before, which was rare for him, and rather hoped to catch up tonight so as to arrive home fresh. To do so exhausted would not evoke compassion, as it had once done, but merely give Frances a chance to question his stamina. This had only happened once but that was quite sufficient to form his resolution. On one of his old Manchester trips he had had an unholy row with Jenkins about delivery dates, which had really knocked the stuffing out of him, and he reached home dead beat. Frances had poured the appropriate drinks and cooked the appropriate food, but then, standing over him as he ate and drank (disguised of course as ministering angel), she had said in a soft, thoughtful voice, 'This job is getting you down rather, isn't it?' and he was certain that behind the apparent concern lay a measure of delight. What she really meant was: Here am I doing a full-time job and running the house with only a few hours' help from Mrs Bailey and cooking and washing and ironing and mending and keeping pace with my marking and still having time to sit down with you in the evening in front of the box, and of course never asking you to help. Because your job exhausts you.

So he must arrive home fresh. On the other hand, a companion for the journey, a chat, and see what develops . . . . Why not? Why pass up a chance? He would stop. But the car was slowing down already: while simultaneously observing the girl and deliberating about her he had taken his foot off the accelerator without even noticing. He changed down and braked.

'D'you want a lift?' He leaned across to speak to her: the windows, on this scorching, oily August day were both already open as far as they would go. As he moved he unstuck the back of his shirt from the leather on which it was roasting and merciful air circulated round it. But warm air. It was impossible to get cool.

'That's what I'm here for,' the girl said. She had a pale face that contrasted with her brown arms. He had stopped for more grateful hitch-hikers but he was not too put-out. He knew kids were cheeky these days; Frances had told him often enough.

'Hop in,' he said, opening the door for her. She picked up her rucksack and pretty well flung it on to the back seat, following it with the jacket which, he saw now, was leather and in quite respectable condition. She got in and slammed the door: a hard, practised slam. Her jeans and shirt were the faded blue of denim and her feet in open sandals were dirty.

'Oh,' he said, suddenly remembering that he usually gave his destination long before this point, 'I'm going to Birmingham. Will that do?'

She shrugged and turned to look at him for the first time. Her eyes were green, but a dirty green, muddied with brown and yellow, and she had black stuff round them to make them appear larger, and the black stuff was smudged by the August heat. 'Anywhere will do,' she said.

He drove off. The girl did not speak again but he was already conscious of the changed quality of the silence. It was always so: if you picked someone up and they said nothing for miles, it was still not the same as the silence you got when you were alone in the car. In a way it meant you were not quite free to think your

own thoughts any more. Though that, of course, could be a bless-
ing as well as a restriction.

Some pick-ups worked hard for their free ride, making bright
chat about the weather, the journey, even their life history. Often
they were students.

'Are you a student?' he asked the girl. She looked the right age
for a student, late teens.

'No.' He heard a faint smile in her voice.

'Been waiting long for a lift?' He was surprised to find himself
talking. Usually he let his passengers make the effort or accepted
their silence. But he wanted to know about the girl.

'Not very long.' Her accent puzzled him: he could not decide if
it was, as he put it, Cockney overlaid with Oxford or (though this
was clearly absurd) Oxford overlaid with Cockney. But there were
definitely two conflicting elements in it; he had noticed that the
first time she opened her mouth. He was sensitive to accents, having worked hard on his own.

'It's a hot day for waiting around.' Immediately he had said
this he thought how silly it sounded. The girl seemed to think so
too; she didn't answer. The silence between them deepened and
spread out, unnerving him. He took cigarettes and a lighter from
the dashboard shelf. 'Cigarette?'

'I'm not smoking today.'

He put one in his mouth and flicked at the lighter. 'Why not
today?' The firm tone amused him. He went on flicking the
lighter, which sparked but would not ignite.

'It doesn't do to get hooked on things.' As she spoke she
reached for the lighter and he let her take it. She had small, tough
hands with short nails, much cleaner than her feet. As their hands
touched he thought, Well, I wouldn't mind. She struck the lighter
savagely with her thumb. It lit at once.

'Aren't you strong?' he said teasingly, to re-establish himself,
make up for his stupid remark about the weather.

'It's a knack.' She studied the lighter. 'The cheap ones are better,' she said critically, and put it down.

'It was a present.' He had forgotten when but he remembered
Frances saying, 'Darling, you are the most difficult man to buy
anything for so I got you this.'

'From your wife.'

This was not quite a question but he treated it as such. 'Yes.'

He did not like the girl being so sure he was married and yet perhaps it was better, safer, that she should know from the beginning. If it was a beginning. He was surprised at himself for fancying, however slightly, a rather dirty, scruffy teenage hitchhiker.

'People spend too much on presents.' The girl yawned and stretched, ending up with her hands clasped behind her head. He glanced at her swiftly and felt a twinge of disappointment that she had rather small breasts. In fact she was decidedly thin all over.

'It gives them pleasure,' he said. He thought the conversation was proceeding oddly but could not pin it down.

'It doesn't give me pleasure,' the girl said. 'So I don't do it.'

He smiled; this was better. 'Do you only do things that give you pleasure then?' It was a good enough philosophy; it would have suited him very well. But only the young could afford it.

'Yes.' Another flat statement, no elaboration. He had already noticed that all her remarks were as brief as possible and that he was asking all the questions. Impossible, however, to reverse the procedure now. He decided to be provocative which, after all, was probably what she wanted. And he had nothing to lose.

'Tell me,' he said, 'some of the things that give you pleasure,' feeling already a slight but growing excitement and wondering if it was ill-founded. He was a little annoyed with himself for getting interested so quickly: it was unlike him and contrary to his rules for self-preservation. He waited for her answer. No doubt she would play safe and say vaguely, Oh, lots of things, and the ball would be back in his court. It was all part of the game and could be stimulating but more often was merely tiresome when you had played it too often.

The girl said, 'Travel, conversation, food and sex.'

The final word hung in the atmosphere. The green light: it could hardly be clearer. Yet still some instinct made him cautious. It was his policy never to risk a rebuff so he never moved until there was no possibility of one. Now he justified this by thinking, Well, she can hardly mean me to pull into a lay-by and rape her in broad daylight and anyway, Christ, in this weather? All the same, it was obviously there, waiting. He was gratified but also slightly let-down. It was too easy: the chase was over. Physically it was more exciting, almost uncomfortably so, but mentally she had cheated him of something by taking the initiative. And yet he admitted he often found the usual drawn-out preliminaries tedious. He threw his cigarette out of the window, annoyed with himself for being illogical.

'Well, we're talking and travelling,' he said, making his voice as suggestive as possible. 'Let's see what we can do about food.'

They had lunch in a pub that he knew and it was his first chance to look at her closely without making a point of it as he must when driving. She had the blank face of youth: nothing had touched it yet. Her hair, parted in the centre, was lank and needed washing; when he stood close to her to hand over her drink he could smell the stale, musty sweetness of it. He knew the smell; it belonged to Frances, too, the day before her weekly shampoo and set and he had always found it oddly endearing. It seemed more like real hair than when it was clean, perfumed and lacquered, and he was not permitted to touch it.

He liked looking at women, even studying them as he might a picture or a building; it was living with them that he found difficult. The girl had thin lips; though her mouth was not small there was nothing generous about her lips, which in women he liked to be full, a taste acquired in his youth when someone told him it meant a voluptuous nature. He was surprised to find the girl's mouth attractive. He wondered what it would feel like.

'How is your bread and cheese?' he asked her. He had chosen a meat pie and a ham sandwich for himself and would claim later for a three-course meal.

Her mouth was crammed with food; in fact she ate as though she were starving. She did not hurry to answer his question or make any sign. She just went on chewing vigorously and when her mouth was at last empty said, 'Fine,' and drank greedily from her glass of beer, getting froth on her top lip. He watched her lick it away with a thin, red tongue. She is sexy, he thought, rather than attractive. That would explain his departure from his usual type. Not that his usual type could normally be found propping up signposts at the kerb-side.

'How long have you been on the road?' he asked her. He still felt the tug of an irresistible curiosity about her that he could not explain to himself. There was nothing about her to justify it. She had given him a more direct invitation than probably any woman he had ever met and yet he still felt she was essentially mysterious.

'Since last summer.' She immediately filled her mouth with bread and cheese again.

'Was that when you last ate?' He wanted to inject some humour into the conversation, to stop himself taking her seriously.

Again she waited until her mouth was empty. But she did not even smile; she let his poor little joke go unregarded. 'No, yesterday,' she said.

He consulted his watch; he was shocked. 'D'you mean you've had nothing to eat all day?'

She drank some more beer. 'That's right.'

'But why ever not?'

She looked at him as if he were mentally deficient. 'Because I haven't any money.'

It was too simple to have occurred to him. In his world no one went out of the house without money, let alone across the country. He found himself saying in amazement, 'None at all?'

'Absolutely none.' She did not seem at all perturbed; she even added with her first flash of humour, 'You can go through my pockets if you like.'

He wondered if her nonchalance was genuine or part of a strategy. Did she in fact mean: I am going to cost you? Would she pinch his lighter (she had already noticed that it was expensive) and cigarette case in the night, if there was a night, empty his wallet and disappear? He never slept with tarts for this reason, amongst others, but aware of the general avarice of women, always bought the current one, however casual, a negligée or a bottle of scent, partly as an insurance against theft, partly to establish himself as the generous type. Besides, it did actually give him pleasure: he enjoyed seeing them unwrap the presents in a fever of impatience, struggling with paper and string; enjoyed hearing their squeals of excitement; enjoyed even the monotony of their initial reaction to the parcel (there was hardly a one who did not say, 'Ooh, what is it?'). And it was undeniably more gracious than slipping two or three quid into a handbag and saying casually, 'Here, buy yourself something pretty.'

Presents, he thought, turned women back into children and he found this intensely attractive. Perhaps it was the enthusiasm: there was something touching and vulnerable about enthusiasm.

Adults ran short of it, learned to suppress it or despise it. When last had he been enthusiastic about anything, other than the product he was paid to enthuse over? When last, for that matter, had there been anything to be enthusiastic about? But enthusiasm was dangerous as well as attractive because it left you open to ridicule.

The girl, however, might be one of the few who preferred money to presents. In any case it seemed ridiculous to give a negligée or a bottle of scent to a hitch-hiker who wore jeans and carried a rucksack and had not a penny in her pocket.

'Maybe I'll give you some money instead,' he said, to check up. Two could play at being obvious.

The girl looked straight back at him with the muddy green eyes which, now he came to study more than their arresting colour, he noticed were set a bit on the slant, giving her face what he termed a slightly Mongolian appearance. This might not be ethnically correct (her face and nose probably needed to be flatter to qualify) but he knew what he meant by it.

'That would be lovely,' she said.

So it was money she wanted. The question now was, how much? In practice he found money more expensive than presents, another good reason for giving presents. Nothing less than five pounds could really be bestowed with aplomb, whereas a three-pound present was often quite stylish. But five pounds was obviously a ridiculous amount to give this girl. In any case, she hadn't done anything to earn it yet. There was time enough later to decide. But he still could not make up his mind if the girl was really on the game or just an ordinary hitch-hiker down on her luck and wanting to make the position clear.

'I'd rather give you a present,' he said, to test her.

She shrugged. 'It would have to be a small one,' she said, 'to fit in my rucksack.' She made it sound as if the only advantage of money was its size.

'Yes,' he said, 'that's a point. Perhaps money would be better. And also if you're not eating . . .' He let the sentence trail away. 'Of course,' he added, 'I shan't be giving you the money until tomorrow morning, shall I?' and smiled at her to be reassuring.

She stared back. 'That's entirely up to you,' she said.

He was suddenly aware that he wanted her, actively, urgently, so that anything he had felt before in the car amounted to positive indifference by comparison, so that he would have given her five pounds, ten pounds even, right that minute if it meant that he was sure of having her that night, or better still in a room upstairs *at once*, only that was out of the question. God almighty, he thought, I must be going mad. And he was terrified that she would guess and, realising the strength of her position, would demand an exorbitant price and, which was worse, get it. But the worst fear of all was that she would realise and refuse.

When she stood up and said, 'I'm going to the lavatory,' he read threatening knowledge and power in her tiny smile and denied it strenuously to himself. As soon as he could he got up and went to the lavatory himself, which mercifully was empty, and while he was there in the loneliness of the smell and the graffiti he thought, Christ, I don't know where she's been, I might catch something, and then he thought of her and then he didn't think at all.

When he got back to his table she was not there, so he lit a cigarette and when his hands stopped shaking went to the bar and got another beer. He returned to the table and she was still not there. He thought, Dear God, she's guessed and she's not coming back, and now instead of the physical pain he got an ache in the region of his heart that made all the pop songs he had ever heard suddenly explode from cliché into truth. He drank his beer and smoked his cigarette and looked at all the other people drinking and smoking and heard their laughter and talk all around him and now seeming excessively loud. He could not look away from the door she had gone through even though he told himself it would only delay her return, as watching a kettle seemed to stop it from boiling. And he went on watching. The door opened and a fat blonde in a short skirt and high heels came out and he cursed her in his head with all the words he knew for not being the girl.

The girl was right behind her. He felt weak and he was sweating absurdly, nothing to do with the weather, but he did not feel excitement or relief or anything he had expected to feel, only a sensation of rightness that the world had clicked back into focus and someone had turned down the volume of the people around him. The girl came up to their table and he heard himself say in quite an ordinary voice, 'How about one for the road?'

She shook her head and sat down. She looked just the same: sticky and unkempt. She had done nothing to herself. But then she had only a rucksack and that was still in the car. He had never known a woman who did not carry a handbag and fuss with her face and hair. The girl would in fact have looked a lot better for doing so, but there was something splendid, he thought, about her not bothering.

'Would you like to have my sandwich?' he asked her. He had quite lost his appetite.

She took it without answering and applied herself energetically to eating. He looked all round the room so as not to look at her and when she had finished and was licking her fingers he said, 'All set?' and she nodded.

When they got back to the car he opened the door for her but she did not get in. She put her hand on the rear door instead. 'I'm going to sleep in the back,' she said.

As he drove he wanted to sing and once she was asleep he did so, but softly, for fear of waking her.

2

SHE WAS still asleep when he reached Birmingham and pulled up outside Jack's hotel. He left her in the car while he went in to sign the register and exchange the usual jokes. The weather was now much cooler and so was he, even beginning to succumb to a feeling that it was all rather pointless and why was he doing it anyway. The exhilaration of the evening had faded with the sun.

'Come on,' he said to the girl. 'We're here.' He spoke loudly; he did not want to touch her to wake her up.

She opened her eyes and sat up without speaking, collected her coat and rucksack and got out of the car.

'I've got the key,' he said. 'We can go straight up.' He got his suitcase out of the boot. 'I'll go first, shall I, as you don't know the way.' He had been given his usual room.

She followed him without a word into the cool, musty foyer and up the stairs. The carpet was threadbare and he found himself thinking irritably, Surely Jack could afford to do this place up a bit. He walked the length of the corridor and stopped outside number nine. 'Here we are,' he said, frowning at the loud, cheerful voice that came out so unexpectedly. He put down his suitcase and took out the key. It jammed in the lock and he thought, If she takes over and makes it work that really will be the end; but at that moment the lock moved and he said with relief, 'Ah, that's got it,' and turned the handle.

The room was exactly the same. Faded pink roses over three walls and Regency stripes on one, brown patterned carpet with (he knew) a bald patch under the beige rug by the bed, cream paint, a pink satin bedspread and green and white checked curtains. You had to pay the earth before you got anything less haphazard. He went in and dumped his suitcase. 'Well, here we are,' he said again, only this time he meant, Take it or leave it.

The girl closed the door behind her, appearing neither impressed nor disappointed by the room. She kicked off her sandals and he saw that the straps had marked a pale imprint through the dust on her feet. He took his shaving kit out of his suitcase and went over to the wash-basin. He wished she would say something. It was so long since she had spoken that he felt they had never exchanged any conversation at all, making their present situation all the more unnatural.

He rolled up his sleeves and plunged his face and hands into the water, hoping all he needed was a wash and shave. He could hardly tell her he had changed his mind. But he watched her curiously in the mirror as he started to lather his face. Surely she could not keep up this silence indefinitely, and as soon as he heard her voice he would know if she too had gone off the idea. Her face, as usual, revealed nothing.

The girl ignored him completely. She undid the straps of the rucksack and lifted it up, emptying the entire contents on to the bed. A strange assortment of objects fell out and his immediate reaction was fury that she was making such a mess of his room. He watched her select a towel, a red dress and a bar of soap from the heap.

'I'm going to have a bath,' she announced, but her voice told him nothing: it was casual, even domestic, as if they had been living together for years.

'It's half-way down the corridor,' he said in the same tone. But now he felt a twinge of interest and annoyance. He wished Jack ran to private bathrooms. A bath might have been fun.

After she had gone he finished shaving, but rather quickly and carelessly because curiosity was overtaking him. He let out the water, gritty with stubble that turned the shaving foam grey, and went over to the bed to examine her things. He did not normally do this and would in ordinary circumstances have considered it both underhand and unnecessary, but then the girls he normally shared rooms with did not carry rucksacks.

There was a bra and a pair of pants, both small, he noted, but surprisingly clean. A headscarf, black. A pair of shoes with absurdly high heels. Sun glasses (why hadn't she worn them today of all days?) in a case, a brush and comb (filthy), a packet of tissues, a waterproof zip bag containing all the usual feminine clutter of cosmetics, and a small notebook, presumably a diary.

But it wasn't, quite. He knew he would not be able to resist it so he didn't wrestle for long with his scruples but settled for a mere token resistance. He opened it, and the indented alphabet letters jumped at him: it was a cheap Woolworth's address book and he smiled, thinking, Ah, the female equivalent of the little black book. He read the first entry.

Adams, John. 35. Fair. Liverpool. July. Took ages (1 & 2). Afraid of impotency. No need. B+.
Arnold, Freddie. 41. Manchester. September. Bang bang, all over. (2.) Going bald.

His smile faded as he read. No pornographic photograph could have given him such a surprise. But he couldn't put it down. He read on, his heart beating rapidly, his throat dry.

*Allingham, Mike. 38. Dark. Jazz fiend. Nottingham. August. (1, 2, 4.) A−. Snores.
Attwood, Hugh. 40. Civil servant. Talked all night. Ungraded. January.
Arthur, Henry. 51. Grey. Got drunk. Couldn't. Cried. Ungraded. October.

He turned the page and it was blank. He went on to B.

Barlow, Peter. 39. June. (1, 2, 3.) B+. Hobby: vintage cars. Afraid his wife is going to leave him. Indigestion.
*Barry, Francis. 40. Actor. Did everything. Super. A−. Insomnia. April.

He went on reading and wished he could stop. He felt naked and embarrassed, as if people were laughing at him. At the same time all his old excitement had returned. He wanted the girl to come back; he wanted to touch her, to hurt her, to punish her. And he also wanted to walk out, to say, You're not putting me in your little black book, my girl. But he couldn't stop reading.
'How far have you got?'
He had not even heard her footsteps in the corridor, let alone her hand on the door. Now she was in the room and had caught him and he was full of justified rage and at the same time, shame.
'You little bitch,' he said, dropping the book. But her appearance pulled him up: she was wrapped only in a towel and her hair was soaking wet, her face wiped clean of make-up. Even in

his wild state of mind he could hear Jack saying, if he saw her like this, 'Jail bait, old man, sheer jail bait. I'll lose my licence,' which made him even wilder because it accorded so ill with the contents of the notebook.

'Some people find it exciting.' Her calmness was enraging and so was the accuracy of her observation. She stared at him pointedly. 'I think you're one of them.'

He was not conscious of crossing the room, only of finding himself suddenly close to her. He slapped her face hard—the first time he had struck a woman—and after that events moved quickly. Her body was pale under him, with sunburnt arms and legs; she did not struggle nor did she respond. He kept getting mouthfuls of wet hair. His consciousness was both dimmed and sharpened as if in a partial blackout: he was aware of her eyes watching him, always watching him, but not aware of his own movements, only of a sensation of violent release far beyond mere pleasure as he finally subsided upon her, spent and gasping and at peace.

He came to himself, breathing warm, dusty air, his face close to the carpet. He felt ridiculous in such a position but intensely good-humoured about it, like a man playing bears to amuse a child. They were lying between the bed and the wardrobe in a tangle of wet towel and his discarded clothing. He raised himself on his elbows and looked at the girl with something akin to friendship.

'I hope I didn't hurt you,' he said.

She shook her head, or turned it rather, from side to side on the floor. 'Oh no,' she said. 'I'm very tough.'

He took deep breaths to steady the pounding of his heart. He was exhausted but full of goodwill instead of the more familiar distaste or detachment. This surprised him. The absurdity of their position on the floor and the speed and high drama of the entire performance struck him as intensely funny.

'Well,' he said, half to himself, 'I suppose we'd better get up.'

'After you,' the girl said gravely, and it was too much. He exploded into laughter and somehow knew that she would understand and not take offence.

'What a fool I am,' he said, sitting back on his haunches.

The girl smiled demurely, a most incongruous smile in view of her nakedness. This pleased him. She sat up slowly and wrapped the wet towel round her head. Turban-like, it gave her a classic, almost Eastern appearance.

'I'm not usually like that,' he said: an explanation not an apology.

She inclined her head. The red weal on her cheek suddenly reminded him.

'I'm extremely sorry I hit you,' he said, and meant it.

'I know,' she said calmly. 'It was the notebook.'

He nodded, then struck by a sudden idea: 'Did you do it on purpose?'

She shrugged pale shoulders, lifting her small breasts. She looked very young. 'A bit,' she said. 'You'd cooled off. I thought it might help.'

'Well, it certainly did.' He stared at her, fascinated. 'You're amazing. D'you know you haven't even told me your name?'

She stood up. She was very thin, her stomach flat, the hip bones sharply prominent. 'It's Ella,' she said.

'I'm Steven.' He got up, collecting his scattered clothes. 'Steven Howarth.'

'Ella Patterson.'

He turned and saw that she was holding out her hand. He took it.

'How do you do?' they both said solemnly, and then, as if at a given signal, collapsed into helpless laughter.

He unpacked and changed and lit a cigarette. Ella put on her clean underwear and then sat by the window, endlessly brushing and combing her hair.

'You look like a mermaid,' he said fondly. He felt extraordinarily comfortable with her.

'I had a mermaid doll as a child,' said Ella. 'I used to take it on holiday with me each year and dip its tail in the sea.'

He smiled. It was her longest speech so far and as such gave him an absurd feeling of triumph. 'I've never seen a mermaid doll,' he said. 'I didn't know you could get them.'

Again she shrugged. It was her most frequent gesture. 'Maybe you can now,' she said, 'but you couldn't then. Mine had to be specially made.'

There was so much he wanted to ask her: who made the doll

for her, what it looked like, what she called it; instead he said, 'How old are you?'

'Nineteen.'

'You look about fifteen like that.'

She nodded. 'It's my eyes without eyeliner.' She went on brushing her hair.

He said, moved by sudden guilt, 'Look, Ella, I know I didn't give you a very good time just now; in fact that's the nearest I've ever come to rape . . .' and laughed slightly on the word to soften it, to prove it was only near and not actual.

She glanced through the window. 'It's early yet,' she said. 'It's only just going dark.'

He felt relief like a warm and comforting drink spread through him and yet he knew it was crazy. Why should he suddenly feel like a man on his honeymoon promising his bride better things?

'That's true,' he said. 'We've got plenty of time. What would you like to do? Shall we go downstairs for a drink or out for a meal?'

She turned her huge eyes on him. 'I'd like to go dancing. I've got a dress in the bathroom, hanging up. All the creases came out in the steam.' She was pleased with her own know-how.

He had not danced for years. 'All right,' he said. 'We'll do that.'

3

'HE'LL BE home tomorrow,' Frances said. The phone was on a long lead so she circled round the room as she talked to Claire. It was nice to be rung up, at any time, particularly when she was alone; it was even nicer in the new house because it helped to establish her identity. (I answer the phone therefore I live here.) But her list of things to do was getting longer every minute. Things kept catching her eye as she moved round; she found a pencil and started adding items to the list she had propped on the mantelpiece. 'Oh yes, absolute chaos,' she said (writing Phone electrician). 'It's surprising the difference it makes not having an extra room. There's nowhere to dump things and forget them.' (Unpack glasses, she wrote, sort books.) The empty shelves yawned at her. 'Oh yes, it will be, when we get straight.' She peered into an overflowing tea-chest and wrote More shelves? 'Yes, I know, but he couldn't really take a week off at the moment and anyway he does so hate moving he's better off out of it.' (Electric floor polisher or carpet? If carpet, new or dye green one? Colour?) 'Well, I told you he was an artist and she was a photographer. Oh, didn't I? I thought I did. Well, we've got this sort of mural in the bedroom—oh, very strange, like a jungle or something—still, we can paint over it or paper it. No, that's not so bad. It's the floor in the living-room that really worries me. I didn't notice before with all the rugs and coffee tables'—(and children's toys)—'but she must have done photography in here because now I come to look at it closely there are funny white stains all over the floor. Must be developer or hypo, whatever they call it, but it's taken the surface right off the wood.' She paused, fiddling with the flex of the phone. 'Oh, would he?' (Find French polisher.) 'Only if not, I'm better off cutting my losses and putting down carpet. Yes. Yes, it is.'

It was pleasant to have someone to share the problem of the floor, yet she also could not help glancing at her watch. Outside it was getting dark and cool at last; she and Claire had already

discussed the fantastic weather, just what August ought to be
and so seldom was. But she had yet to enquire after Claire's children and husband and Claire was now asking about the garden.
'Oh well, that's practically waist high with weeds. I think they
must have played hide and seek in it. But I managed to find a
flower bed. Yes. I fell into it. Oh no. No, I'm counting on Steve
for that. I'm afraid he's in for a very horticultural weekend. How's
Jimmy?' She listened without really hearing. 'And the kids? Oh
good. Yes, I suppose we should. Mm. Sweet of you to phone, love.
I will. That's a joke. Okay. Bye.'

She put down the phone, her ear quite numb and painful from
being pressed too hard against it for too long. The silence was
different after the interruption: fragmented, like water that had
been stirred. Its surface was broken and she could feel it reas-
sembling its particles. Impossible to pick up exactly where she
had left off and she was not sure if she was grateful to Claire or
not. She could probably use a drink if she could find a glass. She
certainly needed a cigarette and would have had one before if she
could remember where she had put them down. I'm tired, she
thought; it's not like me to be so disorganised. I must pull myself
together; I'll have to be straighter than this before Steve gets
home.

She found a glass full of sawdust and newspaper and went
through into the kitchen to wash it. Perhaps it had been a mistake
to start with the kitchen: that was undoubtedly where all her
time had gone. But you had to start somewhere and Steve would
expect a meal when he got in and she couldn't work in an untidy
kitchen. She opened the bottle of whisky, her splendid new cut-
price bottle from the shop across the way which appeared to sell
almost everything you could want and had opened specially to
serve the estate. As she thought the word she smiled and pulled
herself up: Steve would not like her to use it. But what was it
then? Housing development; village? Anyway, the shop was specially for all these particular houses and very convenient. She
had gone in that afternoon to buy cold meat for supper and coffee,
sugar, butter, tea, bread, soap powder, salt and milk: all the things
it seemed impossible to exist without for a day and she had bought
the whisky as well, feeling vaguely disreputable.

She had had to wait at the check-out and heard the girl say
brightly to the woman ahead of her in shorts and sun glasses, 'And

how are you today, madam?' She won't like that, Frances thought;
she is not that kind of woman. You can tell by looking at her. But
the girl is too stupid and well-meaning to let her alone. The
woman turned slightly and Frances saw that her sun glasses revealed nothing of her eyes but reflected back the onlooker's face
and a nasty distortion of it at that. Her mouth, which was large
and shiny red, narrowed thinly and she gave an abrupt nod before picking up her basket. She could hardly have made her feelings clearer but the girl was unabashed. 'Oh good,' she said in
the same excessively cheerful tone. 'You're quite well are you,
madam?'

The whole performance and both players irritated Frances, who
felt she had cause to be hotter and tireder and crosser than either
of them. But she also admired the woman's rudeness and the
girl's nerve and knew she could emulate neither. When her turn
came she answered, 'Fine,' with the smallest smile that good man-
ners allowed and escaped with her basket back into the broiling
afternoon sun and crossed to her own new house. It was then that
she had been caught by her neighbour, a large woman with thick
grey hair in a military crop, whose eyes, Frances felt, immediately
lighted on the whisky bottle.

'I heard your van arrive,' she said in a firm, hearty tone, 'and I
thought you'd be ready for a cup of tea by now. I'm Joan Messenger. We're neighbours.'

Frances held out her hand and noticed how dusty it was. 'I'm
Frances Howarth,' she said. 'I'd love some tea but I have to brew
up for the men first.' The other's grip was strong. 'You know what
it's like.' She invoked the common bond of moving house.

'I should do; I've moved fourteen times myself. My husband
used to be in the army. You come along any time. I'll be in the
garden.' Her skin was harshly red.

So Frances had brewed up for the men who showed their gratitude by entertaining her with their views on the government,
the heavyweight contest and the other houses they had moved
people in and out of. They showed no sign of going until they
had all had two cups each and one had had three and Frances had
poured the tea leaves down the sink and changed the subject to
what she owed them. She paid them and tipped them and they
went, leaving her alone with her house. It was an odd feeling, half
triumph, half anti-climax, and she wished Steve had been there

to share it or improve it. But she could no longer be sure that his presence would be an improvement; it depended on his mood, and on hers too, she supposed.

The house was full of mirrors: wherever she went she could not help catching sight of herself and registering what a mess she looked. She stopped in front of one to comb her hair and powder her shiny face and apply fresh lipstick before going to face Mrs Messenger. She noted that her freckles were increasing, the inevitable result of a good summer, and resented them nevertheless. I wonder if we are going to be happy here, she thought, and set off across the tangled garden.

She saw Mrs Messenger from the gate, stretched out in a deck-chair with the tea things on a tray on the grass. The garden was immaculate, with smooth lawns and trim borders and neatly blooming flowers in orderly beds. The only similarity with her own was the stone patio in front of the French doors. There was an empty canvas chair awaiting her. 'Come along, my dear,' said Mrs Messenger, and she sank into it gratefully, feeling she might never get up.

Mrs Messenger poured tea. 'How did it go?' she asked, and her tone suggested a military operation. I am jumping to conclusions, Frances thought, because she mentioned the army and has that kind of voice.

'Pretty well,' she said. 'I can't believe it's all over.'

'All over bar the clearing up,' said Mrs Messenger. 'Milk or lemon?'

Frances was soothed. 'Oh, lemon please,' she said. 'How nice. And no sugar, thank you.' She took her tea and sipped it, immediately feeling as hot inside as she was outside and reminding herself that it would in the long run make her cooler, or so people always said, than a cold drink.

'They didn't take long,' said Mrs Messenger. 'I think it took Dana longer to move out. She had Henderson's, you know. They're very slow.'

'Oh really,' said Frances. 'I don't know them.'

'Well, they have a good reputation and they trade on it. Poor Dana was quite distracted. The children got so fretful. Do you have children?'

People always asked this question and she ought to be used to

answering it without seeing a speculative look which was probably all in her imagination. 'No, we haven't,' she said.

'Dana had three,' said Mrs Messenger. 'I expect you met them
when you saw the house. Or were they at school?'

'I saw the baby,' Frances said.

'Oh, she's so like Igor, poor little thing. Did you meet Igor?'

A large, bearded man with a thatch of red hair and dark, search-
ing eyes hovered in Frances' memory. 'Yes, once,' she said.

'He's having an exhibition this month,' said Mrs Messenger.
'Such a talented boy. What does your husband do, my dear?"

Frances sipped her tea. Another stock question; she asked it
herself, as everyone did, not out of real interest, only because it
was impossible to ask what do you earn and how old are you and
are you happy, the things people really wanted to know. 'He's a
sales representative,' she said, and then, as she always added once
her childlessness had been established: 'I'm a teacher. I shan't be
working till after Christmas; I think there'll be enough to do in
the house. But I'm hoping to start again after that. Maybe just
part-time.' She hated herself for sounding defensive.

'You will have your hands full,' said Mrs Messenger. 'I find
with the garden and the WVS there aren't enough hours in the
day. If you want a daily woman you better start advertising now.
They're more precious than gold and they know it.'

'Yes, I suppose so. It's the same story everywhere.' She finished
her tea and stood up, smoothing her skirt. 'Well, I suppose I'd
better get back to my packing cases. I want to make some impression on the house before my husband comes home tomorrow.'
She smiled. 'I'm hoping to spur him into starting on the garden
so I'll have to set a good example. Thank you so much for the tea.
It was just what I needed.'

Mrs Messenger waved her off. 'I'm afraid Igor wasn't a gar-
dener, as you can see. And poor Dana was far too busy, of course.'

Well, there isn't much future there, Frances reflected in her
new, tidy kitchen, sipping her watered whisky. She's nice enough
but I doubt if we have much in common. I should think Dana
would have been more interesting. She had noticed this before:
the people who sold you their house were often the ones you
would have preferred as neighbours. Dana and Igor. How extraordinary. I should have told Claire that. I don't care for what

they did to the house but their conversation might have been interesting.

She found her cigarettes under a tea towel and took them and her drink on a tour of the house, somewhat impeded by furniture and trunks that lay everywhere in her path. She had to keep reminding herself that it could and would be beautiful, that it was a sensible size and it was lovely not to have stairs and she would certainly appreciate the central heating in winter, though now it seemed impossible to imagine wanting such a thing, and that as for the décor, white paint would work miracles, it always did. Dana and Igor had solved the problem of dirty finger marks by painting all the woodwork black. To offset this they had emulsioned all the walls in various brilliant colours except for the mural in the main bedroom and the tiny study (nursery) where they had incredibly bounced tennis balls dipped in Indian ink against the severely white walls.

Frances shut the door on the study, repository of trunks and suitcases, and the spare room, where she had made the men dump all the furniture she was not yet sure where to place. Forget it, she told herself; you can't do everything at once. To minimise chaos she had allowed only the bedroom carpet and furniture to go in the bedroom. It was almost respectable already. She had made up the bed before tackling anything else, knowing how important it was to be able to walk straight in and collapse at that moment which usually came in the small hours when you suddenly keeled over from exhaustion. Meanwhile with coffee and whisky and cigarettes she could keep going for a while, though it did seem a long time since she had consumed her cold meat. A familiar light-headedness was overtaking her.

She returned to the living-room, the chief battle area, and began unpacking books and arranging them on the shelves. It would be something to have them all in position before Steve got back, a small triumph and evidence of occupation. Without books it could be anyone's house. She heaved them out, her school books, packed near the top because in use until the last moment, and her college books grouped with them according to subject but some never opened in all the years since finals, she thought guiltily. She became overambitious as she made progress, and attempted to lift too many: the top volume skidded out of her hands and fell on the floor, open, shedding a letter. She sank to her knees and picked it up curiously.

'. . . till Saturday, Fran darling, and then we'll be together. You're not to worry, d'you hear me, and that's an order. I wish I could take the exam for you, I don't want you to go through anything without me, but you'll sail through it, you know you always do, and anyway, d'you think I'd have picked a girl who wasn't clever as well as beautiful? I don't know what I've done to deserve someone as wonderful as you. I suspect there's been a muddle in Somebody's filing system and we'd better keep very quiet so They don't notice. They'd soon give my marching orders. Move along there, Howarth, They'd say, that girl's not for you . . .'

She put it down when the writing started to blur and replaced it in the book. She would have liked to feel nothing and yet she was also saddened that the pain was not as acute as it would once have been. She shook her head and lit a cigarette, knowing that she was not going to allow herself the luxury of tears and depressed by her own good sense. It would have been as futile as crying for somebody dead.

4

'OH YES,' Ella said. 'Oh *yes*.' She closed her eyes and her face assumed an expression of rapturous bliss as if she had seen the beatific vision or found the Holy Grail. It thrilled him and yet the puritan in him was alarmed: there was a touch of blasphemy, of tempting providence about it. He almost expected to be struck down or at least rendered impotent. Not at this precise moment, he urged, please God. As man to man.

'Can you keep that up for ever?' Ella asked, the words coming out of her slowly. Her voice sounded drugged.

'I'll try.' He aimed at diverting his mind to other things like—who was it?—Aly Khan in the Sunday newspapers. And Aly Khan had died young. No connection though.

'Oh . . .' A long drawn out sigh from Ella. He was surprised that she had so much ecstasy left in her; they had done everything possible beforehand and impressed each other with their inventiveness and virtuosity. (Though he would have to accord her the victory since he had had twice as long to learn as she had and yet he could teach her nothing.) Was she perhaps insatiable? I shall die on the job, he thought; policemen friends had told him of many such cases and the woman always saying, 'He was just lying in bed having a cigarette . . .' Whereas by rights there should be a magnificent funeral with banners proclaiming 'A Martyr to the Cause' and a marble headstone with an inscription from the Kama Sutra.

'Mmm . . .' Ella moved her arms upwards and outwards, above her head, clenching her fists; her expression now was of ferocious concentration. He thought, It is only now that I am really seeing her, when she goes off into some private place of her own but only because of what I am doing to her so we are not really separated. Ella in Wonderland, he thought, because she looked so much like a child. But afterwards would she come back to him, would she answer all the questions he wanted to ask, would he know her any better? Or would they be strangers, their transaction over, sleeping, packing, giving and receiving cash? He had seldom felt like this about a woman before and never at such a time when he was usually more concerned about her sensations or his own.

'That's it.' She spoke triumphantly: she might as well have shouted Eureka. She began to move with him. He clung desperately for a few moments to Aly Khan then lost him in what seemed like a turbulent sea.

'Ella,' he said. 'Keep still.'

'I can't,' she said. 'I can't.' And went on moving.

He wanted to be sure she understood: it would be appalling, after all this, to fail. 'I can't keep going for long if you move,' he said. 'I'm nearly there.'

'Me too,' she said. 'Shut up.'

But the conversation broke his rhythm: he was carried backwards on a different wave, away from the shore. Like surfing, he thought, though he had never surfed. He squeezed her breasts in his hands to hurt her just a little, to slow her down. 'I'll stop,' he said teasingly. He was master of the situation now for the first time and drunk with mastery. Her eyes snapped open; she looked furious.

'No,' she said.

'Greedy.' He felt tender towards her, grateful for the power she had given him. 'Don't be in such a hurry.' But everything was mounting again and he could not escape it this time; accelerating and building up, it carried him forward with red and black flashes of colour and heat in his brain, and he saw Ella's eyelids flutter as if under hypnosis and her clenched hands open with that most beautiful gesture of release as they both crashed finally blood pounding in his head with the same cries of delight that was almost pain on to the same beach.

When at last he tried to move she hung on to him, digging her nails into his back. 'Don't go,' she said.

'I can't help it,' he said regretfully. 'I've gone.' He rolled over and reached for cigarettes. 'Will you have one now? It's tomorrow morning.'

She curled herself into a ball, her knees almost touching her chin, her arms clasped round them. 'Mm.'

He lit two and put one in her mouth. She drew on it but made no attempt to hold it so he had to take it out and put it back at appropriate intervals. He wanted to call her silly names: Pussy cat, baby, rabbit.

'Aren't you lazy?' he said tenderly. She made another small, meaningless sound, her face utterly peaceful. He went on feeding her with the cigarette and smoking his own. When they were both finished he stubbed them out. The bed was in a turmoil, sheets and blankets on the floor with their clothes. They would have to remake it before they could sleep in it. He felt a great lassitude, not quite exhaustion but rather the drowsiness of complete relaxation. He leaned over and kissed her forehead.

'Aren't we clever?' he said. He remembered the notebook but without resentment now. 'Do we get high marks?'

She lay curled up like a small animal. 'A—', she said, hardly moving her lips.

He was absurdly disappointed but tried to sound amused. 'Only A—?' He hoped she would think he was teasing her.

'Nobody gets A.' She turned her face into the pillow and it muffled her voice.

'Then it doesn't mean anything. It might as well not exist.'

She shook her head. 'I'm saving it up,' she said. 'Just in case.'

'For what?' He wished he could leave the subject alone. 'What more do you want?'

She answered out of a long silence, so long that he thought she was asleep. 'I don't know,' she said, 'but I will when I get it.'

5

THE TEA-CHEST was empty, the books in place on their new shelves, with fiction in alphabetical order and an overflow pile on the floor. Frances sat back on her heels, exhausted by her achievement but full of the false energy that sometimes comes with exhaustion. It had all taken longer than she had expected though, and she said aloud, 'I really must go to bed,' and frowned at the sound of her own voice. She only talked to herself when Steve was away, but it was a habit she disliked, a weakness. And Mother had started that way, she remembered, a low monologue all over the house but with surprisingly conversational cadences, so that at first Frances had thought she must have someone with her.

She pushed herself up and stumbled, her legs unsteady and tingling with pins and needles. She piled newspaper débris into the tea-chest and dragged it into the hall. It left a satisfying space behind. Another area cleared, however small. I am making progress, she thought. Encouraged, she began unpacking china and cutlery and glasses and carrying them into the kitchen to be washed. She filled the sink with hot soapy water and began washing glasses separately. She had long ago proved that if she put two in the water together she could be sure of cracking one and these were her new glasses and doubly precious, a leaving present from school. The staff had given her a magnificent coffee pot and the school as a whole some gorgeous and (she knew) expensive table mats. But the glasses came from her own form and she could still see the notice on the board: Everyone remember money for Mrs Howarth's present on Friday, and Sally Kirby, her face pink, vigorously wiping it off as Frances came in.

Well, she would find another school and be just as attached to another form in a few months, so there was no point in becoming sentimental. They would forget her as quickly as they had forgotten her predecessor. But this was intellectual comfort. At the moment she still felt that she had been torn from them as by amputation, noisy and self-conscious and typically fourth year as they were. Someone else would have to see them through 'O' level and cope with Linda Jackson's moods and try to get Jill Lawson to concentrate and encourage Pamela Stephens to open her mouth when she knew the answer and was too shy to give it. Someone else would come to them without knowledge and without making allowances, whereas she had taught some of them, despite streaming and restreaming, since first year when they were small and round-faced in their new uniforms and too nervous to talk among themselves even if she was late for a lesson and they had to wait for her. She could have left a dossier on each one; the parents too, some of them, with their over-crowding, their new babies, their bereavements, their relatives 'inside'. 'We're a very mixed area,' the headmistress had said at her interview. 'We get children from every sort of background.' This in itself was an added interest but did not account for her present attitude. Nor did the intensely emotional end of term atmosphere, which was the same in any school. No, they were special because she had been with them when she realised, finally, when suspicion became certainty, that there would never be a child.

And yet it was not that she was excessively maternal. She did not coo over babies or yearn to pick them up. She had never felt the urge to kidnap one from its pram as childless women sometimes did. She thought, certainly, that they became more interesting as they got older and able to talk and listen, but she could not say in truth, 'Yes, I love children,' which was what people wanted to hear when they asked her the question, because she could not love anything en masse. The children she taught (had taught) were all individuals and as such she had resented them and accepted them and warmed to them. Was that love? It was certainly more alive and constructive than anything she had felt for Steve in the past few years. It led somewhere; it was progressive. There was always something new. But surely this could be true of a marriage too, even without children? She had never believed that children were essential to a marriage, that two people could not be vital and fulfilled (how she hated those words, beloved of journalists) without them. If she had, she would not have deliberately postponed them for so long. Now she regretted this. It was not that she would rather children had come—had been allowed to come—at the beginning than not at all; she still believed this would have been a mistake. It was a more painful regret because it was illogical: a primitive, almost superstitious feeling that the unborn were taking their revenge.

She had tried to discuss this once with Steve but he had said sharply, 'Oh, now you're being ridiculous,' and then as if to comfort her with facts: 'It's not as if we didn't take the odd risk now and then anyway.' She tried to explain that it was not the same thing, that they had never accepted them in their minds at that time, and he had exploded: 'Well, if an educated woman like you can believe that sort of rubbish,' and she noticed for the first time that when he referred to her education it was no longer a loving joke. She told herself that his nerves were on edge, his pride injured from too many fertility tests, though surely to God not half as many as she had submitted to. But men were allowed to be more sensitive about such things. And all the embarrassing questions: how often they had intercourse, in what position, at what times in the month, did she enjoy it, did she achieve orgasm, did they indulge in preliminary sex play, was it satisfactory, how long did it last, until she wanted to scream, 'For God's sake, it's *making love* you're talking about.' How did they expect her to frame answers when there were no possible words? Did they think she could say, 'Well, he does this and I do that; or he puts his . . .'? Were there women who could say all that? The young, brisk doctor waiting for her answers and no doubt believing she was prim and frigid; hadn't they taught him in medical school that it was not things you were ashamed of that you couldn't express but things that mattered too much? 'I can't help you, Mrs Howarth, if you don't help me. We really need this information, you see; there's no need to be embarrassed.' And going on disapprovingly, with incomplete answers, regarding her as uncooperative, to her parents, her childhood, her first acquaintance with the facts of life, any early sexual experience, had she had pre-marital intercourse, had she had relations with other men besides her husband, had she indulged in 'prolonged clitoral stimulation which may or not terminate in climax—what the layman calls heavy petting,' all with a bland, matter-of-fact smile to reassure her, as if they were discussing baked beans.

Even Steve emerged somewhat shaken from the cross-examination but he recovered more quickly. 'Oh, they have to ask all those questions, I suppose.' She felt sure it was easier for men; they had the terminology ready, the vocabulary of their jokes, after all, used and familiar. There was no other explanation for his expecting her so soon to resume doing all the things the doctor had wanted her to describe. He did not seem to understand why she felt as if the doctor were there in the room. It was months before they seemed to be alone again; the interviews took so long to fade. And yet he had not always been so insensitive: when they were first married, for instance, he had understood that she could not make love with people, friends or relatives, in the house, and they had never invited anyone for more than a weekend for that reason.

But the worst thing of all was to achieve nothing, to go through all that clinging desperately to the belief, very shaky at times, that it was all worth while, and then at the end to learn nothing. There was no medical reason for their childlessness. Perhaps if they took a holiday or moved or changed jobs or she perhaps didn't work for a while. But she knew after that, even as they tried all these things (and the staying at home was torture, the holiday an expensive catastrophe) that it would make no difference. And it must have been then that her attitude changed. She remembered looking at him once or twice at night when he undressed and thinking, 'It doesn't work. It's useless.' And twelve years of pleasure were cancelled out. She was ashamed of the thought: it was unfair. Since medical science could tell them nothing why should she blame Steve? It was just as likely to be her fault, or no one's fault, just one of those things. The banal little phrase echoed round in her head. She wondered if he, in his turn, blamed her, if he felt she was less a woman. Once on a bus she had heard two women talking about another, and one said contemptuously, 'She can't even give him a child.' She had never forgotten it. Why did they think it was so easy, like making tea? No doubt they had huge families of their own, and all by mistake, and were so proud of their cleverness and abundant fertility that they felt safe to throw stones.

She never knew what he thought because they did not discuss it. It was an area which neither of them felt free to explore and she perversely blamed the doctors for stripping them too naked. Before they had been able to joke: 'Be funny if we can't after all this time,' or: 'How funny if we took all those precautions and they weren't necessary,' and although it was not really funny and they both knew it, at least they were able to say the words. Now they murmured about knowing where they stood and discussed adoption. They did not so much decide against it as allow the subject to lapse. She thought it was a matter of waiting until their relationship was stronger, but it never seemed to get stronger after that; it rather extended itself in a straggly, diffuse kind of way, like a plant left too long in the dark. Their lives became very full, mostly of things they had not thought necessary before, like drink and parties and expensive clothes and holidays. She shed some of her friends too, half-deliberately, half-unconsciously, the ones with children, who knew too much about her, and to the other, newer ones she talked so convincingly that they said to their husbands, 'Oh, Frances is a real career girl.' The few old friends she did keep nearly all had children (it was not easy, at her age, to surround yourself by people without them) and she watched them grapple with the problem of childless Frances. Some were patronising under a cloak of envy: 'You look marvellous in that dress, love; I'm afraid Catherine simply ruined my figure.' Some gathered her into the circle: 'Show Auntie Frances your picture book while I put Jeremy to bed. Frances, would you be an angel and keep her amused?' And some ignored the problem. Since they could not pretend Frances had children they were forced to pretend they hadn't, by entertaining only at night, all toys put away, and talking resolutely of adult matters. Sometimes Frances could see them fairly bursting to mention their children and she would watch the struggle with ironic amusement, for a length of time that varied with her mood, before giving them a decent excuse by her casual enquiry. Then the floodgates would open.

She tried to be fair but mostly she did not think they were happier than they had been without children. They were poorer, certainly, and complained that their husbands went out more often and alone, and the husbands complained of broken nights. She was also willing to admit that they all went easy on the infinite compensations of family life so as not to provoke her into instant suicide. But these were specific facts: it was the atmosphere she wanted to analyse, an atmosphere of routine and acceptance and discontent, all mixed with a certain unmistakable smugness. She was sure that they felt justified by having reproduced themselves, having fulfilled society's and their own expectations. Some were quite unsuited to parenthood and others thrived on it, but all

had, to her, this air of justification. They were self-important because they had crossed the dividing line of the merely married and
entered the big league of mothers and fathers. She recognised the
attitude because she had seen other manifestations of it: at college between virgins and non-virgins, or the engaged and the un-
attached, at school between married and single teachers. It was a
primitive, fundamental thing: she had felt it herself.

But if parenthood did not necessarily make their marriages happier, why should she assume that lack of it had made her own less
happy? Was it not more reasonable to assume that children were
largely irrelevant, making you happier or unhappier in direct pro-
portion to your previous state? Might not the unsatisfactory marriages around her, including her own, be the logical products of
time, the natural state of most marriages that had lasted for ten
or fifteen or twenty years? Perhaps children merely obscured the
issue and by providing an aim, an interest, an obsession even,
postponed the moment when you were forced to take stock and
find out where your marriage was leading. They offered such an
obvious answer that you didn't bother to ask the question until
years later, after they had gone; whereas she and Steve, alone with
each other, were asking it now.

At least, she was. She took her hands out of the soapy water,
tepid now, and rinsed and dried them, regarding the huge pile of
glass and china stacked on the draining board. Perhaps it was the
new house that made her feel like this; she had thought when
they bought it, Well, we must be going to stay together, not that
there had ever been any question of anything else, but buying a
new house was such a united step, much more positive than
merely continuing to live in the old one. And if you were going
to stay together you ought to know why.

It was late. If she didn't go to bed soon it would hardly be
worth going. In a little while she would not be able to fall asleep
because of the birds. But on an impulse she opened the kitchen
door and stepped into the garden. It was cool and dark away from
the reflected light, the only light visible on the whole estate.
Tempting in this mood to regard a new house as a new start. She
would make an effort; she would really try. She must talk to Steve:
they had both been far too busy lately, what with work and the
move, but it was no good to go on like that, amicable enough on
the surface but never really making contact. They had once been

so close, shared so much, had such fun. That was it: it was the fun that she really missed.

She turned to go in, but reluctantly: it meant she would have to sleep. It was years since she had actively missed him when he was away on a trip, except as a warm back in bed or a caustic comment on the television, but now she did. She thought that she saw things more clearly in the small hours of the morning and she was afraid that her vision would not last until tomorrow.

6

SHE WAS all smoothness and warmth. He could explore her without fear of rejection or hostility. He buried his face in her hair and against her skin and breathed the clean, unperfumed scent of shampoo and soap, the smell of a healthy child. He forgot that her words had offended him, or he discounted them. They had both been tired, or he too demanding and she sulky, or both trying to re-establish supremacy after too much exposure. Perhaps they were both takers and unused to giving, least of all themselves. And yet she had already given him so much he had been mad to ask more. She had a right to retreat into herself. She had shown him her pleasure, and in such abundance that it obliterated all the other times when he had failed to give pleasure. She had dressed up for him in the red dress and the crazy shoes, with her hair piled on her head in intricate coils and made him feel the envy of other men's eyes. She had been receptive and experimental and young, and made him all these things too, so that he forgot he was twice her age and had danced half the night and made love more than once in a few hours for the first time in ten years.

'Ella,' he said tentatively. She stirred but did not answer. Asleep. He ran his hand over her body, the brown arms and pale breasts, the hollow of her navel, the dark tuft of hair, the thin legs. Why didn't all women sleep naked? And why did he encourage them not to by buying them stupid bits of nylon as a barrier to skin? Just now, when he woke, he had been stuck to Ella and it seemed an almost closer bond than when he had been inside her.

'Ella,' he said again. He wanted to hear her voice, to be reassured that he was not manufacturing a dream. She stirred; she moved closer, curling herself against him. Most women moved away.

'Go to sleep,' she said, and he was satisfied.

*   *   *

FRANCES slept fitfully, alone in her half of the double bed, and the moonlight poured over the mural, cooling the colours but giving the jungle shadows an added dimension of mystery which had been quite beyond the skill of the painter. When she woke it was six and the birds were screaming, the sunlight rushing through the as yet uncurtained windows. She had a blinding headache and at first could not remember where she was.

7

HE WOKE to see her dressing, disappearing into the blue shirt and jeans and shoving the red dress back into the rucksack. He said, 'Hey, what's the hurry?' as item after item was pushed in, until only the make-up kit remained. She opened it, smeared foundation over her face (it must be that which kept her so pale) and began outlining her eyes.

'We're moving on,' she said, 'aren't we?'

'Well yes, but . . . what time is it?' He looked at his watch. 'It's only eight; what's the rush?'

She continued work on her eyes. It was amazing how it changed her face, her age, her expression. 'I'm hungry,' she said. 'I want my breakfast.'

It was the tone of a petulant child and delighted him. He got up, feeling less tired than he had expected, and went over to her. 'I want *you*,' he said.

Her face in the mirror expressed nothing. 'You've had me,' she said.

He felt an urge to match her toughness. 'Yes, very thoroughly.'

She finished with her eyes and started on her mouth. The lipstick was pale, so pale that yesterday he had not noticed that she was wearing any. He began to shave and tried to watch her reflection at the same time till he nearly cut himself.

'We had a good time, didn't we?' This sounded better than his last remark, still casual but less aggressive. She didn't answer. 'Have you written me up in your little book yet?' He felt a lot more himself: it was true what they said about cold morning light. He could remember feeling uncommonly sentimental during the night.

She paused with the lipstick. 'No. I do that later. What time is breakfast?'

He laughed. 'It's going on now. But don't worry, you won't miss it. Just hang on while I finish shaving. If I'd known you'd be so desperate I'd have got you a few rusks to chew.' He was pleased with his new light-hearted approach.

Ella perched on the bed. He could not see her at all now without turning his head. 'There are one or two things I forgot to tell you,' she said.

'There's a whole lot you forgot to tell me,' he said. 'I hardly know a thing about you.' Except, he thought with an odd pang, that you once had a mermaid doll. 'I've never met such a secretive wench.'

'I mean important things.' He heard her putting the make-up things away. 'For instance, I'm clean.'

'I should think so; you only had a bath last night. And washed your hair.' He could not control these heavy, jocular remarks; it was something to do with her attitude, something also to do with the tepid shaving water and the morning light and the hideous appearance of the room where something too important had almost happened.

'I mean inside,' Ella said in the same non-committal voice. 'You won't get VD. I've just had a check-up. I have them quite often.'

He had never met this before and though he had often considered the matter he found her directness disconcerting. 'Very sensible of you,' he said, 'with all those names in your little black book.' He pulled out the plug in the basin and enveloped his face in a towel. The water gurgled away.

'Yes,' she said calmly. 'Anyway, I thought I should tell you. As you have a wife.'

'Oh, I see,' he said, wiping his face. 'It doesn't matter about me.'

'Well, you might pass it on.' She sat calm and quiet on the bed, hands folded, face blank. 'And she might be pregnant or something.'

'Well, she isn't.' He felt a wave of anger.

'I only thought you should know.' She regarded him unemotionally. 'And I won't be either. That's all taken care of. So you needn't worry.'

He put away the towel. 'I wasn't going to. You seemed to know what you were doing.'

'Oh, not about me,' she said with a tinge of surprise. 'I meant about paternity orders and things.'

'I see.' He felt disorientated. There was something incongruous,

almost painful, about such a detached conversation, like talking to
a doctor or solicitor. He looked at her. Was this really the girl
who had moaned in his arms and moved with him and cried 'Oh
that's it,' and 'I can't'? 'Well, that's a relief,' he said furiously.

She got off the bed. 'Can we have breakfast now?'

He could not let it go at that. 'So we both leave no trace, is
that it?' he said. 'You don't give me VD and I don't give you a
baby. What a splendid arrangement.'

She looked at him with large, painted eyes. 'What's the matter?' she said. 'You don't seem very pleased.'

He turned away. 'No, I'm not.'

'But what did you expect?'

He didn't answer.

'Did you want VD and babies?'

No reply. Then: 'Oh, don't be such a bloody fool, of course I
didn't. It's just your attitude.'

'What's wrong with my attitude?'

He was alarmed to find that he wanted to hit her or at least
take hold of her and shake her. She seemed to provoke a violence
in him that he had not known existed.

'Come on,' he said, making an effort. 'Let's go and have breakfast.'

There were a few other people in the dining-room, lone men
and improbable couples. He chose a table far away from them all.
Ella looked at the menu.

'I'll have everything,' she said. 'Fruit juice, cornflakes, bacon
and tomato, toast and coffee.'

He gave her order to the waitress, peroxided and sulky, and
ordered toast and coffee for himself. He was not hungry.

'What time will you get home?' She made the word sound odd.

'About two, if I step on it. I've got a man to see first.' He lit a
cigarette.

'Will you tell your wife you picked up a girl?'

He was startled. 'I shouldn't think so.'

'Would she mind?' Her curiosity was childish, almost innocent.
He forgot his earlier, baffled rage.

'I don't know.' He tried to answer honestly. 'I suppose so.'

The waitress came and went. Ella drank her fruit juice. 'Is that
why you won't tell her—because she'd mind?'

'Well . . .' The question was odd: too simple. 'It's not the sort of thing you rush home and tell your wife.' He poured coffee for them both since she made no move to do so. 'Sugar?'

'Two. Is it the sort of thing you do often?'

He felt himself somehow on trial. 'Not as often as you, apparently.'

Ella stirred her coffee. 'I'm not married,' she said.

'You're very curious all of a sudden.' Her attitude puzzled him. 'You knew yesterday I was married. Why the sudden interest?' He tasted his coffee: it was stewed and bitter.

'That was yesterday.' She smiled at him. 'Today I'm interested. D'you mind?' The mixed accent was strong.

He felt it would be a sign of weakness to admit that he did and he was very aware of her strength. 'Not at all.'

His toast arrived, and Ella's cornflakes. They both began to eat. 'What's she like, your wife?'

'You mean to look at?' He went on without waiting for an answer; looks were easier to describe. 'She's about your height but not so thin. She has quite a good figure, about average, blue eyes —well, bluish-grey really—and brown hair that's a bit red . . .' He always had difficulty in describing Frances' hair. There was a certain kind of wood that matched it exactly but he did not know the name. He considered his description. It was accurate but it did not conjure up Frances for him.

'How old is she?'

This seemed an impertinent question. Knowing Frances was sensitive about her age he felt that an answer would be disloyal yet a lie or evasion would make him look foolish. 'Thirty-five,' he said.

Ella munched her cornflakes. 'Do you love her?' she asked conversationally.

This was too much, though last night he might have welcomed the question, even spent hours trying to answer it. 'I can't say yes or no to that,' he said heavily. 'It wouldn't mean what I mean. At your age love is a very simple word. At mine it isn't.' This was important. He wanted to say what he meant; it was years since he had tried to express how he felt about Frances.

Ella was watching him. Her gaze was cool, almost clinical. 'You mean you're fond of her,' she said, 'but you don't mind a bit on the side now and then.'

'No, that's not what I mean.' He was furious at the oversimplification, so crudely and casually stated over the breakfast table.

'Well, aren't you fond of her?'

'Yes, of course I am. It's just not as simple as that. I told you.'

'But I *am* a bit on the side.' A small, triumphant smile.

'Oh hell, if you want to put it like that.' He looked round for some way to attack, to make her tire of the game. 'If that's how you think of yourself.'

She finished her cornflakes and pushed away the dish. 'How else can I think of myself? That's how you see me, isn't it? A quick bash, an easy lay, a piece of tail.' She piled phrase upon phrase, watching him flinch.

'Do you have to be so vulgar?' he demanded in a dining-room whisper.

She laughed aloud. One or two heads turned. 'What's the matter?' she said. 'Isn't that what you say to your friends? I met this bird on the road, simply begging for it, fucked like a rabbit. Or am I out of date? You must educate me. What's the current expression?'

He was not mistaken: heads were turning. 'Perhaps you could lower your voice,' he suggested with an icy calm he was far from feeling.

She regarded him curiously. 'Are you ashamed of last night?'

He had no choice but to defend himself. 'No, why should I be?'

'Then why don't you want me to talk about it?' She was persistent, relentless.

'Because I don't like your language,' he said sharply, 'and we're in a public place.'

She laughed again. 'So that's it. You can do what you like as long as nobody knows about it. And it's okay for you to be crude but not for me.'

The waitress returned, eyeing them curiously; she removed Ella's empty dish and put down a plate of bacon and tomatoes. He waited until she had gone, looking round at the quickly bent heads of the other diners.

'I was not aware,' he said, and knew he was sounding pompous, 'that I had been crude.'

She attacked her food at once; nothing seemed to interfere with her appetite. 'No, but you will be,' she said. 'You'll have to boast

about it, won't you? And you're not going to say, "I had an idyllic
night with a wonderful girl," now are you?'

He lit a cigarette and poured himself a fresh cup of coffee. The
toast had gone cold and hard.

'I don't understand,' he said, 'what on earth you're trying to do.'

'Suppose I stood up and shouted,' she said, 'in front of all
these people, something very rude and accurate. How would you
feel?'

He was not even sure that she might not fulfil this threat.
'Embarrassed,' he said briefly.

'But why? If it was all true?'

He was amazed at her obstinacy. 'Because it's not the thing to
do,' he said. 'Surely you can see that.'

She smiled. 'Was last night *the thing to do?*' She made his
words sound old-fashioned. His patience snapped. He half-rose
from the table.

'I think you better finish your breakfast alone.' He thought of
the room upstairs as a sudden haven.

'I'll shout,' Ella said. 'Before you get to the door. Everybody'll
hear.'

He sat down again, despising himself. She had defeated him.

'Don't you want to know what I was going to shout?' she asked,
delighted.

'No,' he said heavily. 'I can imagine.'

She went on eating. 'I've frightened you,' she said. 'Poor Steven.
May I call you Steven?'

He looked at her with something close to loathing. 'You can
do anything you like, can't you?' he said. 'You've just proved that.'

She opened her eyes wide. 'But I was only joking. I didn't mean
it.'

He looked past her, feeling that the humiliation was endless
and there was nowhere he could hide. It was like being a tor-
mented schoolboy again. Memories he had almost suppressed rose
up: the playground, the bigger boys led by Turner, the mockery,
the chase, the feeling that his heart would burst if he drew another breath and yet he must keep on running. The dining-room
swam before his eyes.

'I wouldn't really have shouted,' Ella said. 'I was just teasing
you. Didn't you know that?'

He looked at her with thirty years of hatred. 'Well, you've had your fun,' he said.

Upstairs in his room he packed in a kind of trance. Humiliating was too feeble a word for the discovery that he could still be shit-scared like a kid, that he was only a child in an adult's skin, had learnt nothing in all the years, had achieved nothing with his responsible job, his wife, his pleasant affairs, if a few words from a girl half his age could reduce him to this. He wanted—how he wanted—to forget and yet he kept playing the scene over and over in his mind. Humour. That was it. He should have laughed it off. All his life he had known that. Laughter was the great weapon. Only he never remembered in time.

The more he played back the dialogue the more he cursed himself. There was nothing to it: it need never have reached such proportions. He should have handled it differently from the start. Why had he let her needle him? What was there about her that got under his skin? (But even last night she had started to do that. He pushed the thought away.) However, his real mistake had been to let her see her success. Once they got the scent of blood . . . 'Never let them know you're frightened,' his mother had told him again and again, 'and they'll leave you alone.' And he tried; he tried so hard. 'They only do it because you get upset. If you didn't, it wouldn't be any fun for them and they'd stop.' Oh yes, he believed her; of course she was right, it was logical. But how could you walk all the way to school with a grin on your face, not knowing which bush they were behind, and when they started, really started, how could you manage the miraculous laugh when you only wanted to cry—or fight. Only you couldn't fight them all. So you ran away. But that was no solution, for they always found you.

He heard the door open and the girl's voice saying, 'Are you very cross?' She sounded penitent but a long way off: he was still enmeshed in the past.

'What about?' he said, and heard this strange man's voice that sounded so sure of itself, so unruffled. He had met Turner again years after and they had laughed and joked and bought each other pints like friendly strangers.

'I'm a beast,' the girl said. She came up behind him, putting her arms round his waist. Her fingers played over his ribs. He had not thought to feel desire for her ever again and it appalled him. 'Why don't you hit me?' she said softly, burying her face in his back. 'That's what I deserve.'

He disengaged her hands. 'Don't be silly,' he said, in his fatherly voice. When he was sure that his face was a mask he turned round. 'Why ever should I want to hit you?'

She closed her eyes. 'You can if you like,' she said. 'I don't mind.'

It was not what he wanted to do at all. She looked very small and defenceless in front of him, thin and young in the blue denim, her hair long and loose round her pale face, her absurdly over-painted eyes: like a child play-acting. He could not imagine how she had ever demoralised him. And he had a feeling that if they could only start again it would all be different. But what did he mean by that? There was nothing to start; it was all finished, an interlude, over.

She said plaintively, 'You haven't hit me yet,' and he tapped her lightly on the nose, saying, 'There, will that do?' She opened her eyes at once and to his intense surprise flung her arms round him and kissed him energetically, saying when she had finished, 'Oh, what a pity, what a pity.'

He smiled. 'What is?' But he knew.

'Oh.' She sat on the bed, pouting. 'It's such a pity it's nine o'clock and you're going home and I'm staying here. Where d'you live?' She spoke all in one breath.

'Middlesex.' It was mere reflex action not to be precise. 'What d'you mean, you're staying here?'

She rolled over, lay flat on the bed, her arms and legs outstretched. Memories of the night came back to him. 'Oh, your manager friend has offered me a job.'

He was disturbed and knew he had no right to be. He lit a cigarette and sat down on the bed. 'What sort of job?'

She was gazing up at the ceiling. 'Oh, he's short of staff. He wants someone to double as waitress and chamber-maid and maybe help out a bit in the bar. I met him just now in reception and he offered me the job.' She spoke lightly and casually like a girl trying to convince her father of the absolute safety and propriety of her first continental holiday.

He tried to use the same tone. 'You better watch out. He's an old lecher.'

She smiled. 'So am I.' She looked at him mischievously.

He said, 'No, you're young.' This was how he should have handled it before. But he knew Jack. They had been in the army together. He said with sudden urgency, 'Ella, not with Jack—please.'

She gave him a curious look. 'He hasn't asked me.'

'He will.' She said nothing. He went on with an effort, 'Well, anyway, I was going to give you this,' and took out a five pound note.

'That's pretty,' she said. She made no move to take it. He had to leave it on the bed beside her.

'Well,' he said again, 'you won't be needing a lift then?'

She turned her head towards him. 'No, it's a residential job.'

He was making a mess of the ending. He should have been up and out already with some neat exit line. He stood up. 'I hope you enjoy it.'

She shrugged her shoulders. 'It's a job,' she said indifferently. 'It's money. And I get a room and my keep.'

'Yes, of course. It's very convenient for you.' He made his voice casual: he was alarmed by his own motivation. 'How long d'you think you'll stick it?'

She smiled. Did she read his thoughts? 'Till I get bored.'

There was no help. He looked at his watch. 'Well, I'd better be moving.' His appointment was at ten-thirty.

'Drive carefully,' said Ella. 'And don't pick up any strange girls.'

Her grin was young and cheeky and unmalicious. He smiled back, hoping it all looked as it should: a man leaving, satisfied and uninvolved, the account squared. He picked up his case and walked out of the room, shutting the door behind him. He was alone again.

Downstairs in the bar Jack was polishing glasses. He had started as a bartender and still enjoyed doing menial jobs in his own hotel. He winked at Steve.

'Any time you're passing,' he said, 'do drop in. I can always use an extra waitress.'

8

The day was hot but overcast. Muggy, they had called it when Frances went shopping. Very close, and she nodded. Now she worked in a flared skirt and sleeveless blouse and still felt uncomfortably sticky. She was hungry too; if Steve did not come soon she would grill her own steak and have it alone.

As if in answer to this unspoken threat, the car drew up outside. She went to the door, remembering that he did not yet have a key (he had gone before she collected them from the agent) and opened it. She watched him getting out of the car, a big, good-looking man who should, she always felt, have had an outdoor job in some pioneering environment; in her youth she had dreamed of him as a cowboy or a sheriff with guns and a horse. Looking at him now, she felt with the left-over sensitivity of the previous night, how sad it was that each home-coming could no longer thrill her, that the mere sight of him did not, as it once had, make her heart lift. She snubbed herself: You are being romantic. That stuff is for teenagers or newly-weds. You can't expect it to last.

'You're late,' she called out down the path, and noticed at once that her very first words to him were an accusatory reflex. How long had she been like this? Was she—horror of all text-book horrors—becoming a nagging wife? She would, in her new mood, have to watch herself closely.

He came into the house and put down his case. He kissed her cheek. 'I got hung up with Standish,' he said. 'And the traffic was worse than ever. Have you had lunch?'

She turned and went into the kitchen to switch on the grill. 'No, I waited for you.'

He looked around him at the hall, the living-room. He came and stood in the doorway of the kitchen, whistling admiration. 'You've worked wonders,' he said.

She smiled, gratified. 'I've hardly stopped. I don't know what time it was when I finally got to bed.' She studied him. 'You look tired. How was your trip?'

He turned away. 'Okay. I had a late night too. I stayed at Jack's.'

She laughed; she knew what that meant. 'Oh yes? The old regimental booze-up.'

'As usual.' He lit a cigarette. 'How did the move go? You seem to have coped magnificently.'

Praised, she felt the urge to minimise her achievement. 'Oh, it wasn't too bad. The men were pretty good. And I met our next door neighbour.' She pointed. 'That side. The others seem to be away. A Mrs Messenger. Very much the Colonel's lady, rough-hewn version. She gave me a cup of tea in the garden. Her garden, need I add?'

He followed her gaze. 'All right, I take your point.'

She said hastily, 'I only mean sometime. You know. Only it is——'

'Yes. It is. Do we have any beer?'

'Sorry.' Whatever she bought he always wanted something else. She ought to be used to it. 'Only Scotch.'

'Scotch'll do. Where is it?'

'The shop across the way will have beer. They're open all day and they have an off-licence section.' She could not imagine any-one wanting to drink whisky at ten to three on a hot afternoon.

He shook his head; he was already pouring Scotch and drinking it, she was surprised to see, neat. 'D'you mind if I go and sit down?' He knew she liked company while she cooked.

'No, I'll join you in a minute. This can take care of itself. I did a salad to go with it.'

'Shall I pour you a drink?'

She shook her head. 'I had enough last night.'

He moved into the living-room. 'You, too.'

She peered through the hatch after him. 'Can you find any-where to sit? I'm afraid it's still chaotic.'

He pushed a pile of débris off a chair on to the crowded floor. 'It looks quite respectable.' All his movements were heavy, slow.

Frances turned the steak. 'Have a look at the floor,' she called through the hatch. 'If you can find it. It's got funny white stains all over it.'

He looked briefly. 'Oh yes, so it has.'

'D'you think they'll come out?'

'I expect so.' He leaned back in his chair and drank whisky with concentration, his eyes closed. She left the meat to grill itself and went into the living-room.

'D'you know what they are?'

'No.' He did not sound very interested.

'Then what makes you think they'll come out?' She heard the sharpness creep into her voice. I mustn't, she thought; I really mustn't.

Steve opened his eyes. 'Why, what are they then?'

Frances perched on the edge of a tea-chest. 'I think it's some photographic stuff. I think they used this room as a studio or something. You know she was a photographer.' He nodded. 'Well, that kind of thing may not come out. If it doesn't the floor's ruined and we'll have to carpet it.'

'Oh well,' Steve said, 'we've got enough carpet.' He wondered what all the fuss was about. His head ached; it had ached all the way down in the car. Did Frances have to start on about carpets and floors and the garden the minute he got inside the door?

'I know we have,' she said. 'But that's not the point. It's a beautiful floor—or it *was*—and I don't want it to be ruined.'

He got up. 'Well, maybe it isn't.' He went across to the French doors at the other end of the room. 'We'll get someone to take a look at it.' He stood in the doorway breathing the hot, stale air. What was Ella doing now?

'All right,' Frances said, her patient voice, full of martyred resignation inadequately repressed. 'I'll just go and look at the steak. It should be nearly ready.'

The evening hung heavily. There was no television to watch until the men came to fix the aerial on the roof and they had both worked themselves to a standstill achieving some kind of order in the living-room, which now contained only essential furniture. The result was that the hall and spare room were even more chaotically crowded with containers waiting to be unpacked and objects to be placed or discarded and the incredible amount of newspaper that seemed to be almost created by moving house, an inescapable by-product. Now they merely sat and surveyed their achievement. For some time they had been saying, 'We'd better go to bed,' and making no move to do so.

Steve poured another drink and said, 'For you?'

She shook her head. The bottle was already half empty. 'It won't last very long,' she said, and tried to keep the disapproval out of her voice. What did it really matter, after all, if he had another drink? But he was drinking more than usual. She wondered why.

'It never does.' He surveyed his glass. 'God, I'm tired. I'd forgotten what hell all this is.'

'It was even more hell yesterday.' The words were out before she could stop them. Or was it before she wanted to stop them?

'Yes, of course, you had the worst of it.' He sighed heavily. 'Next time we move I'll have to take my summer holiday, that's all.'

'Oh, I didn't mean that.'

But what did she mean then? What was the point of allowing him—as she had, with a very good grace, full of understanding—to miss the removal, if she was going to reproach him with it immediately afterwards? He drained his glass. The whisky was good, strong and healing.

'No,' she said, 'I meant we've done a lot today. It's much better than yesterday. Only we must expect to be chaotic for quite a while yet; we're bound to be.' She smiled. 'We're just out of practice. It's so long since we moved.'

'Five years.'

'Well, that's a long time.' Their last house had been large and rambling, suitable for the children they had been sure they would have. She had hated leaving it; it seemed a denial of something. She said, 'Does this place seem awfully cramped to you?'

He was staring at his empty glass. 'No, just crowded. It'll be fine when we get it straight.'

'I suppose so.' She had seen the children so clearly in the other house, running about, playing games. She had almost heard their shouts of delight at the space and the freedom, the nooks and crannies to hide in. 'It just seems rather small.'

'Well, it's bound to by comparison. The other one was enormous.' He wondered why they had to have this pointless conversation now. A fine time to start finding fault with the house, the day after moving in, when she had always been as keen on it as he was—keener, if anything. 'Surely four rooms are enough,' he said. 'And you've always wanted central heating.'

She nodded. 'Seems ridiculous now but I suppose it will be cold again.' She thought of her lost house, sold, betrayed, with alien children thundering along its corridors. Not hers.

'I think we can count on that,' Steve said. He stood up. The night was grim and overcast. 'D'you think it's going to rain?'

'I don't know.' She felt tired to the bone. The effort of getting up to go to bed seemed to her insuperable, even though there were no stairs to climb. 'I suppose we're due for some.' She put out a hand. 'I think I will have that drink.'

He poured it for her and another for himself. 'Are you all right?' he said. 'You look awfully tired.' The freckles were standing out sharply on her skin which, when she was tired, had an almost translucent pallor. Without being a true redhead she was never able to tan.

'I'm dead.' She took the drink and added water. She always, he thought irritably, drowned her drinks.

'You'd better take it easy,' he said. 'You've been doing too much.'

'I'll be all right,' she said, sipping her drink. 'I just need a good night's sleep.'

He looked round at the nearly habitable room with its debated floor; at the tangle of garden awaiting his scythe; at his wife, slumped in her chair, white-faced and exhausted from accomplishing miracles of work and organisation. 'Come on,' he said. 'We'd better go to bed.'

They washed simultaneously, he in the bathroom, she in the bedroom wash-basin. The bathroom suite was harmlessly modern but the décor nearly blinded him. What would it be like with a hangover?

'Christ,' he said to Frances, going into the bedroom, 'how can people live like this?'

She pointed at the mural. 'You mean that?'

He shuddered dramatically to please her. 'Well yes, that as well. But I mean the bathroom. How can anyone want an orange bathroom?'

'Oh,' Frances said, 'they were arty people.' When they had first met he had teased her with that word. Now when she tested it there wasn't even a flicker. She sighed.

'They must have been.' He started to undress.

'It only needs paint,' she said. 'Thank God it's not wallpaper or we'd have to strip the walls.'

She was in her slip, brushing her hair in front of the mirror. How sturdy she looked, he thought for the first time. Almost heavily built. And her hair was wiry and coarse.

'Thank God indeed,' he said.

'The study is fantastic, isn't it?' Frances began to undress. 'They dipped tennis balls in Indian ink and bounced them at the walls. They told me.'

'Good God,' he said, 'whatever for?' He watched her undress and thought: I suppose after fourteen years Ella wouldn't excite me either. Or maybe after fourteen days even. But this, he was aware through the whisky, would have been fun to test.

'I've no idea.' Naked, she looked round for her nightdress. He had never succeeded in persuading her to sleep without one except for a few nights in the first year of their marriage when they had both, drowsy with rapture, fallen asleep too suddenly to dress. Now he was glad. Living with her, he had not really looked at her freshly for years. Now he saw that her figure was thickening, an inch, maybe two, all over. It must have happened so gradually that he had not noticed. She pulled the nightdress over her head and immediately looked better. Time, he thought with a certain satisfaction, was unkinder to women than men. He wondered how Ella would look at thirty-five.

Frances got into bed and started creaming her face. He switched out the main light, leaving only the lamp by the bed; it subdued the mural considerably.

'The curtains don't fit, I'm afraid,' said Frances, yawning.

'They'll do till we get new ones.' He got in beside her. Outside there was the first distant rumble of thunder.

'I only put them up this morning. Last night I slept without any; that's why I woke up at six.'

'Poor you,' he said absently.

She stiffened a little as the thunder murmured again. She had spent years training herself not to be frightened, if only because it was unthinkable to show fear in front of the children at school, but the cure was not quite complete. 'Sounds as if we're going to have a storm,' she said, bravely casual.

'It's a long way away. It may pass over.' He knew her fear. Years ago he had enjoyed soothing it away but tonight he did not want to have to touch her. He put out the light and they lay side by side in the darkness, together and apart.

'I found an old letter of yours yesterday,' Frances said. It was easier to talk with the light out; so far she had not said anything she really meant, despite her good resolutions. It had been so hard to recapture her mood of last night: they had been too busy, too tired, too irritable. . . . She didn't know why but the day had not gone at all as she had planned it. She was alarmed that they showed every sign of going on in the same old way in their new house.

'There must be hundreds knocking around,' Steve said. 'We ought to burn them.'

She was appalled. 'Oh, why? I want to keep them all; they're lovely.' The banality of her own words depressed her: it was not mere sentiment that she felt but panic at the thought of destroying the only proof she had that the past really existed.

'I only meant,' Steve said, 'in case somebody found them. Of course we both want to keep them but we'd hate anyone else to read them.' This was not what he meant. Most of all he hated her to read them aloud to him, as she had once or twice after a row, trying to drag a reconciliation out of stale emotion. He loathed being brought face to face with his twenty-three-year old self, vowing eternal fidelity and love. It would not have been so bad if this person had been a stranger to him. But he recognised him only too clearly.

'Someone else?' Frances said. 'Such as who?'

He felt trapped; forced to specify. 'Oh, I don't know. Just people. Visitors.'

'We don't have many visitors.'

'No.'

'And they'd hardly go through our drawers.' But she felt a touch of guilt: the letter had been in a book she might have lent to anyone. So she had to attack. 'You're not ashamed of your letters, are you?'

He shifted uncomfortably. 'No, of course not. They're just private. You know perfectly well what I mean.'

It was all going wrong; still she tried desperately to hang on to it. 'It was a lovely letter,' she said. 'It made me think.' The thunder rumbled again and this time it was a help; she almost wanted to be frightened. She put a hand on his arm. 'Steve, we ought to have a talk.'

'What about?' This was entirely unexpected and alarming. He had counted, he realised now, on having time to think, to adjust, to be alone. No: that was too dramatic, too positive. He had simply counted on normality, on the resumption of everyday life in which Ella was just an incident which would surely fade soon into memory like all the others. There was nothing special about her, he thought, like a man who drinks regularly and moderately and is therefore surprised to find himself suddenly with a hangover.

'Oh, about everything,' Frances said. He was relieved; he had been dreading to hear those fatal, feminine words *about us*.

'If you mean the house,' he said quickly and hopefully, though knowing she didn't, 'don't worry about it. We'll soon get it straight and we'll paint everything and I'll do the garden. I'll start tomorrow if you like. Don't worry. It'll soon be just the way we planned it.' For when they had first seen it they had looked not at what it was but at what they, with their taste and skill, could make it.

'Nothing else is.' Frances found her voice thick and a certain stuffiness and tingling in her nose and eyes that could mean the start of tears. She took a few deep breaths to steady herself; it was not the moment to cry. She had not been aware until now that the danger existed. 'Oh, I started thinking last night. You know how it is when you're alone. I thought how happy we used to be.'

She meant to go on but he said, 'Why, are we bloody miserable now or something?' quite aggressively, and she shrank inside and took her hand away from his arm.

'No, of course not. I just meant . . . well, we used to have more fun. You know. And . . . *talk* to each other more often. Steve'— out it came, suddenly, in an urgent rush—'people can be happy without children, can't they?'

'Lots of people are.' Oh no, he thought, oh Christ, not that again. Not now.

'Yes, well, I know, and I thought we hadn't really faced up to it. I mean, we were both disappointed, naturally, and we just . . . well, we rather let things drift.'

Noisily, to acknowledge the fact that he was not going to be allowed to sleep, he lit a cigarette. 'You mean adoption?' he asked loudly. She was so vague.

'No, I didn't get as far as that. We could discuss it again, I suppose; we never really made a decision. But I meant just things in general, apart from that. What we're going to *do*.'

'You said,' he pointed out, sheltering behind facts, 'that you weren't going to work till January. And you were wondering about part-time.' What did she mean, *do*?

'I'm not talking about jobs.' She closed her eyes, trying hard to concentrate. He was not helping her at all. Outside the thunder sounded again and heavy, steady rain began to fall.

He said, acknowledging the rain, 'Listen. Thank God for that. It should be cooler tomorrow,' and her nerves stretched and snapped.

'Oh, Steve,' she said, but furiously, not at all in the right way, the way she had intended. 'Never mind the bloody rain. I'm talking about us. What are we going to do to be happy?'

He sat up in bed with a jerk. The bed shook. 'You mean,' he said icily, 'that you're asking me for some kind of blueprint?'

She lay frozen, confused between tears and rage, listening to the rain. 'No, of course not.'

'Well, what then?'

She didn't answer.

'Damn it, Fran, I'm trying to understand.' Silence. 'You start a conversation like this in the middle of the night when we're both dead beat. . . .' He snapped on the light—anything to get back to reality—and the mural sprang into life. He was startled; he had forgotten it. 'Oh God,' he said, half to himself, 'that damn thing will have to go for a start.' It gave him a headache just to look at it.

Frances had turned away. She lay on her side, her face in shadow. He could see only her shoulder, the blue of her night-dress and the dull reddish brown of her hair. 'Look, love,' he said, more calm than he felt, 'can't it wait till the morning?'

'It can wait for ever.' She was conscious of her muffled voice, her over-dramatic words. But she did not feel over-dramatic. Only furious at exposing herself and giving him the chance to reject her.

'Oh, now you're being ridiculous.' She felt him get up. 'D'you want a drink? I'm going to have one.'

She didn't answer; then as he reached the door she flung at him, 'You think a drink is the answer to everything.' She felt impossibly violent from forcing herself to lie still and her only relief lay in words. He went out and the door slammed after him, either by intent or the draught from the window. The rain streamed down.

She turned over, suddenly, with a thump, and lay looking first at the ceiling, then at the jungle shadows on the wall. The leaves seemed to move in the soft light; she could imagine that the rain was falling on them. It had a soothing sound.

She sat up and looked round the room. Apart from the bizarre décor everything was normal. Without Steve beside her she felt she had imagined the scene. I must have been mad, she thought, saying all that. We're both tired, it's terribly late, and he's had a lot of whisky. I should have known better. What *did* I hope to achieve?

She got up and wandered in her nightdress into the living-room where he was sitting with a glass in his hand. He looked up with his sulky expression as she entered; she knew it well. It meant: Don't start anything now because I'm ready for you.

'Would you like me to sleep on the couch,' he said, 'since we've cleared it?' And she didn't know if he meant to be funny or dignified.

'Don't be silly,' she said, managing a smile. 'I don't know what got into me.'

He cradled the glass between his knees and she thought how absurd pyjamas looked. She sank into a chair. 'I think I'll have that drink,' she said but he made no move so she leaned across and poured it for herself.

He was studying her with frightening intensity. 'Are you really unhappy?' he said.

Faced with a direct question, she panicked. The moment was wrong, or the mood. It was too soon, or too late. And he had taken the initiative away from her. She made her choice.

'No, of course not,' she said. 'Just tired.'

9

THEY HAD warned her when she phoned that today was a bad day. If Steve had known he would have said, 'Well, why go then? What's the point?' But she had gone nevertheless, because she wanted to and because with all the upheaval of the move her visit was overdue, and also because—perhaps most of all because—it was surely on a bad day that she was most needed. But it had not worked. Now, driving home in commuter traffic, feeling sticky and dirty and harassed by the noise of the cars and the jostling pedestrians, she admitted that she had been wrong. It had been a failure.

'I don't think she even knows me,' she had said to the crisp little nurse who seemed absurdly young for her job, and the girl smiled politely.

'You mustn't worry, Mrs Howarth,' she said. 'They're often like that.'

Frances found the pronoun offensive. Why should the old be grouped together so anonymously just because they were old? If the nurse couldn't see her patients as individuals she was in the wrong job. She hesitated and murmured something about wanting to see Matron.

The girl looked at her watch. 'She's gone to a meeting,' she said. 'She won't be back until six. If you'd care to wait . . .' And she shuffled some cards in an index file to show she was busy.

But Frances couldn't wait. She would already hit the rush hour if she left immediately and there was Steve's meal to get. Yet even as she thought this she wondered if it was an excuse to save her from facing Matron, who was frankly terrifying and reminded her of her first headmistress. What was the point of complaining to Matron who would only say in the end, 'Well, of course, if you're not satisfied, Mrs Howarth, you can always make alternative arrangements. We shall quite understand and as you know we do have a long waiting-list.'

A long waiting-list. Were there so many people then all eagerly queuing up to get their elderly relatives off their hands? The thought was depressing. So many people. Like her. No, like Steve. But she had agreed: she must share the guilt. And anyway, complain about what? What could Matron do, with the best will in the world? She couldn't make Mother young again. If Frances said to her, 'She's not getting enough care, enough attention, enough . . . love,' she would be accusing not Matron but herself.

So she had walked away, down the long drive with its smooth lawns and fine display of roses, and the deck-chairs with a few old people sitting in them, watching time pass. The place looked beautiful as ever, the graceful old house in perfect condition, the well-stocked garden. No wonder it was expensive: so much money must go on upkeep. It was a well-run home—if such a thing was not a contradiction in terms.

The traffic thinned out as Frances neared home. She tried to banish the afternoon from her mind; it had already made her slow at the lights several times, causing people to hoot impatiently behind her. Were they really in such a hurry to get home? Did they have everything they wanted there so that they could hardly wait to get back to it?

Steve was in the garden when she arrived, knee-high in shorn grass. He did not look up but went on scything mechanically in a smooth, unbroken rhythm. Frances stood and watched him for a while. She thought, not for the first time, how odd it was that so many men, big and powerful like him and obviously suited to hard physical work, should earn their living by their wits. When had manual labour ceased to be respectable?

'It looks much better already,' she called to him and he straightened up, wiping his forehead with the back of his hand.

'Another evening should see it through, I think,' he said. He dropped the scythe and began raking the long cut grass into a heap for burning.

Frances went into the house and unpacked her shopping. He would be hungry after working in the garden. She switched on the stove. Steve appeared in the doorway of the kitchen as she started to cook.

'How was she?' he asked.

She knew this was mere politeness as always and as always she resented it accordingly. 'Not too good,' she said, busy with her hands and the food, not looking at him. 'Very vague.'

He came in and began to wash at the sink. 'Oh well, she's getting on. I suppose it's to be expected.'

Something snapped in Frances. 'Is that all you can say?'

He looked up in surprise, reaching for a towel. 'What d'you want me to say?'

She watched him wipe his hands, making dirty marks on the towel. He never rinsed properly but she had given up reminding him. 'You might show a little pity.'

'Well, of course I'm sorry for her. Poor old thing.' He opened the fridge and took out a can of beer. 'God, it's hot. I thought we were in for a cooler spell but it's worse than ever.'

'Yes,' Frances said. 'It is.' She felt edgy and nervous, but in an alarming way, as if her mind were hovering a few inches outside her body. 'I wonder what we'll be like when we're old,' she said.

'Dead, I hope,' Steve said. There was a rush of beer meeting air as he opened the can and poured the frothing liquid into a glass. 'What's for dinner?'

'Mixed grill,' said Frances with heavy emphasis. 'I thought you'd be hungry.' She watched him drink the beer greedily, pouring it down. He had not offered her one and she was glad because it was another instance of his selfishness. 'Yes,' she said reflectively, 'I suppose death is the answer.' A *consummation devoutly to be wished* floated in her head, left over from GCE. 'I wonder how many of the people in that home wish they were dead.'

Steve put down his empty glass and stared at her in surprise. 'Oh, come now,' he said, 'they're the lucky ones, surely, aren't they?'

Frances watched the sizzling chops, bacon and sausages. The heat in the kitchen was unbearable even with the door open. 'Are they?' she said.

'Well, they must be. Think of all the old people living alone in single rooms and all that. Whereas your mother and the rest of them have got every possible amenity.'

'Every possible amenity.' Frances echoed him.

'Well, they have. Compared to some, they're living in the lap of luxury. They've got a beautiful house and trained people to look after them. It's the others I feel sorry for.'

'Do you?' She eyed him curiously. 'Then why do you sound so indignant? Are you sure you don't feel guilty?'

He stood his ground. 'Why should I? Don't tell me your mother isn't better off there than she would be on her own in one room.'

'No,' Frances said. 'That's not what I'm telling you.' She was amazed—it had always amazed her since she first noticed it—how persistently he refused to understand what he did not want to understand.

Now she had cornered him. He shook his head. 'I am not going into all that again,' he said. 'You know how I feel about it. We settled all that years ago. I don't know why you keep bringing it up.'

'Keep?' Frances repeated. 'I haven't mentioned it for months. Years.'

'Well, I don't know why you mention it at all. You know how I feel on the subject.'

'Yes.' She turned the sausages one by one on the wire grill. 'And that's what counts, isn't it? How *you* feel. That's all that does count.'

'That's right,' he said angrily. 'Put all the blame on me. Go ahead—if it makes you feel better.'

The thrust struck home. She said slowly, turning the rashers of bacon, 'Yes, it's my fault too.'

He stood irresolutely in the middle of the kitchen. She knew how he hated rows—was that why she encouraged them? Or was it the only way to involve him in anything important? It seemed so long since they had shared any real, living emotion except that generated by a row. Life had become somehow beige all over, not even grey.

'Look,' he said, and she observed him trying to retreat, to escape from a situation that demanded too much of him, 'it was a joint decision. We discussed it and we agreed that the home was the best place for her, no matter what it cost.'

'Yes,' she said.

'But all right,' he went on sharply, 'I was the one who refused to have her with us. Okay, that's my responsibility. I accept it. That lets you out. You've done your duty.'

The word struck a chill. Was it duty her mother had done for all those years, cooking and washing and cleaning, caring for a family, long after the easy days in India had ended? 'She brought me up,' she said slowly. 'And you say I've done my duty.'

Steve lit a cigarette. 'People don't have children for what they can get out of them. Your mother didn't have you so you could look after her in her old age.'

'No.' She turned the chops, prodding them and watching the blood and pink ooze come out. It was suddenly obscene.

'Well, then. I don't see what you're so worried about. She's perfectly all right, isn't she? She's comfortable and well looked after and she sees you every week. Lots of old people don't get any visitors at all.'

Suddenly it was all too much for her. 'I don't think she even knew me today,' she said, and started to cry.

Steve put his arm round her. 'Come on,' he said inadequately. 'It's not as bad as all that.'

Frances tried to fight back the tears but it was hopeless, like trying to squeeze toothpaste back into the tube. 'She just kept rambling,' she said shakily, 'on and on about the past, about Daddy and India and all that. She kept saying the same things over and over again.'

His arm tightened on her shoulders. 'Don't worry. Lots of old people live in the past. It's more real to them than the present.'

'Yes, I know.' Frances took a deep breath. 'But why is it? Don't you think it might be because they haven't got a present? If we made the present real enough for them, they could live in it. Couldn't they?'

Now that she seemed calmer, regardless of her actual words Steve took his arm away and she found time to think, I mishandled that. If I'd sobbed on his shoulder or hugged him or said, 'Oh Steve, help me . . .' before realising that she hadn't even wanted to.

'I don't know,' he said. 'You'd need a doctor to tell you that.'

The moment had gone. She blew her nose loudly, feeling a fool, and pulled out the grill. The food was cooked: more than cooked. 'Come on,' she said, 'we'd better eat this. What's left of it.'

10

IT ONLY took Steve a few days at the office to realise how much he liked being on the road. It was always so, but he forgot. Travelling in all weathers, meeting people constantly, fitting in with their schedules and eating too much or too little at irregular intervals, he often cursed his trade and yearned for a nine to five job. But in the intervals when he had one he was reminded how false this yearning was. Even a new office, with new subordinates and superiors, a new routine and environment and the satisfaction of promotion were not enough. He needed to be out on his own, away from everyone, in transit, free. Although he knew this freedom was illusory—there was, after all, always someone who paid his salary and therefore called the tune—he still treasured it. He cherished the image of himself as his own boss because nobody knew to the exact minute where he was and what he was doing; yet at the same time he recognised that he was deceiving himself. I am, he thought wryly, little better than a glorified long-distance lorry driver. And he could not explain why he loved his job, could not justify in logical terms the happiness it brought him. For it was more than mere satisfaction. Sometimes he felt that it was only when he was on the move that he could be really himself. And yet he did not know what he meant by this.

He thought it suited Frances better too. During this week he had been at home, longer than usual, she had been so tense and irritable—neurotic, he would almost have said if he had not known her so well. Whatever you thought of Frances, you could not call her neurotic. 'My wife is a very capable woman' would be an accurate description of her, if only it did not sound a little chilly, respectful rather than appreciative, and suggesting, however slightly, that he was less capable. For years she had done a job and run the house, both with perfect efficiency, making him feel he had almost imagined the absent-minded teenager who had been always late for lectures, worried about her work, living in a perpetual muddle, shy and awe-struck with her more Bohemian contemporaries and relying on him with his easy bonhomie to make friends for both of them. She had been so dependent, whereas now she was merely demanding. If that was the difference between youth and maturity it was a pity she had ever grown up.

He checked himself with a charge of unfairness. She was always, he remembered, a little frayed at the end of term and especially so when that involved leaving a school where she had been happy. And this time there was the added burden of moving, the new house and all that entailed. It was perfectly reasonable that she should be a little below par—only to be expected really. Still, it irked him. To be tired was one thing, to be demanding constant help in the house and garden was legitimate, but not to reopen the old issues of childlessness and her pathetic mother. The old woman was perfectly all right—a lot better off than most and certainly a lot happier than she would be in a house where she was unwelcome. It was not his fault that he didn't want her: it was asking a lot of any man to take an elderly relative, even his own, into his home, and his own, thank God, were not alive to be taken in—or left out. It was unreasonable of Frances to bring up the subject again when it had been settled, conclusively he thought, so long ago. It meant that she had never accepted his decision in her heart and that was galling: an instance of attempted domination. But what was the point of a trial of strength if she was unhappy when he stood firm and yet would surely despise him if he gave in to her? And anyway, the arrangement simply would not work.

The question of children was a different matter altogether, though this too he had thought was settled. In a way it would have been easier if the medics had been able to pin down the reason, to discover the fault (he hated this emotive word but could, in his hurried thoughts, find no other) in one or other of them, no matter which. It would at least have put an end to the unspoken accusations, the tacit apportioning of blame (another emotive word). He wondered if it was this uncertainty that had stood in the way of adoption, making each of them draw back with the silent thought: If I wasn't married to *you* I could have a child of my own.

For it was not the same to him. He would not have been able to look at the child and think: You are mine. I created you. He would not have been able to see himself in his son or daughter, in a turn of the head, in a gesture, in a tone of voice. Despite all they said about environment and imitation, it was not the same as knowing that this new being had come from you, that it resembled you because it could not help itself, because you had given it life. You would only have given it a home and your name. None of these feelings could be put into words and so it was a subject he preferred not to discuss. The emotions were too primitive and as such a little ridiculous.

He supposed that Frances felt the same. She would not have carried the child inside her, would not have been through the pregnancy and childbirth, whatever that meant to a woman. But he did not know for sure how she felt, since he had never asked her. He would have been perfectly willing to go ahead with adoption if that would have made her happy, but he preferred that the impetus should come from her. It was not his place to agitate for it when it was apparently *her* thwarted maternal instincts that were causing distress. He did not want to need anything so badly that lack of it could seriously affect his life; it was a sign of weakness and as such made you vulnerable. And once you were vulnerable you were done for. In his experience, discussing a problem generally only succeeded in magnifying it: it was better to think out, alone in your own mind, how you felt and then express a decision. Too much verbal analysis could uncover facts that were better hidden. If you could not change something it was better not to know too much about it.

In any case, he could not see how adoption would improve their basic relationship. Here, too, Frances had changed imperceptibly, just as she had put on weight. She was more often agreeable than eager for sex, and more often disinclined than agreeable. He did not want to think that this was because he had failed to give her a child; after all, she was not less attractive to him because she had failed to produce one. Less attractive she certainly was, however, but he put that down to the passage of time. No woman could retain her original sexual magnetism for fourteen years, particularly one who did not see the necessity for experimentation to off-set the inevitable monotony of repetition. But even this attitude of hers, which had disturbed him at first, brought its own rewards. It provided easy justification of his experiments away from home, which sent him back to her refreshed and tolerant.

Crawling home through the rush-hour traffic he looked with comfortable scorn at the other commuters for whom this ordeal would go on day in and year out. It was the weekend again. On Monday he would be back on the road.

11

'I THINK I shall do everything white to begin with,' Frances said, 'and then we can decide where we want colour.'

'Good idea,' Steve said. They were sitting in front of the television, now fixed, which they had switched off at the end of the evening. They had had a good dinner and were mellow from a bottle of wine and several whiskies: it was their usual practice, never stated but always adhered to, to make each evening before a trip into a little festivity. He approved of this: it meant that they separated on good terms and he could devote his entire mind to the interviews ahead without any untidy remnants of argument to clutter his brain. And besides, he basically preferred harmony. Disagreements were messy and usually achieved nothing.

'I'll try to get it done while you're away,' Frances said. She yawned and slid her feet out of her shoes.

'I'll be back on Wednesday,' he said. 'It's only a quick trip.' The prospect of it warmed him; he felt alert and benevolent towards the whole world. 'Don't work too hard,' he said to her. 'I'll give you a hand when I get back.'

'Okay,' Frances said. 'I'll just do what I can. Then on Thursday maybe we can discuss colours.' She preferred him in this mood too, come to that, but she wished that they could more often achieve it without alcohol. She was never sure that goodwill created by drinking was really genuine; this, she supposed, was a leftover streak of Puritanism which she ought to eradicate. 'Do you think we should give a house-warming party?' she asked. She liked asking his advice at times like this.

'Oh, I suppose so. But we can decide that later.'

'All right. Only we owe an awful lot of people dinner already. We didn't have anyone round for weeks while we were packing and we went out quite a bit.' She ticked them off on her fingers. 'There's Claire and Jimmy, Jan and Peter, Freddy and Pam,

John and Susan, the Harpers . . . oh, heaps more. So a party might be the easiest way.'

Steve nodded. 'Yes, it might. It'll cost a packet though; still, I suppose we can afford it.'

'Oh, I think so.' She laughed. 'I feel rather reckless.'

Getting up to pour himself a fresh drink he paused in front of her chair. 'How reckless?'

'Oh, it's just my August salary,' she said quickly. 'It always takes me that way, don't you remember? The illusion of wealth. I forget how long it's got to last. Longer, this time.'

He stroked her knee. 'Oh, you'll soon get another job,' he said, 'a clever girl like you.'

She knew what the stroking meant and shifted her legs. 'Shall we go to bed then?' she said in case the movement seemed discouraging.

But Steve did not move. He crouched in front of her chair, the whisky swaying perilously in its glass. 'Why?' he said. 'What's wrong with right here?' Completely sober, he would not have attempted this, having had many rejections; after a few drinks he forgot her resistance to unconventional places. In any case he liked to make love to Frances the night before a trip: it seemed appropriate. Ideally, he thought they should have lived during a war, with the added danger involved in each parting to give spice to the proceedings. At the very least he should have been a sailor. If I'd had the guts, he thought ironically.

Frances moved uncomfortably. She did not like his hand up her skirt and wished he would remember that. It reminded her too much of their courting days and all the mingled emotions of guilty excitement and furtive watchfulness. Surely it was these very feelings that you escaped in marriage? 'It's so much more comfortable in bed,' she said, standing up.

He stood up with her and she said, 'Oh, careful,' a second before he spilt some of his drink. He caught her round the waist.

'What's wrong with the floor?' he said. 'I bet the previous owners used it.' He laughed. 'That's probably what your famous white marks are.'

'Oh Steve, really.' Frances disengaged herself. She hated vulgarity: it seemed to have so little to do with love.

'All right,' he said, offended, draining his glass. 'Have it your own way.' He followed her into the bedroom. 'You generally do.'

'That's not fair.' She looked round her vaguely, as if for help. 'It's not my way or your way—it's our way. Or it should be.'

'Yes, it should.' He looked grim.

'Steve.' She put out a placatory hand; she hated to quarrel just before he went away. 'Darling?' she said hopefully.

He pulled her down on the bed. It was a long time since they had made love with their clothes on and this, because novel, could be exciting, as exciting in its way as nakedness with a new partner. He hung on to this thought as they began; it was a help. And there was the spontaneity of it. He wished he could make Frances see the importance of spontaneity in marriage. Anything to get away from the deadly routine of ritual undressing, washing and teeth-cleaning.

It's as if we weren't married at all, Frances thought. She closed her eyes and all the years of security fell away. She remembered the powerful, energetic young man her parents had considered 'a bit on the rough side' and how he had seemed to her twice as alive as anyone she knew, with his unlimited vitality and self-assurance. Even his accent, before he tamed it, had been an added attraction. And the fact that he had a job, and a highly competitive one, made him a member of the real world, far removed from the pale academics who escorted her friends. He had given her an extra dimension.

She kept her eyes shut against the light. She really preferred darkness: it was more romantic and made it easier to concentrate. He was big and heavy on top of her. She wanted to respond; she did respond. But there was something missing: an element of danger. She was ashamed of herself for feeling this. It was not his fault but they ought to have been able to talk about it. Making love should bring them so close that they could talk about anything, unhampered by masculine pride or feminine reticence. If they could have reaffirmed their love for each other, the importance of their marriage as an end in itself. . . .

It was all over. They rolled apart and had cigarettes. Why couldn't she show more pleasure? Steve wondered. Didn't she know how vital it was to him to see that he had given her something? He smoked in silence, staring up at the ceiling.

'That was nice,' Frances said. She hoped he had enjoyed himself. It had been tempting to open her eyes, but that was a two-way traffic and he took it as a personal affront if she was not visibly in ecstasy. It was easier with her eyes closed. Why did he have to have such high standards? In the early years it had been such a luxurious experience, full of love; now it seemed a constant athletic striving after some impossible perfection.

'Mm.'

He sounded sleepy; she raised herself on one elbow to look at him and noticed that he immediately closed his eyes. 'Are you tired?'

'Mm.' He sighed. 'Got a big day ahead.'

She got up heavily and began to undress. After a moment he did the same.

12

HE HAD not meant to go there at all. At least, if he had, the thought had been too deeply buried to be noticeable. He had not been thinking of her, had not thought of her for days, though at first this had taken a conscious effort. And the motorway had lent itself to the deception: for the greater part of his journey he had been heading for both destinations, so there was no decision involved. Even when he had finally taken the wrong fork it had been subconsciously, almost as if he hoped he would not notice and when he did . . . well, it was not much out of his way, there was all the bother of being in the right lane to change direction, and he could do with a break and a cup of tea: one place was as good as another.

It was only now as he stood in the foyer that the full import of his action came home to him. The place was deserted, looking more seedy and downbeat than ever; there was still time to retreat. But after a moment's hesitation he walked up to the desk and pressed the bell. It sounded and ceased. He waited in the peculiarly heavy silence of afternoon in an hotel. Nobody came. It was only then that he realised he had been expecting Ella to emerge instantly and, what was more, be surprised and pleased to see him. He rang again, longer this time, keeping his finger on the bell. A girl appeared, the same blonde, sulky girl who had served their breakfast.

'Yes?' she said, in a tone that questioned his right to be there at all, let alone demanding her presence in such a peremptory manner.

He said, 'Are you serving afternoon tea?' though he knew perfectly well that she would have to if he insisted. It was one of Jack's eccentricities that despite the somewhat squalid appearance of his hotel it offered amenities normally provided only by more opulent establishments. It was curious, he said, how many of his tea customers stayed for bed and breakfast and since his staff were on duty anyway they might as well be working.

The girl consulted her watch as a formality. 'I s'pose so,' she said with reluctance.

He made his voice as pleasant as possible. 'Thank you very much.' And walked into the dining-room. It was empty, the grubby white table-cloths laid for dinner. The girl followed him and stood in the doorway.

'D'you like to order now?' she said loudly.

He looked round for a menu but there wasn't one. 'A pot of tea and some cake,' he said, but her expression was so uncomprehending that he added, 'or some biscuits. Whatever you've got; I'm not fussy.' He smiled at her; her goodwill might be his only bridge to Ella.

She sniffed and picked at a tooth with a varnished finger nail. 'Just as well,' she said and stalked out. The doors swung violently after her.

He waited. He looked round, half expecting Ella, or at any rate Jack, to come in. He had a cigarette. The place was funereal, shrouded in silence. Ten minutes passed, slowly. Christ, he thought irritably, how long does it take to boil a kettle and open a packet of buns?

The girl reappeared, kicking the door open and shooting quickly through it before it closed in her face. She carried a tray bearing tea, milk and sugar, a cup and saucer, and two plates, one containing an assortment of four cakes. These items she unloaded one by one, putting them down on the table with a great deal of noise.

'That'll be three and six,' she said in a weary voice. 'D'you like to pay now?'

This was his opportunity. He took out five shillings and gave it to her, saying warmly, 'Keep the change.'

She spun on her heel and turned away. He added casually, as if he had just thought of it, 'Oh, is Mr Roberts anywhere about? I'm a friend of his.' It would help if Jack was out; he could do without his comments.

The girl half turned. He noticed the dark roots of her hair, the sudden draught of stale sweat. Now you, he thought, I really might kick out of bed.

'He's out,' she said.

So far so good. 'Oh. Never mind. Is Miss Patterson around?'

She stared at him vacantly and his stomach gave an annoying, ominous lurch. 'Who?' she said.

He tried again. 'Ella Patterson.'

Her expression cleared slightly but now it took on a hint of curiosity. 'Oh. Yeah. She's in the office.'

The accent was curious: local overlaid with pop American. 'Could I see her for a minute?' He began pouring tea to give himself something to do.

The girl frowned. 'I dunno. She's typing.'

Suddenly it took a great effort to be civil. 'Well, could you ask her to spare me a minute?'

Her gaze became insolent. She had small blue eyes, like a china doll, and each lash stood out separately, stiff with black mascara, giving her a wide-eyed, startled appearance. I wouldn't employ you for long, my girl, he thought. Was this an example of the staff problem Jack was always talking about?

'You a friend of hers?' she asked, not moving.

The description struck him as quaint but it obviously had to be accepted. 'Yes.'

She turned on her heel. 'Okay, I'll tell her.' And disappeared.

He drank his tea and surveyed the cakes. They formed a singularly unappetising group and he realised that he had lost whatever appetite he'd had. There was a rock bun that defied the pressure of his fingers, an almond slice, a fairy cake bright yellow and studded with small black currants, and something else covered in sticky pink icing embedded with white shredded coconut. He selected the almond slice.

He ate slowly but he was on his second cup of tea before Ella appeared. He heard her footsteps approaching and knew they were not those of the other girl. He forced himself not to watch the swing doors. She came in and walked over to his table before speaking.

'Well,' she said softly.

He looked up. She was just the same and he felt a quite ridiculous pleasure at seeing her: the long hair tied back with a velvet bow, the dark-painted, greenish eyes, the pale, thin lips.

'Marcia said I had a friend waiting to see me,' she said. 'Only I haven't got any friends. So I came right away.'

He collected the opening he had planned. 'I was passing so I thought I'd give you a surprise.' It sounded trite in the extreme.

She smiled and the smile suggested that she knew all about his taking the wrong fork without noticing. 'Well, you did that all right.' She pulled out a chair and sat down opposite him. She was wearing the same outfit as the other girl but it could hardly have looked more different.

'You look very nice in your uniform,' he said in his cheerful, just-passing tone.

She accepted the compliment. 'Yes. I always look good in black. Isn't that lucky?'

What it was, he thought, to have such confidence, and at her age. 'Very lucky,' he agreed.

She was studying him. 'I didn't expect to see you again,' she said, but with neither regret nor relief.

'Oh well,' he said casually. 'I come up this way pretty often.'

She clasped her small brown hands in front of her on the table. Her face was still as pale as ever. 'Where are you heading for this time?' she said.

The truth was easier than a lie but he still felt foolish. 'Manchester.'

She raised her eyebrows. 'Oh. Aren't you a bit out of your way?'

'Not much.' He hesitated. 'I felt like a cup of tea.' Then he looked at her, fair and square, and suddenly they both laughed and he felt better.

'Is it stewed?' she said. 'I bet it is. Marcia makes it at four o'clock and just leaves it on the hot-plate.'

He smiled. 'That's what it tastes like.'

'Then I won't have any. I'll have a cake though.'

He felt absurd relief that her appetite remained the same. 'They're all yours,' he said, 'but you eat at your own risk.'

Ella plunged her teeth into the rock bun. He watched her and thought there was something predatory, almost carnivorous, about the way she ate. He half-expected to see blood dripping from her mouth. She was, he thought, the only girl he had ever seen who could make eating into a sexy act. The vigour with which she did it suggested all kinds of energy for other things. 'Is it nice?' he said.

She waited until her mouth was empty. 'It's awful,' she said, 'but I only had a sandwich for lunch.' She started on the fairy cake.

'Jack ought to feed his staff better than that.'

She shrugged. 'Oh, he does. Only we were busy and by the time I got my lunch I didn't want it. There's something about serving dozens of people with meat and two veg that puts you right off.'

The Cockney was uppermost today. He found himself listening for nuances of Oxford or Kensington, whatever it was. 'How's the job going?'

She brushed crumbs from her fingers. 'It's all right. A bit hard on the feet.'

He looked at her feet, sandalled but clean. Her legs were brown and bare and she had hitched up her uniform skirt to a fashionable level. 'Marcia'—he made fun of the so appropriate name with his voice—'said you were doing some typing. That must be easier.'

'Oh yes, it is.' She had finished eating and was watching him again.

'I didn't know you could type. It must be one of your many hidden talents.' He badly wanted to establish this kind of mood.

'It is. Well, not really. I mean I'm not a typist. I just type better than Marcia or Jack.'

So it was Jack already. He should have known; he had expected it really. But not the sinking heart it caused. 'So you got the job,' he said.

She nodded. 'Actually, I'd better be getting back. There's a hell of a lot to do. Jack's frightfully behind with letters and the accounts are in an awful mess.'

The tone of efficiency was both alarming and attractive. He said, wanting to keep her and not knowing how, 'Well, surely you can have a cigarette first. Or is this one of your non-smoking days?'

'No.' She took one. He hoped that she would steady his hand as he lit it for her; he would have liked even that much contact with her. But she did not. He decided to be blunt.

'What time do you get off duty?'

She watched him for a long time before answering. 'Eight o'clock. Why?'

'I thought I might take you out to dinner.'

She smiled. 'Is that what you thought?'

'Well . . .' He let it go. 'I know what a hungry girl you are.'

She looked at him, uncomfortably calculating. 'Are you hungry too?'

He let his eyes give the real answer. 'I always like to eat well when I can.'

'Can't you eat well in Manchester?' she said.

'Oh yes,' he said. 'But not when I happen to be in Birmingham.'

She looked at him for a long, appraising moment, squashing her cigarette half-smoked into the crumby, sticky cake paper. A charred smell arose.

'Well, I'm off duty at eight,' she said, and got up suddenly. She was out of the room before he could think of a parting remark.

He went to a news theatre and saw the programme round twice.

13

WHEN HE got back Jack was in the bar, which was fairly crowded, and they exchanged a few obligatory remarks about Ella with a lot of laughter that was not, on Steve's part at least, entirely sincere. Even Jack did not seem quite as cocky as usual; his final comment, as Ella came down the stairs, was delivered in an undertone and struck Steve as oddly out of character and therefore disturbing. 'She's a funny girl,' Jack said, busy with glasses, not quite looking at Steve. 'Sometimes I get the feeling she could eat the pair of us for breakfast.' And his laugh, which was probably meant to be full of bravado, sounded uneasy.

Steve finished his whisky and got up to meet Ella. He was surprised to see that she was wearing her original shirt and jeans, her hair hanging loose. 'Where d'you want to eat?' he asked. He had planned on taking her somewhere quite smart and her clothes disappointed him.

'We can eat at the fair,' she said.

'The fair?' At first he thought it was a new restaurant he didn't know. Or a discothèque or something similar that would doubtless make him feel very old.

'Mm. There's a fair on.' Her eyes were dancing; he had never seen her so animated. 'I love fairs. I was planning to go before you turned up.'

They walked to the door. 'Oh well,' he said, 'far be it from me to interfere with your arrangements.'

'Well,' she said placidly, 'you should have given me more notice.' Outside on the pavement she turned round and smiled at him. 'Poor Steven,' she said, 'have I upset all your plans?'

'Not at all,' he said stiffly. 'I just thought you might enjoy a good dinner at a decent restaurant.'

'And I turn up looking like a tramp.' He opened the door for her and they got into the car. To his surprise she leaned across and kissed him, very lightly, her lips hardly brushing his mouth.

Her hair swung across him as she moved. 'It's not your idea of fun, is it?' she said. 'Are you afraid there won't be time for bed?'

He started the car. 'Well,' he said, 'it'll be a pity if there isn't but that's not the only thing I came for.'

'Isn't it?' She sounded surprised. 'What did you come for then?'

'To see you.' The truth and the simplicity of this perturbed him: it seemed to suggest a need far greater and more dangerous than sex.

'Gosh,' she said.

They drove for a while in silence and then he said, 'Look, this is ridiculous. You really must direct me.'

'It's all right,' she said. 'We're nearly there. First left, then right, then right again.'

The fair was in full cry, shrill with teenagers and small children with harassed parents. 'Aeroplanes' swung out above their heads. The Big Wheel, its seats rocking in the wind, revolved slowly. Thumping collisions resounded from the Dodgem Cars where a lot of lads about Ella's age were systematically bumping into each other. The low green Caterpiller rolled back its skin and some rather dishevelled people emerged. Various stallholders shouted the respective merits of Hoop-la, Houdini, ladies sawn in half and the Tunnel of Love. Above it all came the piercing shrieks of the pleasantly terrified occupants of the Big Dipper as they hurtled up and down. The noise mingled with a blare of pop and honky tonk music from all over the ground.

They walked round, not speaking, and surveyed it all. The grass was soft and muddy beneath their feet, thick with bottles, cigarette packets, ice cream cartons and candy floss sticks. Ella breathed a deep sigh.

'Isn't it wonderful?' she said. 'I want to go on everything.'

*

In the Dive Bomber he felt quite sick as they seemed to turn over in two directions at once. Ella fell against him and he held on to her but wondered if it should not really be the other way round.

'I never went to that big fair,' she said. 'Did you? The one in London—oh, years ago.'

He shook his head. The machine gave another sickening lurch and spun round on itself. He shut his eyes.

'They had something there that revolved,' she said, 'like a
drum, and when it got to a certain speed they took the floor
away. Everyone thought they'd fall but they didn't: they were
pinned to the wall. It was scientific.'

*

On the Merry-go-round he felt exceedingly silly astride a gar-
ishly painted horse. Ella in front of him patted her mount affectionately.

'I never had a horse,' she said. She turned round. 'Never ever.
Isn't that sad?'

'Very,' he said. He was amazed that she seemed to enjoy the
sedate motion just as much as the jerky revolutions of the Dive
Bomber.

His expression was tragic. 'And now it's too late,' she said.

*

She insisted on candy floss. Steve watched her consume it, her
face almost concealed behind the huge pink mass.

'I don't know how you can eat that stuff,' he said indulgently.
He felt slightly better now that his feet were back on the ground,
though he doubted if that would last long.

'You forget,' Ella said. 'I'm the girl who can eat anything.'

*

In the Ghost Train he said to her, 'Is this really your idea of a
good time?'

She giggled without answering and reached out a hand to start
something he felt bound to stop.

'Don't be so stuffy,' she said. A skeleton glowing with phos-
phorescent paint swung out and nearly touched their faces.

'It's a short ride,' he told her severely.

'I only meant it as an hors-d'œuvre.'

*

He failed abysmally to win her a coconut or anything else at
the Hoop-la stall. He threw eighteen humiliating rings, one after
the other, because Ella kept urging him to have another go.
Everyone else at the stall was about fifteen and the owner kept
looking at him with shrew, amused eyes. Finally Steve said, 'I may

as well give up.' He smiled at her, wanting to walk away, if possible to sit down, most of all wanting a drink, but she said, 'Oh, I *must* try,' in tones of such passion that he could not argue with her. The first ring went wildly astray. The second hung tantalisingly for a moment before falling off. It was then that he realised he did not entirely want her to succeed. The third ring caught and held.

Ella let out a shriek of excitement and jumped up and down. 'I've won, I've won,' she shouted in ecstasy.

'So you have,' Steve said.

She ignored him, giving her whole attention to the difficult matter of choice, as the stall owner, much amused, said, 'What'll you have, luv?' She looked all round the prizes for a long minute and finally pointed.

'I'll have that.'

The man detached a bright pink rabbit with floppy ears and a check waistcoat and handed it to her.

'Oh,' she breathed, holding it reverently and turning to Steve. 'Isn't it lovely?'

He pulled her away, embarrassed by the stares and smiles of the other competitors. 'D'you really like it?' he said. 'It's really rather hideous, isn't it?' And despised himself for not being more gracious and for wishing he had won the absurd thing for her.

'Of course it's hideous,' she said, stroking the nylon fur. 'But I love it. I wanted it all along.' She pressed the rabbit against her face. 'It's just like one I had in hospital when I was six.'

They were walking away from the stall across the squelchy ground. 'What were you in hospital for?' he asked.

Absorbed in the rabbit, she took some time to answer. 'Tonsils,' she said eventually. 'They put a funny sort of oilskin thing on me and when I asked why the nurse said, "Oh, we're going out in the rain." I was ever so surprised. When I woke up there was blood all over the sheet.'

*

The only way he could get to sit down was by taking her to see a man who sawed his partner in half. Ella watched intently until her fascination annoyed him.

'It's all a trick,' he said.

'Well, of course.'

'No, I meant surely you've seen it before.' He began to explain to her how it was done but she did not appear to be listening. When the performance was over she turned to him, her eyes shining.

'Wouldn't it be lovely,' she said, 'if you could really do that?'

*

She was just as enthralled by a man who squeezed pennies from his partner's nose and ears. The audience was full of children—the age group had dropped considerably—and they squealed appreciatively as each penny fell with a resounding clang into a tin box. Then the man called up one of the boys and proceeded to squeeze pennies from *his* nose and ears. The squeals became shriller and even more appreciative.

'Funny how much they love it,' Steve said. He felt safe because the audience was so young. 'They must know how it's done but they still love it.'

Ella turned her head. She looked cross. 'Shut up,' she said. 'You're only jealous.'

*

They went on the Big Wheel and it stopped when their seat was at the top. Ella swung her legs and the seat began to move gently.

'Don't,' Steve said. He had been keeping still on purpose.

'Are you frightened?' Ella said mischievously. She looked down, leaning so far over the side that he thought she would fall out. 'It's like looking over the edge of the world,' she said.

Steve mentally cursed his age, his stomach, his attitude and most of all the fair for being there. 'It certainly is,' he agreed. He nerved himself to glance below: it was getting dark and the many-coloured lights of the fair glittered beneath them and the music rose thinly through the air. 'It's rather beautiful,' he admitted. He wanted very much to share her enjoyment but he also felt that she wanted him to drop a façade he was not yet prepared to do without.

The wheel remained motionless. They could hardly have been more isolated. The whole scene took on a curiously unreal intensity for him and he thought that Ella must be feeling it too for she looked at him suddenly and said, 'Steven, can't you enjoy yourself? What's the good of being all uninhibited in bed if you don't know how to have fun?'

He looked at her. They were both quite serious and very gentle.

'I'd like to,' he said, 'but I'm twice your age. Maybe I've forgotten.'

'Then let me remind you.' As he spoke the wheel began to move again. 'Come on,' she said. 'Relax. Let's live a little.'

*

He found, once he stopped fighting whatever it was, that it was surprisingly easy to share her enthusiasm. They climbed into a Dodgem Car and bumped energetically into everyone in sight. It was almost therapeutic. I must, he thought, be a very savage driver at heart, however well I suppress it. Coming after the curious peace of the Big Wheel it seemed appropriate. When they got off he felt mean and said, 'Would you like another go?'

She shook her head.

'I meant so you can drive,' he said.

She smiled. 'You really enjoyed that, didn't you?' she said. 'You see? It's not so difficult, is it?'

'What?'

'To have fun.'

The whole situation suddenly choked him and he looked away. 'Would *you* like another go?' she said.

He pulled himself together. 'No. We haven't been on everything once yet.'

*

They drank fizzy drinks. They ate crisps and sausage rolls and bars of chocolate. They went on the Big Dipper and nearly lost their stomachs as they zoomed up and down. The noise of the machine on the rails was deafening and it moved with such violence that it seemed they must either be thrown out or derailed. They staggered off at the end and fell into the calm of the Caterpiller. When the cover went over them he kissed Ella in the greenish gloom. She smiled at him and said, 'You're getting younger all the time.' They wasted sixpence after sixpence on the One-armed Bandits and were about to go dismally on to pennies when at the final tug there came a tinkling gush of money.

'There,' said Ella triumphantly. 'Isn't that the most beautiful
sound in the world?' And to Steve, who until then would have
voted for champagne corks, it suddenly was. They scooped out
their winnings and counted them. 'Has it paid for everything?'
Ella asked. 'Have we made a profit?' She was hopping from one
foot to the other and still clutching the pink rabbit. 'We've won
seven and six,' he told her, and she skipped all the way to the
Tunnel of Love until she got so far ahead that he had to run
after her. The crowds were thinning out; people were going home.
He realised that he had no idea of the time and did not want to
look at his watch. His eleven o'clock appointment in Manchester
the next morning seemed very remote. In the darkness of the tunnel they hugged each other like all the other couples and she
kissed him long and hard and deep. 'Come on,' she said. 'Let's
go back to the hotel.'

14

'You were quite different tonight,' he told her.

'Same girl, different angle.' Her voice was muffled in the pillow.

He stroked her back. It had been different, at once less exciting and more satisfying, but that was not what he meant. 'No, at the fair,' he said. He kissed her shoulder blades; he felt immensely contented and at peace. The world outside had receded to an enormous distance. With a little luck it might not be there at all.

'Tell me,' she said.

'Oh . . .' He spoke slowly; his whole mood was lazy and relaxed. 'You were so much younger. Like a child. I mean that as a compliment.'

'Of course.' One eye looked at him mischievously through a curtain of hair.

'Oh . . .' He put an arm round her shoulders. 'You're gorgeous. D'you know that? Would you be insulted if I said I felt like your father?'

She turned her head and grinned at him. 'You're a bit incestuous,' she said. 'Dad.'

He shook her gently. 'I meant at the fair.'

'Oh, the fair.' She spoke as if it was already remote. 'You quite enjoyed it, didn't you? After all.'

'Yes, I did.' He smiled. 'You were quite right.'

'Don't you have any children?' she asked thoughtfully.

'No.' He considered the question. 'Is it so obvious?' Her skin was smooth and warm under his hand.

'Well, if you had you'd take them to fairs, wouldn't you?'

'Yes,' he said. 'I suppose I would.'

'Maybe that's why you felt like my father,' she said, with satisfaction at a problem solved.

'Come to that,' he said, 'don't you have parents?'

Her shoulders moved as she tried to shrug while lying on her stomach. 'Somewhere. They were in London when I saw them last.'

'And when was that?'

She shook her head. 'A year ago. Maybe more.'

'What are they like?'

Again the attempted shrug. 'Oh, you know. A mother and a father.'

'Aren't they worried about you?'

'I don't know. Maybe they were at first but I expect they've got over it by now.' She smiled. 'I send them postcards from time to time. You know. "Having a good time, glad you're not here." That kind of thing.'

'So you ran away from home,' he said softly.

'No. I walked out.'

'All right.' The effort at dignity touched him. 'But why? Were they so awful?'

'No. Not at all.'

'Then why?'

'Oh . . . I didn't want to stay there, that's all.'

'But you must have had a reason.'

He felt her body stiffen under his hand. 'Let's say I wanted to live my own life.'

'And they would have stopped you?'

'Well . . . it was difficult for them. I mean with the neighbours and all that jazz. "What's your daughter doing these days?"— "Oh, she's a tramp, didn't you know? She's getting on very well."'

'Yes,' he said. 'I see. And that was all you wanted to do?'

'What? Tramping?'

The dual connotation bothered him. 'Well . . . being on the road?'

'It's fun.'

'Is it really?'

'You should try it,' she said defiantly. 'But you won't, will you? You're too secure and comfortable with your nice house and your good job and your steady income and your wife.'

'Yes,' he said equably. 'That's all true. And I'm also too old.'

'I don't think you were ever young enough,' she said. She sat up and her hair fell forward over her pale breasts. 'I think you were always too old.'

'Don't be angry,' he said, pulling her down again. 'We can't all be as young as you. It's not our fault, you know.'

'Whose fault is it then?'

'Oh, I don't know.' He pushed the subject away. 'Don't go on. You'll have me talking about life in a minute. Life with a capital L.' He smiled. 'And then I shall get pompous and maudlin and you'll be bored.'

'All right.' She rested her head on his chest, her sharp little chin digging into his ribs. 'How about death then? D'you get pompous and maudlin about that?'

He shifted uncomfortably. 'I hardly ever think about it.'

'Deliberately?'

'Well . . .' He considered. 'Yes, I suppose so.'

'Why?'

The sharp, persistent questioning struck him as typical of youth. 'It's not exactly a pleasant subject.'

'It's interesting. That's why I think about it. It doesn't matter if it's pleasant or not.'

'Oh well,' he said. 'That's a point of view.'

'Does it frighten you?' She turned her face to look at him, relieving the pressure on his ribs.

He tried to be honest though he could feel his mind reluctantly approaching the problem and trying to slide round it. 'Yes, I suppose it does.'

'Poor Steven.'

'There's no need to sound so smug. You're not immortal either.'

'I know.' She was almost purring. 'But it doesn't frighten me.'

'Then you're very lucky. Or maybe it's just too far away to seem real.'

'No.' She sat up again, suddenly very alert. 'It never seems real; it can't. I mean it's an impossible thing to believe in, really. You know. It can't happen to me. That kind of thing.' He nodded. 'But that's not why it doesn't frighten me. It can't frighten me because I know when it comes I shan't have missed anything.'

He reached for cigarettes. 'Go on.'

'Well.' Her face was alive, wide awake. 'I had a boy friend ages ago and we used to meet in the churchyard. We went round all the graveyards in the district; we used to make love on the tombstones and all that jazz.'

'Delightful,' he said ironically.

'It was exciting. Anyway, apart from that, we used to wander round and read all the inscriptions and wonder what the people were like and what sort of lives they'd led and I thought, Yes, that would be the only awful thing that could happen, to die with things left out. And I sort of pictured my tombstone saying: "Here Lies Ella Patterson who died before she'd done everything," and it was so terrible I vowed I'd never let it happen. And I was never afraid of death again.'

'But,' he said, half-chilled, half-enchanted by her speech, 'you *can't* do everything.'

She shook her head. 'Not everything there is, no. But everything you want to do. That's what I meant.'

The egotism of youth, he thought. But he was not sure if it was mere youth or simply Ella herself. 'You're very ambitious,' he said.

'Not really.'

'Well, confident then.'

She smiled. 'That's rule number one,' she said. 'If you don't believe in yourself how can you expect anyone else to?'

'Oh well,' he said, 'with an attitude like that, I expect you *will* do everything you want to.'

'There you are.' She looked triumphant. 'You see? You believe in me already. You've proved my theory. But do you see why it's not ambitious?'

'No. You tell me.'

'Well.' She was clearly enjoying herself. 'It's not a matter of how much or how little you do; it's just a matter of deciding *what* you want to do and doing *that*. So if you wanted to work in a bank, say, and you did, they could put on your tombstone "He worked in a bank all his life." And that would be all right.'

'I see.'

'Do you? Really?'

'I think so.'

She relaxed. 'It's nice, isn't it? It's something to hold on to.'

There was something here that eluded him. 'D'you mean . . . like religion?'

'Oh no.' She seemed surprised. 'More like a tow-rope. Anyway, that's it. I don't think I want to talk about it any more.'

'And that means you won't.'

'That's right.'

'Yes, of course. You told me that when we first met.'

'Mm.' She yawned. 'I probably did.'

'It's a lovely philosophy.'

She shrugged. 'You could have it too.'

He let that go. 'Well, at least everyone knows where they stand with you—if you never do anything against your will.'

'You mean, like sex?' She looked at him sharply.

'Among other things.'

'But that was what you meant.' She frowned. 'It's on your mind a lot, isn't it?'

He laughed, disconcerted. 'You make it sound like an obsession.'

'Well, you do think about it a lot, don't you?'

He gave in. 'A fair amount, I suppose.'

'Mm. I could tell straightaway. You were thinking about it all the way in the car, that first time. Then when we got to the hotel you went off it. Do you want some more now?'

She might have been offering him a second cup of coffee. He shook his head. 'I'm very tired and I have to get up at dawn.'

'You'd sleep better. But it's funny you thinking about it so much. I never think about it. I mean it's lovely to do but it's boring to think about. It's not an interesting subject. You couldn't walk round thinking about food all the time.' She paused. 'Unless you were starving, of course.' She looked at him intently. 'Are you?'

'Hardly.'

'Oh, I don't mean now. Usually. At home for instance. Doesn't your wife like it?'

'Yes, of course.'

'It's not of course.' She brooded. 'I wonder what you do wrong.'

'Charming. I like the way you're so sure it's my fault.'

'Then there *is* something wrong.' She pounced like a cat.

'Oh, Ella,' he said. 'Leave it alone.'

'Maybe it's your other girls. Like me. Maybe that puts her off.'

'Don't be silly,' he said sharply. 'She doesn't know.'

'I wonder. Well, maybe that's the trouble. Maybe she'd find you more attractive if she did know.'

'Ella,' he said patiently, 'don't you think you're a little young to play marriage guidance counsellor?'

She grinned, challenging him. 'If you're making a mess of it at your age, who are you to tell me I'm too young to know better?'

'*All* right.' He gave up. 'You've got me. I'm sure there's a perfect answer to that, only I'm too tired to think of it.' He swung his legs over the edge of the bed with great reluctance. 'I'll have to be going. I'll only get about three hours' sleep as it is.'

She looked up, all the challenge and arrogance gone. 'You can sleep here.'

'I can't sleep with anyone in a single bed.' (She had made him come to her room.) 'Not even you.' He touched her face. 'I'm sorry.'

She pouted.

'Next time you must come to my room.' He hesitated. 'I hope there will be a next time. I'd like to see you again.'

She watched him dressing. 'Why?'

He laughed. 'Why indeed? To be told I'm stuffy, too old, unhappily married, obsessed with sex and afraid of death. I can't imagine why I should want to see you again. But I do.'

She bounced up and down on the bed and made various obscene gestures. 'Is this the reason?'

'That's part of it. But only part.' (He nearly added 'I'm afraid.') 'It seems, in spite of all I've just said, that I still find you fun to be with.'

'Well, well.' She was eyeing him closely.

'So now you know.' He smiled at her, hoping he had not said too much, and glanced at his watch. 'And I really must go to bed. Be a good girl till Daddy gets back.'

'Wait.' She jumped off the bed. 'I'll come with you if you like.'

'Yes, I would like.' He waited for her to dress but she went and stood by the door like an eager terrier. 'Not like that,' he said.

'Why not?'

'Well, you can't walk through the hotel with nothing on.'

'Stark naked,' she said. Her accent suddenly became extremely refined. 'Harry Starkers.'

He laughed against his will. 'Come on, Ella. Put something on. I must get to bed.'

She struck a dramatic pose and did some swift, incomprehensible mime. 'I come like this or not at all.'

'Oh, all right,' he said grudgingly. 'But what if we meet someone in the corridor?'

'You walk in front,' she suggested, 'and pretend you're not with me.'

Once safely behind the door of his room they fell on the bed and exploded with foolish mirth, although they had met no one.

'And how,' he said, 'are you going to manage in the morning when there *will* be people about?'

She shrugged and began to undress him. 'I'm not on duty till twelve tomorrow,' she said. 'And anyway it'll probably be good for trade. See Ella, the nude waitress, at no extra charge,' she added in a brochure voice.

'I dare you,' he said on a sudden impulse, 'to go into the dining-room like that.'

Her eyes gleamed and narrowed. 'Do you really?'

'Oh no, no,' he said hastily. 'Of course not.' He felt enormous goodwill towards her now that the small adventure was over. 'You *are* an idiot,' he said affectionately. Time was still suspended and the world held in check; the whole night might have taken place on an island or a ship.

'Go to sleep,' Ella told him. 'You said you were tired.' He shut his eyes obediently and found her face imprinted on his eyelids like a snapshot. 'I want to try a little experiment to see how tired you are. Just ignore me.'

It very quickly became unendurable. He opened his eyes and found her watching him.

'Don't you like it?' she said innocently.

'On the contrary, I like it very much.'

When it was over (finally, excruciatingly, deliciously over) he said, 'Now where did you learn that?'

She yawned. 'I don't remember. But it's a well-known cure for insomnia.'

'It certainly is,' he said. 'I'm asleep already.' And he must have been, for although he heard her next remark, it was merely as a sound from the body curled up beside him. He could not distinguish the words. He breathed hair and shoulder and slept.

*   *   *

In the morning she did not even stir as he washed and dressed and left the hotel in a daze of exhaustion as powerful as a hangover. It was only as he was driving out of town, too far to turn back, that he remembered he had not left her any money this time, whatever that might mean.

15

THE HOUSE reeked with the smell of emulsion paint which, Frances had been repeatedly telling herself for some time, was a pleasant, clean sort of smell. Startlingly white walls now sprang at her from all directions: she had worked hard in the two days since Steve's departure and she hoped he would be duly impressed by the transformation. However, at the moment she herself felt that it was just a little too much of a good thing. Doubtless the addition of carpets, curtains and furniture would add all the colour needed, but at the moment the hall and spare room, being so crowded with boxes and suitcases, assumed the air of the left luggage office at some surrealist railway station. Perhaps a little discreet wall-paper, she thought, just on one wall. But that could be decided later.

She put down her brush and went into the kitchen to wash her hands and put on the kettle for tea. Despite the smell which pervaded the whole house she felt relaxed and contented. She had always found painting a soothing occupation. It was peaceful to use your hands instead of your brain for a change; she could see why some men (not Steve, unfortunately) gardened fanatically in their spare time. There was a sense of accomplishment, of creating something, as in dress-making, only easier. At the moment she was glad that she had decided to take a term off, although she knew that by the first week in September she would feel restless and strange. Fourteen years of teaching had implanted a rhythm that would probably be with her always. But since Steve's promotion had forced her to move and leave a good job, she might as well have a change, if not a rest, before looking for another. Ideally, she thought, she should aim at having the house more or less finished by the end of October, thereby giving herself two clear months in which to recharge, to broaden her outlook, catch up on her reading. It was all too easy to become stale and mechanical when working for too long under continual pressure and though she hoped this had not happened to her yet, it would be beneficial to approach a new job in a refreshed and vigorous frame of mind. And she must remember to order *The Times* Ed. from the local newsagent.

She drank her tea on the lawn, now smooth from its recent mowing. It was a warm day but not oppressive. She closed her eyes, enjoying the sun on her face, and began to make plans, but in a drowsy, relaxed way, without finality. If the house *was* ready by the end of October and they *did* decide to give a house-warming party, they could make it a Hallowe'en party which might be fun. Or perhaps a Guy Fawkes party would be better, with a barbecue round the bonfire and lots of fireworks. She loved fireworks but it had always seemed silly to buy them just for two adults. To invite all their friends, though, would be sufficient excuse and fireworks and a bonfire would make the party spectacular and festive. She began to see the blaze and the storms of colour. That settled it. Better than Hallowe'en; at once more dramatic and less complicated, with no laborious cutting out of cats and witches, no spooky decorations to arrange, and no risk of drunken guests running amok in masks and costumes.

She was so engrossed in the vision that she failed to hear the first knock at the front door. The second time she did hear it and got up reluctantly. The bread delivery perhaps, or a neighbour wanting to borrow something. She went into the house, through the hall, its white walls nearly blinding her, and opened the door.

A girl in blue jeans and shirt was standing there, a black leather jacket slung over her shoulder. She looked at Frances and put down her rucksack. 'Mrs Howarth,' she said.

16

FRANCES THOUGHT immediately that she must have taught her, somewhere, at some time. She racked her brain to put a name to the face. The girl was pale, with enormous green eyes and dark hair in two plaits. She wore no make-up and looked about sixteen. But it was useless: try as she might, nothing came.

Frances smiled at the girl, trying to look as if she recognised her. 'I'm sorry,' she said. 'I can't remember your name.'

The girl looked at her steadily. She did not appear at all put out. 'Ella Patterson,' she said.

Frances tried again, but it was hopeless. She shook her head. 'I'm afraid it doesn't ring a bell.' After all she had taught hundreds of girls. But still she had prided herself on her memory.

'It won't,' said the girl. 'We've never met.'

'Oh.' Frances was at once relieved and disconcerted. 'Well, that explains it. But . . .' She stopped, not wishing to seem rude or inhospitable to a stranger.

The girl smiled. 'What am I doing here?' she said.

Frances felt grateful to her for making it easy. 'Well, yes.'

The girl looked apologetic. 'Oh, it's awful cheek really. I hope you don't mind. But I met Mr Howarth the other week—he gave me a lift when I was hitch-hiking—and he said if ever I was passing I could call in. So here I am.'

'I see.' Frances was considerably taken aback. 'Well . . .'

'It's all right,' the girl assured her quickly, picking up the rucksack again. 'I can pass right on again. It doesn't matter.'

'No, of course not,' Frances said. 'Do come in. You must be tired.' She held the door wide open and the girl stepped into the hall. 'I've just made a cup of tea. Would you like one?'

But the girl was staring at the walls. 'Oh, how super,' she said. 'All white.'

Frances laughed. 'Yes, it is rather dazzling. We've only just moved in; that's why everything's so chaotic.'

'But you've done wonders.' The girl was motionless, her arms very brown against the paint. 'It's terrific.'

Her admiration disarmed Frances and diverted her mind from the question of why Steve had not mentioned picking up a hitch-hiker and giving her their address. 'Well, thank you. It's nice to be reassured. I was beginning to wonder if it was a bit much.'

'Oh no,' said the girl. 'Don't change a thing.'

And there the conversation abruptly lapsed, leaving them both in a great sudden silence, surveying the brilliant white walls. Frances was the first to speak, feeling rather silly to be staring at her own home in company with a perfect stranger. 'Well, I'll get your tea,' she said.

The girl followed her into the kitchen and looked round. 'Gosh,' she said. 'This is quite something.'

Frances busied herself with cup and saucer. 'Yes, it's nice,' she agreed. 'Milk and sugar?'

'Oh, please.' The girl watched her pour. 'This *is* kind of you,' she said. 'After all, you don't know me from Adam.'

Frances handed her the cup. 'Well, Eve.'

'Oh yes.' She smiled politely.

'I was having mine in the garden,' Frances said after a pause. 'Would you like to join me?'

The girl looked enchanted at the idea. 'Oh, how lovely.' She followed Frances on to the lawn.

The solitary deckchair looked unwelcoming. 'Shall I get you something to sit on?' Frances offered, but the girl shook her head.

'I'll sit on the grass,' she said. 'I'd rather. I love grass.'

Frances resumed her seat and the girl sank down gracefully, almost at her feet. 'I suppose I ought to explain,' Frances said, suddenly remembering, 'why I thought I should know you. I'm a teacher and I naturally assumed that anyone of your age on my doorstep must be an ex-pupil.'

The girl nodded. 'Yes, Mr Howarth told me that. He said as you were a teacher you wouldn't mind if I turned up. I was a bit surprised actually. I thought you'd probably have had enough of teenagers.'

'Oh no.' Put like that, it was hard to answer; she did not want to sound absurdly dedicated. 'I like young people,' she said hesitantly.

The girl was rubbing her feet. 'D'you mind if I take my shoes off?' she said. Frances shook her head. 'It would be so lovely to feel the grass in my toes.' She slid off the sandals and continued the massage. 'I'm afraid I've got blisters,' she added thoughtfully.

Frances looked. 'They're enormous,' she said. 'How very nasty for you. Have you walked a long way?' The blisters stood up alarmingly on the dusty feet.

'I ran out of lifts,' the girl said. 'People just weren't in the mood. It happens like that sometimes.' She sounded quite philosophical about it.

Frances said, 'Have you come a long way today?'

'From Birmingham. I was trying to get right into London but I couldn't get a lift past Barnet. If I had I wouldn't be here.'

Frances felt bound to say, 'Well, I'm glad you are.' She thought about it. 'You surely don't mean you walked all the way from Barnet?'

The girl nodded. She appeared to take it all for granted.

'But it's *miles*,' said Frances, horrified.

The girl shrugged. 'I'm used to walking,' she said, wriggling her toes on the grass.

Frances was still shocked. 'Couldn't you get a bus?' she said. 'Or a tube?' She could not take her eyes from the appalling blisters.

The girl shook her head. For the first time she appeared embarrassed. 'Not really,' she said, almost mumbling the words.

'But why ever not?'

'Oh . . .' She looked away with a cross expression. 'I couldn't afford it,' she said at length, both reluctant and defiant.

Frances was concerned. 'Are you very hard up?' It did not seem impertinent to question a girl of this age, she was so much like any pupil.

'Mm.' Again a hesitation. 'I'm broke actually.'

'Good heavens.' Frances had never met anyone in this predicament. 'Where are you trying to get to?'

'Oh, just into town.' The girl sipped her tea.

'Do you have relatives there?'

The girl's mouth set tightly. Finally she said, 'Yes, but I might as well not have.'

She sounded so bitter that Frances did not like to pursue this line of enquiry. 'Well, have you got a job to go to?'

The girl put down her cup. 'That's it. I was hoping to get one in London. In an hotel. That's what I was doing in Birmingham. It's very handy because it gives you somewhere to sleep as well.'

Frances frowned. 'Yes, I see that. But didn't you have any money left from your wages?' She was at a loss to understand how the situation had arisen.

'I got paid on Thursdays,' the girl said. 'So I'm always broke on Wednesdays.'

Frances considered this. 'Well, then, wouldn't it have been more sensible to wait till tomorrow before leaving? And what about notice?' She wondered how many of the girls she had taught might have this casual attitude to their employers. It disturbed her: she did not like the younger generation to be irresponsible. It reflected on their teachers as well as their parents.

The girl was shaking her head. 'I gave notice last week. But he wouldn't pay me. He said he'd pay me this week. Then he started . . .' Her chin began to tremble; she tried again—'he kept coming to my room and—and I just had to leave.' Suddenly, to Frances' horror, she burst into floods of tears, pressing her fists against her eyes like a child.

Frances leaned forward and patted her shoulder. The howling redoubled. 'It's all right,' she said. 'Calm down. I quite understand.'

The girl went on sobbing. At the same time she was struggling to get her sandals back on to her blistered feet. 'Please can I go now?' she said presently, like a girl kept in after school, and raised a tear-streaked face.

'Look here,' said Frances gently. 'You can't possibly go like this.' She felt in her pocket for a tissue (she kept them handy for paint smears) and gave it to the girl who blew her nose loudly.

'Thank you very much,' she said in a muffled voice. She wiped her eyes roughly as if to deny that tears had ever appeared. The gesture touched Frances: she too hated a stranger to see her cry.

'Now you listen to me,' she said in a firm comforting tone. 'There's no question of your going, at least not yet. I wouldn't hear of it. I'm going to start cooking soon and I'm sure you could do with a meal. I could certainly do with some company. I hate eating alone and my husband won't be home till late tonight. Why don't you have a bath while I'm cooking, then I'll put some plaster on those blisters and we'll eat? Then you can tell me all about everything—if you like,' she added, noting a look of panic.

'You don't have to. If you'd rather forget about . . . your employer and his appalling behaviour I shall quite understand. Though I really think something should be done about him,' she ended sharply.

The girl shook her head; she looked more alarmed than ever. 'Oh please,' she said, and stopped.

'Please what?' said Frances encouragingly.

The girl hesitated, then said all in a rush, 'Oh, please don't tell Mr Howarth what I told you, please don't.'

Her agitation was intense. Frances said gently, 'Why not?'

The girl screwed up the used tissue, now a soggy mess, in her fist. She seemed extremely reluctant to speak. 'I just don't want —oh, you mustn't tell him. He got me the job. He—he was so kind. When he gave me the lift I told him I was out of work and he—he said this friend of his had an hotel and always needed waitresses and—oh, please don't tell him, he was doing his best and he didn't know it would turn out . . .' She suddenly began to cry again. 'Like this,' she added presently between sobs.

Frances waited until she was calmer. 'I see,' she said.

'He meant well,' the girl said, wiping her eyes with her fingers. 'He was trying to help me.'

'Yes,' Frances said. 'I'm sure he was.'

'So you won't tell him, will you?' The girl's eyes pleaded with her.

'Well, I don't know; I'll have to think about it.' She hardly knew what to say.

'And there's something else.' The girl paused; she looked flushed and uncomfortable. 'I must tell you because you've been so kind. That's why I feel so awful now. You see, when I knocked on your door I was really hoping to borrow five bob.'

Frances stared at her, unable to see the horror of this admission.

'Oh, I would have paid it back,' the girl said rapidly. 'Really I would. As soon as I got a job.'

'I'm sure you would,' Frances said. 'And what's so terrible about wanting to borrow five bob?' She smiled, trying to cheer the girl up. 'I think I could run to that.'

'But I didn't tell you,' the girl said. She seemed very distressed. 'I knocked on your door and I let you ask me in and give me tea and I told you I was broke and I just sat around. I should have

asked you straight off and gone away. I'm sorry,' she said finally.
'I didn't know how to say it. I felt so mean when you'd been so
kind already and you didn't know I just wanted to sponge on
you.'

'Now you're just being silly,' Frances said in her classroom
voice. 'Borrowing five bob is *not* sponging. You've had a very
nasty experience at work and you're naturally upset. I'm very
glad indeed that you did call here. But I'm appalled that a friend
of my husband's could behave in the way you've described. I assume it *was* Jack Roberts.'

'Mr Roberts,' the girl said. 'Yes.'

Frances sighed. 'I had no idea he was that kind of man.'

The girl shook her head as if puzzled. 'He seemed very nice at
first,' she said.

'Well, I really owe you an apology,' said Frances, 'on his behalf.
And so does my husband.'

Again the look of panic. 'Oh no. You're not going to tell him?'

'Look,' Frances said. 'I really think I'll have to. After all, as he
got you the job he's partly responsible for what happened.'

'Oh *no.*' A most vehement denial. 'That's why I don't want
you to tell him. I don't want him to feel responsible.'

'But he is.' She said it as gently as possible. 'And anyway, it
might happen again, to somebody else. You must think of that.'

'Yes, I suppose so.' The girl spoke slowly. 'I suppose it could.'

'Well, then. You see why I have to tell him.' There was silence
which she interpreted as agreement. 'Now don't you think about
it any more. I'm going to run your bath.'

17

THE NOTE was brief and to the point, typed on the office machine. 'I'm off,' it announced. 'I've taken the money you owe me for the week so we're square. Ella.'

Steve had no sympathy to spare for Jack. He was conscious only of first surprise and then an intense disappointment that made him feel almost physically sick. It was alarming to realise how much he had counted on her being there, on his being able to see her any time he called.

'And no forwarding address?' he said stupidly. He was stunned with shock and it slowed his brain, making him like a man who continues to look in the same place over and over again because he cannot believe that the precious object is no longer there.

Jack gave him an impatient glance. 'What do you think?' He screwed up the note in his fist. 'Bloody little thief. Just stuck her hand in the till and buggered off before anybody was up.'

'Didn't you owe her the money?' Steve asked. Jack's annoyance was so violent that he wondered briefly if it was directed more at a lost mistress than a missing waitress.

'Well, in a manner of speaking. It's pay day tomorrow. But just to help herself like that. . . . Why the hell couldn't she wait till tomorrow or at least give notice like any normal person?' He stared at Steve suspiciously. 'Are you sure you didn't give her a lift somewhere?'

'Don't be a bloody fool,' Steve said, wishing he had. 'I left here at six and went straight to Manchester.'

Jack took a long draught of Scotch. The bar was nearly empty and the blonde girl behind it stared at them with dull curiosity.

'Well, she must have left soon after.' Jack was sullen, like a thwarted detective stockpiling useless evidence.

'She was still asleep when I left,' Steve said. He could see her so clearly in his mind. The picture hurt.

Jack snorted. 'Huh. Planning her getaway.' He turned to the bar. 'Two more, Marcia love.'

'No, really,' Steve said. 'I must be on my way.'

'Back to your ever-loving.' Jack's solitary—and brief—experience of married life had left him sour. 'Well, give her my regards. Maybe Ella's done *her* a favour, anyway.'

'Oh, come off it,' said Steve, accepting the glass that Marcia handed across the bar. He looked at Jack and realised with unpleasant surprise: He'd like to make trouble for me. Christ, after all these years. Now why?

'Well, she's gone,' said Jack with a certain glum satisfaction. 'She could be anywhere.' He drank some more whisky.

'Yes.' Steve could not repress the thought, I'll never see her again, and did not know which disturbed him most: the pain of the thought or the realisation that it was so painful. He was no longer in charge of himself; perhaps had not been fully so since meeting Ella, only he had not admitted it. It negated all the cold manoeuvring, the manipulation of people that he practised in his job and which gave him the satisfaction of power. He could speak lines not his own and be the person each client wanted him to be. It was like amateur theatricals, only the applause came in cash. But not with Ella.

'Well, I must be going,' he said, draining his glass. 'Thanks for the drink.' He stood up and added with quite an effort, 'I'll see what I can do about your staff problem next time I'm up here.'

Jack grinned at him. But the unmistakable sexual rivalry was still there. 'Don't bother,' he said. 'Unless she's fifty and after a pension.'

Back in the car, on his way home, Steve felt he was on a long, lonely journey. He played the facts over in his mind. Wherever she was, she would be all right; that much was certain. She would get another lift, find another job. But where, with whom? He heard her voice, full of teasing sympathy. 'Poor Steven. Have I upset all your plans?' And he admitted that she had. But what plans? He had had no plans. He only knew that he had not expected it to end like this.

So how had he expected it to end?

18

'Now you'll have to stay the night,' Frances said. This had in fact been obvious to her as she started running the bath though she had not mentioned it before. Since it was Steve's fault, his misplaced kindness, that the girl was in such a mess, the least they could do was offer her accommodation. The only alternative was to press two or three pounds into her hand and turn her out in search of a hostel or something and that at nine o'clock at night, if not impossible, was clearly un-Christian.

'It's awfully kind of you,' Ella said. She was curled up in her chair and wearing an old dressing gown of Frances'. 'But I can easily get dressed and move on. Really. My feet are ever so much better and after that lovely meal I feel fine. Honestly. I'll find somewhere to go.'

'Not at this hour,' Frances said firmly. No matter what the girl said, she did not look well. She was deathly pale and all her movements were slow with exhaustion. 'I wouldn't hear of you going,' Frances said. 'You look absolutely worn out.'

'Oh dear,' Ella said. 'Is it so obvious?'

'Yes, I'm afraid it is.' Frances smiled at her. 'So no arguments please. I'm going to make you a milk drink and you can take a couple of aspirins with it. A good night's sleep is what you need.'

The girl shook her head. She seemed on the verge of tears again. 'You're so kind,' she said in a low voice.

'Nonsense,' said Frances briskly. 'Anyone would do the same. Mind you, I'm not saying you wouldn't be more comfortable in a hostel. You haven't seen our spare room yet. Still, there *is* a bed and I've made it up, so if you can manage to climb over all the trunks and packing cases you should be all right.'

Ella smiled. 'It sounds wonderful,' she said, and was immediately engulfed in an enormous yawn. 'Gosh,' she said apologetically. 'Just hearing about it makes me sleepy.'

Frances warmed to her appreciation. 'If you like,' she said, 'you can go straight to bed now and I'll bring your drink in to you.'

Ella stood up very slowly, uncurling herself. 'Could I?' she said. 'That would be marvellous.' She picked up her rucksack and jacket from the floor.

Frances looked at it. 'Do you want to borrow anything?' she said.

The girl shook her head. 'No, thank you. I've got everything I need in here.'

It seemed pathetically small. Frances said, 'How ever do you manage to travel so light? I can never go anywhere without a suitcase at least.'

'Oh, it's easy,' Ella said. 'I only carry what I need and I don't need very much.'

Frances showed her the spare room and apologised for it, but the rucksack still haunted her as she went into the kitchen to make the warm drink. When she returned to the bedroom with the mug in her hand Ella was already in bed, looking very small and young and defenceless. 'Oh, thank you,' she said.

Frances put the drink down beside her. 'Ella,' she said, using her name for the first time, 'what about your parents?'

Ella turned her face away and did not reply. Frances tried again. 'They are alive, aren't they?'

'Mm.' A small, reluctant sound.

'Are they your relatives in London?'

Ella turned her face back to look at Frances. 'D'you mean you want to ring them up?'

Frances sat on the edge of the bed. She still had the aspirin bottle in her hand. 'No,' she said, 'not if you don't want me to.'

'Please don't.' The voice was very firm and serious.

'Well, I can't, can I?' Frances tried to lighten the atmosphere. 'Unless I work through all the Pattersons in the book. But I do think they should know where you are.'

Ella leaned on one elbow and began sipping her drink. 'No, really,' she said.

'Do they know what you're doing—hitch-hiking and working in hotels?'

Ella nodded. 'Sort of.'

Frances sighed. 'And don't they mind?' She waited but no answer came. 'All right,' she said. 'It's your own affair. You don't have to tell me if you don't want to.'

Ella put down the mug. 'Oh, I'd like to,' she said. 'But I can't. I just can't.'

Frances hesitated. 'Was it . . . boy friend trouble?' she said. Ella shook her head violently.

'All right,' Frances said again. She shook out two aspirins and gave them to the girl. 'Here. You take these and go to sleep. I'm not going to bother you any more. In the morning, after breakfast, we can have a talk. If you feel like it.'

She said goodnight as she crossed the room, picking her way through the jungle of suitcases. At the door Ella's voice stopped her. 'Mrs Howarth.'

Frances turned round. There were dark patches under the green eyes that watched her from across the room. She felt a surprisingly protective surge of feeling. 'Yes?'

'Are you going far away?'

This was unexpected and strangely moving. 'No, only into the next room.'

The girl smiled and lay down. 'That's good,' she said contentedly, and her eyes closed as her head touched the pillow.

Having turned out the light and closed the door, Frances returned to the living-room and poured herself a stiffer than usual Scotch. 'Well, well,' she said aloud, looking round the room. The hours since Ella's arrival had passed so swiftly that it was only now when she was alone that she could collect them into some sort of pattern. Here she was, quite suddenly it seemed, giving shelter to a lonely, weary teenager who for all her evident courage in travelling alone showed signs of extreme vulnerability underneath and who, thanks to Steve's 'help', had nearly been attacked by Jack Roberts.

'I'll have something to say about that,' she thought. She lit a cigarette and settled down to wait for Steve's return.

19

IT WAS nearly eleven when Steve drove into the garage. He had stopped for a meal and a drink on the way home, less from the urge to eat and drink than from the sheer necessity to sort out his thoughts. It seemed impossible to drive straight from Jack's hotel to his home, to go from the discovery that Ella had disappeared from his life to the resumption of his life with Frances. He needed something to intervene. A traffic jam, even a collision (his thoughts alarmed him) would have been welcome, would have given him something else to think and talk about, put another look on his face.

He sat for a moment or two in the garage with the car door open and looked at his face in the driving mirror. He thought he saw a beaten, defeated expression, but that was surely in his imagination. All the same, as he got out and slammed the door, he was conscious of deliberately assuming the cheerful, confident look he used for clients. He did not need to see it; he knew the muscle movements well enough. But he had never used it for Frances until now.

He went in through the kitchen and into the living-room where the light was on. Frances, sitting on the couch with her feet up, looked up as he entered. He was so busy with his own performance that he did not notice the look on her face.

'Hullo,' he said, and heard his professional voice. 'How are you? Got a drink for me? God, I'm tired.'

He sank down into a chair and lit a cigarette. Frances got up and slowly poured him a drink. He took it from her.

'Been busy?' he said cheerfully. Then he noticed that she was moving oddly round the room and coming to rest in the empty fireplace, her elbow on the mantelpiece. She too had a drink in her hand. He remembered this posture: it heralded some important conversation. In the past she had discussed her mother like this, and adoption. There was something very considered about it and from long experience it made him uneasy.

'You didn't tell me,' she said, using the measured tones that went with the pose, 'that you picked up a hitch-hiker on your last trip.'

His brain froze and he was very keenly aware of the feel of the glass in his hand. He drank from it gratefully. 'Hitch-hiker,' he said vaguely and his frozen brain could only produce one thought: That bastard Jack has rung her up. Christ, what a bastard.

'Ella Patterson,' Frances said.

He could feel the muscles of his face working hard to keep his expression good-humoured and unconcerned, as with an awkward client. (So he'd given her the name. And what else?) 'Oh yes, Ella Patterson. I forgot all about it. Why?' It was all he could do not to shout: What do you know about her? The pause before Frances spoke again, though probably infinitesimal, seemed unendurably long.

'She's here,' Frances said, and with that began to walk around the room again.

A small part of his mind told him he could afford to relax, though the rest was still icy with horror. Frances, he knew, remained motionless until she had delivered her trump card (he sometimes wondered if it was a technique developed in the classroom) so now that she was moving round again the worst must be over. The fact that Ella was here (*Here?* He could not take it in) was the biggest shock she had in store for him. But then what had Jack done? Sent her here? Typed the note himself? For Christ's sake, what?

'Here?' he said, and felt profound relief that his voice expressed only extreme surprise when it might easily have come out as a croak of panic-stricken horror.

'In the spare room,' Frances said, pausing in her progress along the carpet. She glanced at her watch. 'Fast asleep by now, I should think.'

Steve took another large gulp of whisky. He felt outmanoeuvred in a sitting position but it probably looked more relaxed and anyway it would be too ridiculous for them both to march up and down. They would end up passing each other like soldiers on parade. They might as well salute. He felt the onrush of hysteria and made a big effort to curb it.

'What on earth,' he said, 'is she doing in the spare room?'

'That's just it,' Frances said, pacing a bit more and stopping in front of his chair. 'I'm afraid it's all your doing.'

'Mine?' Perhaps it was nothing to do with Jack after all. 'Why?

What d'you mean?' The whole situation must be played most carefully by ear; he was on the thinnest ice of his life.

Frances sighed and suddenly to his great surprise and relief sat down in the opposite chair. 'Well, that job you got her. Oh, I know you must have meant it well but I'm afraid it didn't turn out like that.' She was turning her glass round and round in her fingers. 'Oh, Steve, didn't you have any idea that Jack was that sort of man?'

Steve rapidly assembled the slender facts as they emerged. He, it appeared, had got Ella her job with Jack and Jack had apparently done something awful. 'What sort of man?'

Frances put down her glass. 'Have you got a cigarette?' she said. 'I've run out.'

He was delighted to be of service. He took out cigarettes and lit one for her and another for himself. Though the conversation was still obscure he was obviously—so far—in the clear. Perhaps it was the time to risk a speech more ambitious than a mere echo.

'What did he do?' he said, letting himself frown and lean forward anxiously. 'For God's sake, Frances, tell me. I thought I was doing her a favour. She needed a job.' Steady now, he added to himself, don't overdo it.

Frances drew on her cigarette. 'He made a pass at her,' she said. 'She's terribly upset, poor kid, and no wonder. He refused to pay her wages and he kept going to her room and in the end . . . well, she just ran away without any money. She hitch-hiked all the way from Birmingham.' She paused. 'And, d'you know, she actually *walked* all the way here from Barnet.'

'Good God,' said Steve faintly.

'Yes. We were the only people she could call on.' She made a gesture of disgust. 'Well, there's your precious friend Jack for you.'

'Good God,' said Steve like a gramophone record.

Frances finished her drink. 'Yes, well. Now do you see why it's really your fault?'

Steve took a deep breath. 'Well, yes, I suppose it is. But I couldn't be more surprised.' That much was true, even understated. What the hell was Ella doing in his house, asleep in his spare room, having got Frances all steamed up with a tale of attempted rape? If the situation were not so potentially dangerous —for him—it would have been comic: Ella fleeing from Jack's unwelcome attentions. But, concerned as he was for his own safety, he was still aware of a flash of satisfied excitement. At least he now knew where she was (though in the last place on earth he would have wished her to be) and he would see her again.

Frances was saying, 'You really had no idea Jack was like that?'

'Well, no. Of course not. Otherwise I'd hardly have got her the job, would I?'

'No.' Frances sighed. 'You really owe her an apology, don't you?'

The ludicrous aspect of this remark nearly made him snort with laughter. 'I suppose so. Well, I'll do that at breakfast. I imagine I'll see her then before she pushes off.'

There was a pause before Frances spoke again and it made him uneasy. Something was hanging over his head and he could not identify it. Finally she said rather slowly and hesitantly, 'Steve, she hasn't any money.'

'Oh, hasn't she?' He waited a moment, then ventured, 'I'm not surprised; she was broke when I gave her a lift. It seems to be a habit.'

But Frances did not appear to be listening. 'She's got terrible blisters on her feet,' she said.

Steve began to detest the whole conversation, his lines being delivered as they were by the prompter at very short notice. 'Poor kid,' he said. Violence was rising in him again. That's not the only place she should have blisters, he thought. I'd like to tan the arse off her. What the hell is she doing in my house? It maddened him that he could not march at once into the spare room and demand an answer to the question that very minute. (And after that?) He stubbed out his cigarette and lit another.

'And it's your fault she's broke,' Frances said.

'Is it?'

'I told you. Your friend Jack refused to pay her.'

'Oh yes, of course. Well, I suppose we'll have to lend her some cash.' He sighed heavily. 'Oh hell. It's a bit much, isn't it?'

Frances looked at him, he thought, rather coldly. 'What is?'

'Well, turning up here. Needing money and a bed for the night.' He groped for an acceptable way to put it. 'Imposing on us like this.'

'I asked her to stay,' Frances said pointedly.

'Yes, of course you did. But she must have made you feel you had to.'

'Not at all.'

He was furious that she had made such a thorough job of gaining Frances' sympathy. 'Oh well, you always were absurdly kind-hearted.'

'Was I?' Frances said. 'You never told me that before. When?'

He was floored. 'Oh well, you know. Over those kids of yours. At school.'

'Oh, that,' said Frances, as if it were a long time ago.

He tried again. 'Well, it's very sweet of you to take her in, love, but I still call it a bit of an imposition, her turning up here.'

'Not really,' said Frances. 'After all, you did give her our address.'

'Yes, well.' How the hell had she got it? He never put his full address in the register. She must—yes, she must—have gone through his pockets in the night. Or asked Jack. Would Jack have told her? Perhaps the whole thing was a giant conspiracy between them. But for what?

'Steve,' Frances said, 'why *did* you give her our address?'

He shrugged and scratched his head, trying to appear puzzled and casual. He felt more than ever like an actor in a very bad play on which no one had the sense to ring down a merciful curtain. 'I don't know really. It was just one of those silly things you do. You know. If you're passing you must look us up. That kind of nonsense. You never dream they really will.'

'I think you might have told me,' Frances said. 'After all, you must have known the odds were you'd be away when she turned up. I felt such a fool. I even pretended to recognise her at first. I thought she must be a girl from some old school I'd forgotten.'

He was longing now to be let off the hook. To be allowed to go quietly to bed, in darkness and silence, was the summit of his immediate ambition. 'I'm sorry, love, I just forgot all about it.'

'Well, another time,' Frances said, 'do try to remember.'

'Good heavens'—he was suddenly exhausted but tried to manage a laugh—'there won't *be* another time. After all, I'm not in the habit of picking up hitch-hikers. Let alone telling them to look us up any time they're passing.'

'No,' said Frances, smiling at him in a way that he suddenly found extremely chilling. 'I didn't think you were.'

20

In the morning Frances got up first as usual and he lay, very much more awake than usual, pondering the question of how he could get a moment's conversation alone with Ella. The disadvantages of a bungalow were apparent to him for the first time. He listened to the sounds of breakfast preparations and then, to his incredulous relief, the gods played right into his hands. He heard Frances say, 'Damn,' to herself, slam the fridge door and march through the hall. A moment later the front door banged. He shot out of bed and saw from a discreet vantage point her retreating back as she went down the path, apparently heading for the shop across the road. He had to risk it; there would be no other chance.

He was in Ella's room in a flash, aware that he had only two or three minutes to play with. She was awake and looked up at him with her most innocent, guileless smile.

'Hi, Dad,' she said.

He repressed an urge to whip the covers off her and belt her soundly. 'What the hell are you up to?' The events of the evening were only too clear in his mind; in fact the morning light had brought no relief. The situation was every bit as bad as he remembered it.

'Just visiting,' she said demurely.

Her manner increased his fury to such an extent that he found it quite difficult to speak. 'Look,' he said in a funny, thick voice, 'you've told my wife a pack of lies and got yourself a bed for the night but that's *it*. I want you out of here first thing after breakfast.'

She appeared surprised. 'A pack of lies?' she said. 'Would you rather I'd told her the truth?'

'You know what I mean.' He was incensed beyond endurance. 'Damn it, Ella, what the hell are you playing at?'

To his amazement she held up her arms to him. 'I wanted to see you again,' she said.

Before he could even frame a reply to this he heard the creak
of the front gate. They looked at each other for another second
or two before he gave in to the inevitable. 'Oh Christ,' he said
in despair, and shot into the bathroom just a moment before
Frances put her key in the front door.

Normally he took a quick shower, shaved, cleaned his teeth
and was out again in ten minutes flat. Today he ran a bath and
sat in it doggedly for fifteen minutes. Twenty. Frances rapped on
the door and called, 'Breakfast,' and he answered, 'Coming.' But
he went on sitting in the water, unable even to go through the
mechanics of washing and occasionally slapping the water with
the flat of his hand and wishing it was Ella's face. What in God's
name was she up to and what—which was more to the point—
could he do about it? Then he forced himself, with a huge effort,
to calm down. She would at least be gone by the time he came
home. But where? And would he ever see her again? Simultaneously he was furious with himself for even wanting to, after she
had caused him so much trouble.

He stood up with a sudden movement and wrenched the plug
violently out of the hole. He rubbed a towel over himself and,
still slightly damp, put on his clothes. The day, and Frances,
would have to be faced.

Frances was at the breakfast table when he emerged.

'You're going to be late,' she said. 'Your breakfast's under the
grill.'

He went to fetch it, the fried egg already hardening, and sat
down at the table.

'I had to go to the shop,' Frances said, buttering a piece of
toast for herself. 'I'm afraid Ella had your bacon and egg last
night.'

'Oh, hell,' he said, letting out some of his pent-up violence.

'It's all right,' Frances said mildly. 'I got you some more. That's
it.'

They ate in silence. He could hardly make the food go down
he was so conscious of her presence and of Ella in the spare room.
As if Frances read his thought she said, 'I looked in the spare
room just now but she's still asleep. So I left her. She can have
breakfast later on.'

'You're spoiling her,' he said abruptly. He felt Frances was watching him, waiting for him to make a mistake. He froze at the thought. It was impossible: she could not suspect anything. Why should she? It was merely his own guilt. If he went on feeling like that he *would* begin to act suspiciously. But he had never felt guilty before. Damn Ella. Why did she have to come to the house?

'Oh well,' Frances said, 'she may as well get all the sleep she can. She obviously needs it.'

He went on trying to eat but the effort nearly choked him. Finally he resolved the issue with a glance at his watch, a groan, 'Hell,' and a quick gulp of coffee. 'You're right,' he said. 'I will be late.' He got up and pecked at her cheek. 'Bye, love. See you tonight. Hope you get our visitor off all right.'

Frances looked up from her toast. Her face was a mask or was that merely his fevered imagination? 'Bye,' she said.

He could not linger; there was nothing to say. But much as he wanted to be outside in the air and alone, he hated leaving the unfinished situation behind.

Reluctantly, but with a great show of haste, he left the house.

21

AFTER HE had gone Frances sat for a long time over a second cup of coffee and a cigarette, although she did not usually smoke so early in the day. She surveyed Steve's half-eaten breakfast and though she normally started to wash up almost before the grease could congeal on the plate, this morning she felt no urge to do so. She glanced at the paper which Steve in his haste had forgotten to take with him, but it did not seem very interesting and she put it down. The house was extremely quiet.

Finally, rousing herself, she got up and began to clear the table. Her mind was at once very active and curiously blank: it seemed to be ticking over with great energy, yet not producing actual thoughts.

When she had finished washing up, which did not take long, she returned to her bedroom to make the bed and tidy up, but paused on catching sight of herself in the mirror. She examined herself critically for several minutes and then, with an air of decision, sat down at the dressing-table to put make-up on her face. She took more care than usual, attempting to camouflage her freckles with a thicker layer of foundation; she dug in a drawer for mascara and applied it to her naturally sandy eyelashes. The effect startled her: she was not sure if it was an improvement on her usual quick lipstick and powder routine. Perhaps it was just that she was unaccustomed to anything more. She got up and walked away, then turned round quickly as if to catch herself unawares for an unbiased judgment. A stranger's face stared back at her. She played with the idea of washing it all off but at the last moment shrugged and returned to the kitchen to make coffee for Ella. Despite the odd and disturbing circumstances of her arrival, she was someone to look after, however briefly, and this, Frances was surprised to find, was a pleasant change. Surely, she thought, I am not becoming bored and lonely already, a housebound, suburban housewife and after only three weeks of the school holidays. But the knowledge that she was not returning to school, any school, until January had made her recuperate more quickly than usual and the hard physical work on the house had relaxed her still further.

She took coffee and orange juice on a tray into the spare room and found Ella awake. At the sight of Frances and the tray she immediately looked guilty.

'Sleep well?' Frances asked.

'Oh yes. I should have got up before.' She jumped out of bed, drawing the curtains as if to make amends and Frances saw that what had last night appeared to be a nightdress was in fact a slip. She put down the tray.

'Not at all,' she said. 'I wanted you to sleep. But I could have lent you a nightdress. Why ever didn't you ask me?'

'Oh gosh,' Ella said. 'I couldn't ask you for anything *else*.' She picked up the glass of orange juice and drank it thirstily. 'I'm perfectly all right like this,' she added. 'I told you I travel light.'

'You certainly do.' Frances surveyed the few garments hanging over a chair. 'Is that all you've got?'

'Oh yes.' The girl seemed quite unconcerned. 'A rucksack doesn't hold very much and that's all I need. In summer anyway.' She started on the coffee. 'This is marvellous.'

'Breakfast,' Frances said. 'What would you like?'

The other's face clouded. 'Nothing, really,' she said. 'Thank you very much.'

'Oh, you must have something.'

Ella shook her head. 'No, honestly, I couldn't. But I would like . . .' She hesitated—'could I possibly have a bath?'

'Quite possibly,' said Frances. 'In fact, why not?' She felt suddenly flippant and frivolous.

'Well . . . you know. Using all your hot water.'

Frances laughed. 'Good heavens,' she said. 'That's one thing we've plenty of.'

*   *   *

Ella was a long time in the bathroom. When she emerged her skin was red and damp, and Frances, painting in the hall, saw moisture on the bathroom walls.

'You take very hot baths,' she remarked conversationally.

Ella said, 'Yes,' in a flat voice. She was dressed in her shirt and jeans again but her hair was still loose and unplaited. She stood around in the hall for a moment watching Frances, then suddenly said, 'Have you got another brush?'

'Yes,' Frances said. 'Why?'

'Can I do some painting before I go?' The request seemed peculiarly urgent.

Frances hesitated. 'Well, you can. But there's no need. I can manage.'

'Oh please let me. I'd like to. If—if I had any money I'd buy you some flowers.'

End of term pangs hit Frances all over again. 'Go on,' she said. 'Get the brush. It's under the kitchen sink.'

She decanted some paint into an empty tin for Ella and the girl started painting. She seemed excited, like a child whose mother had allowed her to 'help' make pastry; Frances caught herself wishing briefly that Steve was such an enthusiastic participant in household chores.

'Oh, it's super,' Ella said. She was both quick and careful: an unusual combination, Frances thought. She herself was slow and painstaking, Steve—when she could persuade him to join in—fast and messy, much given to swearing and wiping gobs of paint off the floor and smearing them over his clothes.

'You're very good,' she said to Ella.

'It's easy.' She negotiated a corner with speed and accuracy. 'And besides, I like it.'

'Oh well,' Frances said. 'That's half the battle.'

'Mm,' Ella said, concentrating. 'I'd like to paint the whole house. D'you think anyone would hire me as a painter?' She giggled. 'I'd love that.'

'I could hire you,' Frances said in the same light-hearted tone. 'This whole house has got to be painted.'

Ella was silent for a few minutes. They both went on painting. There was, Frances thought, something companionable about working with someone, even a stranger, something that made it easier to talk to them.

'Ella,' she said presently, her eyes on her brush and the wall, 'have you thought any more about what we said yesterday? About your parents?'

Ella shook her head. She seemed very absorbed in her work.

Frances said gently, 'I really think you should get in touch with them.'

Ella dipped her brush in the paint. 'I know, Mrs Howarth. And you're probably right. But I can't.'

'I see,' Frances said. 'Would you care to tell me why?'

Again a long silence. Finally, with reluctance: 'I suppose I owe you that.'

'Not at all,' Frances said. 'You don't owe me anything.'

'Oh yes I do.' She spoke rapidly. 'I owe you a meal and two baths and a bed and I know Mr Howarth doesn't want me here.' It all came out in a rush.

Frances put down her brush. 'Whatever d'you mean?' she said. 'He doesn't mind a bit.'

'I'm sorry,' Ella said, painting rapidly. 'But I woke up last night and heard him talking to you. I wasn't trying to hear but he sounded awfully cross.'

Frances considered this for a moment. 'What thin walls we must have,' she said lightly.

'I shouldn't have come,' Ella said. 'I should've known he didn't mean what he said about dropping in. No one ever does. I should've known that.'

'Nonsense,' said Frances briskly. 'He was cross about the way his friend Jack Roberts behaved, that's all.'

'Oh God,' said Ella. 'You told him.'

'Well,' Frances said, 'I warned you I'd have to.'

'Yes.'

'And I still think your parents should know. After all, you've been in considerable moral danger and they have a right to know about that, whatever your reasons for leaving home.'

Ella was shaking her head slowly from side to side. Frances looked at her closely and saw that she was crying.

'Hey,' she said, 'you're watering the paint.'

The crying went on. Frances got up and went over to the girl, putting a hand on her shoulder. 'Come on,' she said. 'What's the matter? You can tell me.'

The girl shook beneath her hand. Presently she said in the funny up and down voice produced by tears, 'I've caused you enough trouble already.'

'Trouble,' Frances repeated. 'What trouble? You haven't done anything of the sort.'

Ella wiped her nose on the back of her hand and Frances gave her a tissue from her pocket. She blew on it loudly.

'I shouldn't have come here,' she said, 'but I didn't know where else to go.'

'Now stop that,' Frances said firmly. 'I don't want to hear that again. I'm glad you came here.'

'But Mr Howarth isn't.'

'Well . . .' Frances half-admitted the truth of this statement and hurried on. 'We're not talking about Mr Howarth. I'm very glad you came. But I do want to know what this is all about.'

Ella blew her nose again. She seemed suddenly calmer but fatalistic almost: like someone facing a firing squad and realising at last that there is no way out. She sat back on her heels beside the paint pot and her voice when she spoke again was flat and dead.

'I think I'm going to have a baby,' she said.

22

STEVE, RETURNING from work at six o'clock, was surprised to see Frances waiting at the gate. He waved and got out of the car, leaving it outside the house.

'Hi,' he said. She said nothing; she did not even smile. 'You look very sombre,' he added brightly. His neck prickled with sudden suspicion.

'We've got to have a talk,' Frances said.

There was no mistaking the ominous tone. He followed her into the house and stopped, shocked, on the threshold of the living-room. A rucksack lay on the couch.

'Good God,' he said, 'don't tell me she's still here.'

Frances did not reply. She poured two drinks and handed him one. 'You'd better sit down,' she said. 'This is serious.'

He had never felt less like sitting down. In fact he wondered if it was even politic to remain in the room. She must have found out. Everything.

'Oh God,' Frances said, abruptly sitting down herself. 'I thought you'd never get home. I wanted to ring you at the office but I'm sure those damned switchboard girls listen in to every word.'

The sitting down was reassuring; the speech was not. He lit a cigarette and Frances put out her hand for one, so he gave her his and lit another for himself. 'Just *tell* me,' he said, 'what this is all about.'

'You'll have to go and see Jack Roberts,' Frances said rapidly, smoking as if her life depended upon it. 'It's criminal. It's—oh, God, what I could do to that man.'

Her agitation was so intense that Steve saw no other way of getting through to her than by shouting. He shouted. 'What the hell has he done now?' and Frances leapt to her feet.

'Don't *shout*,' she said fiercely. 'She already thinks you don't want her here.'

'She's damn right I don't.' He looked round. 'Where is she? It's time I had a word with that young lady.'

Frances walked round him and closed the door quietly and firmly, then stood with her back against it.

'Shut up and listen,' she said savagely. The words shocked him; she had never spoken like that to him before. 'And get a grip on yourself. I don't want you talking to Ella in that mood. She's very upset.'

The protective speech enraged him further but he made a great effort. 'Just tell me,' he said with assumed calm but his voice still threatening violence, 'what this is all about.'

Frances shook her head and took a gulp of whisky. It suddenly struck Steve that she was not so much angry as extremely upset. He risked a gentler tone. 'Darling, what is it?'

'Oh Steve.' She looked round the room as if for help. 'She thinks she's pregnant.'

The word thudded into his consciousness like a dart hitting its target. For a second any reaction was impossible. Then:

'*What?*'

Frances nodded. 'Yes. Now do you see why I'm so upset? She told me this morning. She's frantic. She even tried to run away.'

'Pity she didn't make it.' It was out before he could stop it.

'*Steve.*'

'Well . . .' He groped for the right words. 'I mean . . . what are *we* supposed to do?'

Frances' mouth tightened. 'You seem to forget,' she said. 'It's our fault if she is. You sent her to that place.'

'Our fault,' he repeated. 'You mean it's *my* fault.'

'All right,' Frances said. 'I suppose I do. If you hadn't taken her to Jack's hotel this would never have happened.'

'If it has.'

'Yes, if it has.'

'Well . . .' He clung to the main issue. 'That's the first thing to find out. Can't she have a test or something?'

Frances sat down. She looked suddenly exhausted. 'I suppose so.'

'Aren't you sure? Couldn't you have found out?'

'Oh, not *yet*.' She closed her eyes for a moment. 'Can't you imagine what sort of day I've had?'

'Yes, of course.' He softened his tone while his brain went on working rapidly. The little bitch. What a stunt to pull. But Frances. Comfort Frances. Keep calm. He did not trust himself to touch her so he put out his hand for her glass. 'Come on. I'll get you another drink.'

She handed over the glass mechanically and he poured two stiff whiskies.

'Oh *Steve*, I'm so worried.'

He gave her the drink and downed half his own at one go. 'Don't worry. There may be nothing to worry about. Let's find out first before we get in a state.'

'You've got to go and see him,' Frances said.

He was startled. 'Who, Jack?'

'Yes, of course.'

'Oh, now look. Let's find out first.'

Frances shook her head obstinately. 'Of course it's worse if she's pregnant. But either way, you've got to talk to him. Oh, Steve, she's so young. It's awful.'

'She's nineteen.'

'Is she? Are you sure? She looks younger to me.'

'Well, she told me she was nineteen.'

'Oh well,' said Frances wearily. 'It doesn't really matter. Except that if she's under sixteen it's a criminal offence on top of everything else. It probably is anyway.'

This really annoyed him. 'Oh, of course she's not under sixteen.'

'All right,' Frances said. 'We'll ask her.' And seemed about to call out.

'Hang on,' said Steve. 'Don't bring her into it yet. We haven't thought of everything. Suppose . . .' He stopped. Careful: watch what you say.

'Suppose what?' Frances said dully.

'Well . . .' He spoke slowly and thoughtfully. 'Suppose she was pregnant when I picked her up and she's just . . . saying it was Jack.'

Frances looked at him. 'Why should she?'

'Any number of reasons. If she couldn't find the father. If she doesn't even know who he is.'

'Oh, Steve.' Frances seemed shocked. 'She's not that kind of girl.'

'Isn't she? How do we know? We don't know anything about her.'

Frances finished her drink and put down the glass. 'I'm surprised,' she said. 'It's not like you to be so hard.'

'*Hard?*'

'Yes. You're being so unsympathetic.'

'Not at all. If the girl really is pregnant and Jack's responsible, of course I'm sorry for her. Damn sorry. But we don't know yet, do we? Hell, she only met him two weeks ago. Don't you see, it's much more likely to be someone else. Someone she met months ago,' he added hastily.

'No, I don't think so,' Frances said.

Her certainty chilled him and for the first time the suspicion crossed—or was allowed to cross—his mind. What if she really is pregnant and it's mine? What if I made her pregnant? And he did not know which was uppermost: the panic at having this situation under his own roof or a sudden rush of power at his achievement.

'Why don't you think so?' he asked.

'She's a week late,' Frances said. But she spoke reluctantly and he was aware of a certain feminine withdrawal, as if she hated speaking of such intimate matters to him, a man. Good God, he thought, women. She's on Ella's side. If his own position had been more secure he could have laughed at it all.

'Oh well,' he said, 'a week's nothing. You've often been a week late.'

'Yes.' A fleeting expression of distaste, as if the analogy were unwelcome. 'But she hasn't.' Again a hesitation; the feminine mystique. 'She tells me she's always on time. That's why she's so worried.' A pause, then she faced him with it squarely. 'Look, Steve, she met Jack two weeks ago and that's when it happened, her second night there. And now she's a week late. No wonder she's worried.'

'Yes,' he said, 'that's what she says.'

A look of surprise. 'And you don't believe her?'

It was all much too tricky and getting trickier. He lit a cigarette. 'I don't know, that's all. I agree it all fits. But it could also fit with some old boy friend she's lost track of.' Even as he spoke he realised that he was not sure what he wanted to be true. He only knew that he wanted to talk to Ella—but not in front of Frances.

'I'm surprised,' Frances said, 'that you think she's that kind of girl. She doesn't seem like that to me at all.'

'I don't think so,' he said patiently. 'I don't know. I'm only saying it's possible and we ought to consider each possibility. Look, why don't you get supper and let me have a talk with her?'

Frances sat for a moment without speaking. 'All right,' she said finally. 'If you think it will help.'

23

ELLA CAME silently into the room, her eyes red. He immediately closed the door behind her.

'Now look here,' he said in a low voice. 'We've got to have this thing out.'

She sat down at once and folded her hands in her lap. She looked very small and young. It was clear at least why Frances had taken her for sixteen: she was not wearing any make-up.

'Are you very angry?' she said quietly.

Alone with her, his anger evaporated and he felt only an alarming urge to touch her.

'I just want the truth,' he said. 'Why have you told Frances this cock and bull story?'

She looked up, her eyes wide: he could have sworn she was genuinely outraged. 'It isn't.'

'Look,' he said. 'You're *not* pregnant, are you?'

She went on looking at him. Sayings flashed through his mind: never trust anyone who won't look you in the eye. But then an accomplished liar would be bound to look directly at you. Useless.

'I don't know,' she said. 'I think so.'

He sat down opposite her. 'You can't be,' he said. 'You told me you couldn't be.'

'I know.' She looked very helpless. 'I must have made a mistake.'

He shook his head. 'Not you.' But this new Ella frightened him. The old confidence was gone and he wanted it back, even if it meant mockery and triumph and malice. 'You're just playing a game,' he said, trying to revive her former self. 'I know you. You want to make trouble for me.'

To his horror she began to cry. He was used to Frances' tears and they no longer had the power to move him. But Ella in tears was a terrifying sight.

'Now then,' he said, against all his instincts, 'none of that. There's no point in turning on the tap. It won't cut any ice with me.' But he had to admit that, if it was false, she did it awfully well.

'I'm not,' she said. And went on crying.

He thought of shouting at her to startle her out of it, but with Frances in the kitchen he had to keep his voice low.

'This morning,' he said, 'when I saw you, you were disgustingly cheerful. So why the big act? You can save that for Frances.'

Ella sniffed. She had never looked so unattractive and he had never—to his amazement and concern—wanted so much to kiss her. 'She's been awfully kind,' she said.

'Well, of course she has. She believes that yarn you've spun her. But I don't, so there's no point in all the waterworks. I'm not impressed.' It was extraordinarily difficult to keep up this line of attack.

She sniffed again; she produced a grubby tissue from the pocket of her jeans and blew her nose on it.

'You don't believe me,' she said.

'I certainly don't.'

She put away the tissue and looked at him with a gleam of defiance. 'You will when I have the baby.'

The words sent a strange thrill through him.

'If you do have a baby, which I very much doubt, it won't be mine.'

'It will.' She stuck out her bottom lip and he suddenly thought that they were like two children playing a game: Yes I am, No you're not, Yes I *am*, and so on, into infinity.

'Why me?' he said. 'Why not Jack, like you told Frances? Or any one of a hundred others, I should think. I doubt if you even *know* who it is.' And then he noticed that by saying this he was acknowledging the possibility of a pregnancy.

'I had to tell her it was Jack,' she said. 'What else could I say? But it isn't.'

'Why isn't it? I should think that's as likely as anything else.'

She shook her head. 'I didn't sleep with him.'

He was startled. He fought back a surge of pleasure. 'Oh, come off it. You can't expect me to believe that. He as good as told me all about it.'

She nodded. 'I thought he would.'

'Well then.' He turned on her.

'He was bound to. Because he was so annoyed when I wouldn't.'

Impasse. He sighed heavily and sat and looked at his hands.

'And if I ask him . . .' he said finally, knowing the answer.

She looked resigned. 'Oh, he'll say he did. But he didn't.'

It was hopeless. Steve got up and began to pace about, unconsciously imitating Frances.

'Look,' he said, feeling enmeshed like a man in a labyrinth, 'if you are pregnant—which I doubt—are you sure you weren't pregnant when I met you?'

She nodded decisively.

'How? How can you be sure?'

She smiled at him for the first time in the interview. 'Because you're the only one,' she said, 'since my last period. And now I'm a week late.'

'Yes, I know all about that,' he said irritably.

'Well.' She was silent.

He paced up and down for a while.

'And you seriously expect me to believe all this?' he said at last.

'Oh no.'

He turned to look at her. She was very calm.

'I was afraid you wouldn't. But I hoped you might.'

'I'm sorry,' he said, not even noticing that he was apologising to her. 'I just don't see why I should.'

She sighed. 'Can I have a cigarette, please?'

He lit two and gave her one. He felt very tired and quite unable to proceed in any direction.

'Look,' Ella said. 'You've asked me a lot of questions. Can I ask you one?'

The politeness was unnerving. 'Go ahead.'

'Well.' She hesitated. 'If I'm not pregnant, or if I am but it's not yours, then why am I here?'

He shrugged. 'That's what I'd like to know.'

'Well, can you think of any reason?'

'No. Except to make trouble.'

'Is that what you think of me?'

He was annoyed, manoeuvred into a corner. 'What else can I think?'

'Only that I'm telling the truth.'

'Yes, well . . .' He latched on to that. 'We'll soon find that out —well, half of it, anyway. You must have a pregnancy test as soon as possible.'

'Oh yes,' she said. 'I will.'

'And then, if you're not pregnant, that's that. And if you are, well, there's still the question of whose it is.'

'If I am pregnant,' she said, 'there's no question of whose it is. It's yours.'

Again the strange thrill of conquest. 'Don't be ridiculous,' he said sharply.

She regarded him with open curiosity. 'Why are you sure it can't be? Because you haven't got any children?'

'Well,' he said, resenting the remark but committed to answering it, 'that does make it less likely to be mine. If you *are* pregnant,' he added as part of the ritual, and thought how entirely circular the whole conversation was.

As if she read his thought, she smiled with the first hint of her former mischief. 'Which you doubt,' she said.

'Yes, I do.'

'I've never been pregnant before,' she said.

'Really? Well, you probably aren't now.'

'I think I am,' she said.

'Don't be silly. You can't possibly tell yet.'

She shrugged. 'It's just a feeling.'

Suddenly the whole thing was too much for him, the endless revolutions, the superb act—if it was an act. He turned to her, holding out his hands, almost in supplication.

'Ella,' he said urgently. 'Tell me the truth.'

She looked straight back at him and he felt he was drowning in muddy green water as he tried to drag some gleam of truth from her eyes. 'I've told you,' she said. 'Now you tell me. If I'm having your baby—and we'll know soon—what do you want me to do about it? Get rid of it?'

'No.' The answer came abruptly, unwilled and unpremeditated.

'Then what?' she said.

The door opened and Frances appeared with plates of food on a tray.

24

THE EVENING had been interminable. Even now Steve could hardly believe that he was at last in bed, vaguely watching Frances cream her face before joining him and putting out the light. They had all watched television together in a sort of exhausted silence and what they would have done without television he hated to imagine: his mind reeled at a picture of playing cards or chess or Monopoly. They made few comments on what they saw but those they made were strictly social and superficial, delivered in light, bright voices, like people in a railway carriage forcing themselves to discuss the weather. It was a relief now not to talk: he felt they had all been discussing Ella and 'the situation' for about forty-eight hours non-stop, but at the same time he got an alarming glimpse of a new pattern of life. A stranger had invaded their home; it was, in a way, almost the same as importing Frances' mother. They were not free to talk—or to ignore each other. Not that he particularly wanted to do either but it was odd to know that he couldn't.

Odd, also, to have his wife and his mistress together in one room. (He had never thought of Ella as his mistress before: the word seemed too permanent.) It struck him that the irony of the position should be shared with somebody or other, but there was no one to whom he would dare to communicate it. He knew a great many people but was not in the habit of confiding in any of them. And he was not sure if he would appear absurd or triumphant to any hypothetical friend. The situation was explosive, certainly, but might yet be turned to his advantage. He had an almost physical sensation of treading on thin ice: the expression suddenly assumed real meaning for him. His every move must be made with the utmost care and delicacy. But he was unsure which way he wanted to go.

It was a relief when Frances got into bed and switched off the light. After the silence of the evening all the sounds she made seemed too loud and the lamp too bright. But lying there in the dark he soon began to feel uncomfortably conscious of Ella's presence in the spare room. He imagined he could hear her breathing, though he knew that was impossible. What was she thinking? Was she asleep? Had she told him the truth after all? And when would he *know?*

'Steve.'

He almost shushed Frances; he felt Ella was there in the room. How thin were the walls? Would she hear them talking? 'What?'

'D'you think we should get the police in?'

'The *what?*' He was shaken and spoke too loudly. 'Whatever for?' he added in a lower voice.

'Well . . .' Her voice, disembodied in the dark, sounded odd. 'I suppose it's technically rape. Isn't it?'

'Good Lord,' he said. 'Of course not. No one ever gets raped in an hotel. She probably asked for it.'

'She told me she was afraid to scream,' Frances said. 'She tried to get rid of him but he wouldn't go and she was afraid to make a fuss and wake everyone.' She shivered. 'It's pretty horrible, isn't it?'

'It's a pretty thin story.'

Frances shifted in bed as if to look at him, though in the dark that was obviously impossible. 'Steve. Why are you so against her?'

'I'm not,' he said. 'Am I?'

'You seem to be.'

'Well.' He chose his words slowly. 'I just don't know what to think.'

'Did she tell you any more . . . when you talked to her?'

'No. No more than she'd told you.'

There was a pause. Then: 'What's going to happen,' Frances said, 'if she *is* pregnant?'

What indeed? 'I've no idea.'

Frances said decisively, 'You'll have to go and see Jack. He'll have to give her some money at least.'

The idea of the errand produced equal urges to laughter and panic. 'What d'you mean . . . at least?'

'Well . . .' She hesitated. 'I don't know. I suppose that's all I mean. I suppose that's all he can do, really.'

What was she suggesting? 'You surely don't mean he should marry her?'

'Oh no. I don't imagine she'd want him to anyway.'

'Well, not if he raped her.' He managed a short laugh.

'It's not funny,' Frances said.

'No, of course not.'

'You men,' she said with sudden bitterness. 'How you stick together.'

He was surprised. 'Whatever do you mean?'

'Well, you won't believe he's guilty and at the same time if he is you seem to think it's amusing. Your clever friend getting a schoolgirl pregnant.'

'Don't be silly,' he said. 'I don't think anything of the sort. And anyway, she's hardly a schoolgirl; she's nineteen.'

'I've taught girls of her age,' Frances said sharply.

'Well, you know what I mean.'

'No, I'm not sure I do. I don't understand your attitude.'

'Oh, Fran,' he said, wearied and alarmed by this new attack, 'can't we get some sleep? We've got enough on our plates without talking about it half the night.'

There was a moment's silence and he thought she was sulking and even that was more welcome than speech. His own brain was revolving so rapidly that he felt he could almost see it, like wheels in the dark. Then:

'Steve, are you sure you're not . . . in this with Jack?'

She had guessed; she knew everything. Automatically he made himself very calm. 'In what?'

'Oh—you know. On his side. Are you sure you didn't know what he was doing?'

Relief. At least he supposed it was relief. There was also something else though: a frustrated violent impulse to shout, to 'have it out once and for all', to say, 'All right, so you know, you can stop playing cat and mouse. It's all true, so what? What are you going to do about it?' To unlock years of . . . something in one enormous scene. And then what? 'Know?' he said. 'How could I possibly know?'

'You were in the same hotel.'

'You said it happened her second night there.' He grabbed at the recollection.

'Oh yes.' Did he detect disappointment? 'Of course. I'd forgotten.'

'Well then. How could I know what was happening?' Did he sound too innocent?

'Mm.' But she went on with it. 'When you went on your last trip though. Did you see Jack then?'

He froze. So far he had not been called upon for a direct lie. And suppose she checked with Ella. Would he get a chance to square her first? No. Was she more likely to lie or tell the truth, then? He had only seconds to decide.

'I was in Manchester,' he said, 'last time. Don't you remember?'

'I thought you might have called in,' she said in a neutral tone.

'Why should I?'

'You did before.'

'Yes, for the night. When I couldn't get home.' He had trained her to accept that he would not drive huge distances in order to get home to sleep. 'But it's a bit out of my way to call in for a chat, if that's what you mean.' Was that enough? Would she drop it now? Something came dimly back to him. Attack. Attack was the best form of defence. He put a shade of indignation into his voice. 'D'you really imagine I keep calling in so Jack can tell me all about his latest conquest?'

'Well,' she said. 'Men do, don't they?'

He disliked the generalisation. 'Do what?'

'Tell each other about their latest conquests.'

For a moment Ella's voice came back to him. ('You'll have to boast about it, won't you?' But he hadn't. Not really. Only as a formality with Jack. Not meaning it.) Did all women fear this? 'Sometimes,' he said. 'Some men.'

'Well, I'm sure Jack's one of them,' she said.

'I'll call in next trip and find out.'

'You'll have to do that anyway.'

'Yes,' he said. 'I suppose I will.'

He thought it was over but she went on. 'Steve, what'll happen . . . about the baby?'

He said hastily, 'We don't know there is one yet.'

'Well, all right. If there is. What's she going to do?'

What indeed? His brain churned with the effort of thinking and talking along two different tracks at once. 'There are . . . homes for unmarried mothers, aren't there?'

Frances let out an exasperated sigh. 'You're very good at putting people into homes, aren't you? Any home but yours.'

It seemed an extraordinary moment to invoke her mother. 'Oh, Fran. Don't start all that again.'

But she continued. 'So you'd just turn her out. If she's pregnant you'll just send her off to a . . . home and wash your hands of the whole affair.'

Not if it's my child, he found himself thinking. At the same time he noted the degree of scorn she put into the word home. 'Well, she can't stay here, can she?' he said lightly. But he meant it. Pregnant or not, with his child or not, this was the last place he wanted her to be, right under Frances' nose where he couldn't lay a finger on her.

'Can't she?' Frances said in a queer, thoughtful voice. 'Why not?'

25

THE HALL was finished. So was the study. Ella put her brush carefully in to soak and stood back to admire her handiwork. 'We've finished,' she said appreciatively. 'Doesn't it look great?'

Frances had to smile at her enthusiasm. 'It's pretty good,' she said. 'You've done very well.'

'It's a very professional job,' said Ella with satisfaction. She spun round triumphantly. 'Aren't we clever?'

'You did most of it.' Frances had woken with a headache after thinking for most of the night and her painting had been even slower than usual.

'I *loved* doing it.' She sighed with pleasure. '*Now*. Shall I get lunch? What are we having?'

'Oh no,' said Frances. 'I'll get it.'

Ella shook her head. 'You ought to sit down and have some more aspirin. Do let me cook. I'm not bad, only I don't often get the chance to try.'

The offer was attractive in itself and, coupled with the headache, almost irresistible. 'All right.' She led the way to the kitchen and itemised the food. She thought she was choosing easy things but Ella cut in. 'Have we got mince? Could we have spaghetti bolognese? I'm very good at that.'

'I'm sure you are,' Frances said, touched by her eagerness. 'You seem to be good at lots of things.'

Ella's face clouded momentarily. 'Except taking care of myself.' Then she brightened again before Frances could speak. 'Anyway, shall I make spaghetti?'

They shopped briefly for what they needed and Frances sat on a stool and watched Ella cook. She seemed very competent and it was a change to be waited on.

'Did you learn cooking at school?' Frances asked.

Ella laughed. 'Not this sort. Rock buns and things. Nothing you could actually *eat*. I learnt more at home. My mother and I used to try out recipes from *The Observer* every week. It was fun.'

Frances asked gently, 'Do you miss your mother?'

'Sometimes. But she's all right. She's got my father and she doesn't care how he treats her. Only I did care. That's why I had to leave home.' She paused, then went on stirring. 'There. Now I've told you.'

'I'm sorry,' said Frances, 'if I made you feel you had to.'

'No. You didn't. It just came out.' A hesitation. 'You must be easy to talk to. I'm not used to that.'

Frances looked at the pale, childish face with its look of intense concentration on the food, the long dark hair parted in the centre and hanging loose, the small, capable hands holding the wooden spoon. 'How old are you, Ella?'

'Nineteen.'

So Steve was right. 'You look younger.'

'I know. It's because I haven't got my eyes on. D'you wear all that stuff when you go out?'

'No,' Frances said. 'Not often.'

'It's fun. We used to practise at school in the dinner hour when we were in the first form. Idiotic little kids smearing eye liner all over ourselves. Now I hardly ever go out without it. I guess it's something to hide behind.'

'In that case,' Frances said, 'I ought to wear it. At my age I need something to hide behind.'

Ella shook her head. 'It's not an age thing. It's just how you feel. Maybe you don't need to hide.'

'I don't know,' Frances said. 'Maybe I do.' She watched the meal developing and thought, She's a strange girl. Why do I feel so drawn to her? 'Why do you need to hide then?'

'Oh . . . probably because I'm not too sure who I am.'

This was the sort of prepared answer that Frances mocked when it came from pretentious young men on television, yet from Ella she was willing to take it seriously. It even struck a chord in herself. For who indeed was she? Steve's wife? 4H's ex-form mistress? Her mother's daughter? She was all these people and yet where was the real Frances who had been a student and then a bride? What was there left of her that existed independently? And who was the person who took an unknown girl in trouble into her home despite all doubts that were almost too small and shadowy to be really there and much too minute to be analysed?

'I don't think any of us really know,' she said.

Ella was studying her. 'Did you talk like this to the kids you taught?'

'Not really. It didn't crop up.' Perhaps she should have done? But with exams to get through, there was never enough time as it was.

'Our teachers didn't either. We didn't give them the chance. Poor devils, we were always playing them up.'

Frances caught the scent of old battles. 'Tell me about your school.' This was sure-fire; something you had in common with everyone you met, only intensified by having fought on both sides.

'It was big. A comprehensive. My parents could have paid for me to go somewhere posh but they were good Socialists and they wanted me to mix.' She smiled. 'It wasn't till I came home talking broad Cockney that they realised quite what mixing meant.'

'You've lost it,' Frances said, thinking, Most of it, anyway.

'Oh, I learnt to be bi-lingual. Only sometimes I get confused. Usually I can choose: to be frightfully refined or dead common.' She made her voice do appropriate things. 'Just now and then I get mixed up and people don't know what to think. People go a lot on accent, don't they?'

Frances said, 'Yes. I'm afraid they do.'

'Oh well. It isn't any worse than clothes or something else. It's a short cut really, isn't it? Because they haven't time to get to know you.'

Frances thought about it. 'I suppose so.'

'That's why it's so hard to make friends. It takes so long to get to know people and you haven't got time. Especially if you keep moving on like me.'

'Do you like moving on?'

'Well. I've done it for a year now. It's been fun. Just sometimes I feel I'd like to have friends, to be settled again. You know. I'm not sure really. Till I got in this mess I hadn't thought about it much.'

Frances tried to keep her voice casual. 'Have you considered at all what you want to do . . . about the baby?'

Ella went on stirring. 'Get rid of it,' she said evenly.

Frances said, 'Oh.' Her heart was pounding and she kept very still.

Ella said, 'Have I shocked you? I'm sorry; I wanted to tell you the truth.'

Frances made an effort. 'No, you haven't shocked me. And of course you must tell me the truth. It's just that I don't really approve of abortion. But maybe I'm prejudiced.' She managed to smile. 'You see? Now I'm telling you the truth.'

'It's nearly ready.' Ella stopped fussing over the food. 'Why are you prejudiced? D'you think it's murder or something?'

'Well . . .' Frances considered. 'Yes, I suppose I do. But it's not just that.' This was difficult to say. 'It seems . . . so unnecessary, when there are more people wanting to adopt children than there are children to be adopted.' She was shaking inside.

'Ah,' said Ella. 'But they don't all get adopted, do they?'

'No,' Frances said. 'They don't.'

'Well then,' Ella said. 'Why is that?'

'I don't know.' Why indeed? 'I suppose all the people who want to adopt aren't suitable. And the children aren't suitable either.' She hated the word suitable but could find no other.

'There you are,' Ella said. 'So what's the good of having a baby if it's going to sit in an orphanage all its life?'

'But it might not. In fact it probably wouldn't. It's'—she began to hate herself for saying this—'the ones who are hard to place that don't get adopted.'

Ella said simply, 'Suppose my baby was hard to place.'

'But . . . it wouldn't be.'

'Suppose there was something wrong with it. Then nobody'd want it, would they?'

'Well.' Frances paused. 'It would be more difficult. But there's no reason why you shouldn't have a perfectly healthy baby, no reason at all.'

'It's still a risk,' Ella said. 'And so is adoption. I mean you don't know who's getting your baby. How d'you know it's all right?'

'The odds are . . .' Frances said slowly. 'They go into it all very carefully. That's why some people who want to adopt are turned down.'

'So then there aren't enough to go round.'

'Well . . . I suppose there aren't.'

'So some quite normal babies get stuck in orphanages.'

How relentlessly she pursued the point. Frances said slowly, 'Yes, I suppose so. But only a few, I should think.'

'Well.' Ella turned back to the food. 'I'd rather not risk it. Hey, this is ready. We can eat.'

The food was excellent, though the conversation had robbed Frances of some of her appetite. 'You're a very good cook,' she said.

Ella looked pleased. 'Maybe I should become an *au pair*. I could travel then, couldn't I? I could go anywhere.'

Frances said, 'Yes. You could go anywhere.' She ate a little more. 'Ella, are you determined not to have this baby? Even if you were sure it would have a good home?'

'I don't know,' Ella said. 'How could I be sure?'

'Well . . . if you knew the people.'

'Oh.' A long pause. 'That might be different. But—oh, it's so messy, isn't it, the whole thing? I mean I'll have to find a job and somewhere to live and I'll get fat and maybe feel ill and then when I have it, suppose I want to keep it? Suppose I got fond of it and keep it and ruin its life?'

'I don't think you would,' Frances said gently.

'What? Get fond of it? Or keep it and ruin its life?'

'Oh, I'm sure you'd be fond of it,' Frances said. 'But I don't think you'd keep it unless you were sure it was the best thing to do.'

'I don't know.' She frowned, 'People go funny when they have babies, don't they?'

'Some people,' Frances said. 'Sometimes.'

'Well, suppose I was one of them?'

Frances put down her spoon and fork. 'Look, Ella. You're supposing all the bad things. Why not suppose you have a perfectly healthy baby and it goes to a good home and you miss it for a while, of course, but you know you've done your best for it. That's much more likely.'

Ella went on eating. 'I suppose so,' she said. 'But it's still messy.'

'How do you mean—messy?'

'Well . . .' She gestured with one hand. 'How long could I work? Where would I live when I couldn't earn any more money?'

Frances took a deep breath. The whole conversation had gone a lot further than she had expected. 'Suppose I could help you with all that?' she said.

Ella looked her straight in the eye with startling directness. 'Why should you?' she said.

Frances said, 'I'd like to.'

'But why? Is it because of Jack? Because that's not your fault. Okay, Mr Howarth got me the job, but that's the end of it. I could have screamed. I could have woken everybody up and made a fuss. Look, Mrs Howarth, I've had boy friends before. I mean I'm not a kid. I knew what I was doing.'

Frances said, 'Did you?'

Ella said defiantly, 'Well, I wasn't a virgin.'

The word fell between them like a gauntlet thrown down. Frances said evenly, 'I see.'

Ella went on looking at her steadily. 'Do you want to throw me out now?'

The moment was electric. Frances said, 'No, of course not.'

'I wouldn't blame you,' Ella said. But Frances could see her relaxing.

'It's not a matter of what you've done before,' she said. 'It's the situation as it is now. And I want to help.'

26

ELLA FITTED into their lives with amazing ease. On Friday evening she cooked dinner for them all when Steve came home, making him feel like a guest in his own house, and they all watched television again. On Saturday he worked in the garden while Ella and Frances went on painting the house and rearranging the furniture. In the evening he felt so hemmed in by women that he went off to the pub and left them deep in a discussion of curtains and French polish. He had not yet had time to acquire drinking companions in the neighbourhood and sat in a corner by himself, turning his glass in his hand. The situation was fantastic. A week ago if anyone had told him this could happen he would have laughed at them. Incredible enough that Ella should be in the same house with Frances and he himself caught between them. Yet perhaps more incredible that his mind should be capable of functioning on two levels at once. All his thoughts ran in double and contradictory harness. He wanted to break down Ella's act, to expose and discredit her; he wanted to believe and accept her and . . . take some kind of action. All ideas were prefaced with conflicting conditions: If Ella is pregnant. If Ella isn't pregnant. If it's my child. If it isn't.

His work, he knew, was suffering. At the office he was vague; sometimes people even had to repeat what they said to him. Sometimes he looked up to find his secretary staring at him; evidently he had paused in his dictation, whereas normally she had trouble in keeping up. It was hard to compose a letter in his head with all the if's and but's that were floating there, and Ella's face. He found himself sitting for hours over reports or reading the same page twice without absorbing any of it. He took too long for lunch when formerly he had been punctilious over his precise hour because he believed in example and had made a practice of being back in the office on time so as to jump on those who were not. None of this had ever happened before.

Frances informed him that she had telephoned, with Ella's

consent, some laboratory in London that undertook pregnancy tests by return of post, and they had said that to obtain a reliable result Ella must be at least two weeks late before sending a urine sample. He was not surprised, though he had had no idea what to expect, but the prospect of another week's suspense struck him with sickening force, like a blow in the stomach. And with everything that Frances did or said he found himself asking: Does she suspect me? Meanwhile with Ella in the house it was almost unendurable to have to treat her like an unfortunate stranger he was forced to befriend. There was no let-up. He was to be at the office for another week.

But on Sunday he got an unexpected break. Frances was going to visit her mother; she had not liked, she said, to go before as it meant leaving Ella alone in the house. Her tone suggested unspeakable, suicidal dangers that he did not like to go into. He said yes, of course, and almost held his breath. Was she really presenting him with an afternoon alone with Ella?

She went. He stood at the window and watched her drive away and for a mad moment he thought: She knows and she's going for good. I'll never see her again. He knew this was mad and yet at the same time it seemed quite logical that she should not come back, and a way out of all their difficulties. He turned round and saw Ella staring at him. She was wearing an old dress of Frances' because all her clothes had been washed. It was much too big for her and she looked somehow touching and small, like a film heroine swamped in the hero's pyjamas.

'We're all alone,' he said.

'Yes.'

They went on looking at each other. He had been longing for this but now he could not move. The space between them was immeasurable.

'Well,' she said, and waited.

He lit a cigarette. 'She'll be at least two hours,' he said. 'Maybe three.'

In the end it was Ella who moved. She came across to him and took the cigarette out of his hand. 'You don't really want that,' she said, 'do you?' and suddenly it was all surprisingly easy. She was just as he remembered her, warm and soft and astonishingly eager, and the long wait and the painful proximity put an excruciating and delightful edge upon everything they did, until the very end when he suddenly remembered and wanted to be gentle because of the child. He was only dimly aware of a smell of burning. Afterwards they found a nasty mark on the floor where the cigarette had burned away.

'Oh hell,' he said, 'look at that.' And they both laughed foolishly, leaning against each other. The afternoon sun poured into the room; they had not drawn the curtains in their haste and anyone could have looked in.

'I'll scrub it,' she said. 'We'll get some stuff from the kitchen and scrub all over the floor and say we were trying to get the white marks off.'

This seemed a very good idea. They went to get the equipment and worked on the floor in a breathless silence like conspirators. Occasionally they laughed, at nothing in particular. Finally they stopped scrubbing and surveyed their achievement.

'I don't know,' Ella said, her head on one side. 'I think it looks worse.'

'It does,' Steve said, 'but it all looks worse. At least it's not just one cigarette burn.'

Ella got up and took the kitchen things away. He sat in a chair feeling warm and comfortable and oddly disembodied. It was all so easy: why could it not always be like this?

Ella came back. 'You know,' she said, 'we could always have said we just dropped a cigarette.'

He laughed. 'Yes, we could.'

'I mean, it's not incriminating exactly, is it?'

'No.'

She sighed. 'I wonder why liars automatically tell lies even when they're not necessary. Just habit, I guess.' She sat on the scratched floor at his feet. 'Steven, I think she wants to adopt the baby.'

He was shaken. 'Frances?'

'Who else?'

'Did she say so?'

'Not exactly. But she hinted.'

He brooded over this. In a way it did not surprise him and it was certainly one solution. But . . .

Ella said, 'If she mentions it to you, what will you say?'

'I don't know. Play for time, I suppose. Stall.'

Ella said slowly, 'She must be very keen to have children.'

'Yes, she is.'

'Then why didn't you adopt before?'

'I don't know. We discussed it. It just . . . never got further than that.'

'Were you as keen as she was?'

'Maybe not.' He tried to be honest.

'But this would be different,' Ella said, 'wouldn't it?'

He didn't answer. His mind was crowded with a picture of himself and Frances with Ella's child. His child. And Ella? Where would she be? Back on the road, in some other hotel, making entries in her little black book?

'Steven,' Ella said abruptly, 'I've told her I want an abortion. And I do. Can you get me one?'

He stared at her. 'I told you,' he said, 'I don't want that.' He put a hand on her hair. 'It's silly and dangerous.' Her hair was thick and silky. He stroked it.

'Maybe,' she said steadily, 'but it's a way out. And I want a way out. Not her way out. Mine.'

'No,' he said.

She looked up at him, her eyes green and hard. 'You can't stop me.'

'No, but I'm certainly not going to help you.'

She stood up. 'All right,' she said, 'I'll do it alone. There are people who'll help. I'll just have to find them.'

'No,' he said again.

She drew back, tightening the belt on Frances' dress. 'Why not?'

He made a helpless gesture. 'I don't know why not. But I don't want you to.' He made the words as emphatic as possible.

'I see,' Ella said. 'It doesn't matter about me. This may be your only chance to have a child of your own. Is that it?'

He felt uncomfortable. 'Something like that,' he said, 'I suppose. But you're wrong. It does matter about you.'

She laughed and moved away. 'Oh, does it?' she said. 'So what do I get out if it? I'm just a kind of incubator, aren't I? Growing a baby for you and Frances because you can't grow your own. Charming.'

He could not bear her scorn. 'It's not like that.'

'Isn't it? Then what is it like?' She scuffed at the floor with her bare feet.

Steve said, 'Look, Ella, this is awfully difficult.'

She laughed harshly. 'You're telling me.'

'No, shut up and listen. Please. I'm trying to explain. Frances and I have been married a long time and it's not as good as it was. I don't know how much of that is not having children. We didn't want them at first and then when we did, it just didn't work out. They couldn't tell us why. We had all the tests, the usual routine, drew a blank.'

'So?'

'So here we are. Not happy, not unhappy exactly.'

'Just married,' Ella said. 'Like my parents. So what's so difficult? It happens to millions of people.'

'It's difficult,' he said patiently, 'to tell Frances you're having my child.'

She looked at him. 'But I'm not asking you to,' she said. 'I'm pretending it's Jack's specially to help you out—isn't that obvious? I'm only asking you to get me an abortion.'

'But I can't,' he said desperately, and found himself saying words he had never expected to hear. 'I can't help you kill my child.'

Her eyes were very cold. 'It's mine too,' she said. 'And I don't want it. And Frances wouldn't either if she knew.'

'What's that?' he said sharply. 'Blackmail?'

'No. Just facts. It's two to one, Steven.'

He got up. 'Nonsense,' he said. 'It's nothing of the sort. It's just . . . tricky. We've got to think.'

'I've thought,' Ella said, 'and I want an abortion.'

*   *   *

They made, as is usual in a quandary, tea. They sat and drank it in the living-room, looking at the floor, the walls, the furniture, anywhere but at each other.

Steve said eventually, 'Look, Ella. If I found you somewhere to live and paid your rent, whether you were working or not. Somewhere you could keep the baby and I could see you now and then.' He was trying to provide an acceptable alternative to abortion and also to find out what he himself really wanted. The idea of Ella and his child in a flat somewhere between home and the office so he could call in every day (except when he was on trips) struck him as extremely attractive. 'How about that?'

'You must be joking.' She sounded really amused.

'No, why?'

She turned her head. 'You seriously expect me to sit tight in a crummy little love nest somewhere and wait for you to call and have a quick bash and pat the baby on its head. If that isn't funny I don't know what is.'

He said with irritation, 'You put things so charmingly.'

'I'm realistic, that's all.' She banged down her tea cup. 'Look, Steven, I meant what I said to you in Birmingham. I want a life of my own. I was all right till I met you and you knocked me up. I was having fun. Why should I settle for being tucked away in a corner somewhere with a baby because it suits you to pop in now and then?'

'You'd still be free,' he said helplessly. 'I wouldn't expect . . .' He stopped.

'You wouldn't expect what? Me to be faithful—is that what you were going to say? My God! That's marvellous. Am I supposed to be grateful?'

'It was just a suggestion.' But he felt a little ashamed; he had been asking a lot.

'Well, you know what you can do with it.' She poured herself a second cup of tea with quick, noisy movements.

'All right,' he said. 'What do you want?'

'I've told you.' She stirred the tea. 'An abortion. And the sooner the better. I can't go on staying here. Your wife's being so kind to me I could choke.'

'Abortions cost money,' he said unkindly. 'And you're broke. Or have you still got the money you pinched from Jack? That won't get you very far.'

'He owed it me. Anyway, I can soon make some more. You gave me a fiver that first time, don't you remember? How much does an abortion cost? Fifty pounds? A hundred? Ten fivers. Or twenty.' She snapped her fingers. 'Simple.'

'No.'

'No, what?'

'I know I can't stop you,' he said urgently, 'but I'm asking you not to.'

'But you haven't come up with an alternative yet. Not one I fancy anyway.'

'How can I?' But his brain was moving slowly, with alarming logic, in an unforeseen direction.

'I'm not hanging about here for another week,' Ella said, 'waiting for that test. Hell, it's bound to be positive. Every day makes it more likely.' Suddenly to his surprise she got up and came across to his chair, gripping his shoulders with both hands. 'Oh, Steven—oh hell—it was good in Birmingham, wasn't it?'

He looked up at her, strangely moved. 'Yes,' he said, 'it was. It was the best thing that ever happened to me.'

'Better than Frances?' she said in a muffled voice. 'I mean at the beginning.'

'Oh God yes.' But he could hardly remember. The smell of her skin was like perfume, drugging him. He put his arms round her waist. 'Ella, listen. If—if I was free, if we could—be together all the time, would that make a difference?'

She slid down till she was kneeling on the floor, her face on a level with his. 'What d'you mean?'

He tried again. Something alien inside his head seemed to have taken over and he could not control it. But he hardly wanted to. 'If we could live together . . . would you have the baby?'

The brown-green eyes were troubled. 'Do you want to live with me?'

'I think so.'

'But why?'

'I don't know.' All the words were hackneyed: everything he thought of to say seemed to have come from a cheap song. 'You've made . . . quite an impression.'

'But you can't say you love me exactly.' She went on looking at him intently.

He shook his head. 'I don't know any more what that means. What's the point of saying it? I just know I want you round.'

'Because of the baby?'

'Partly. More so, yes. But it was the same in Birmingham. I wanted to see you again. When I heard you'd gone and I didn't know where you were, it was'—he managed to smile—'pretty rough.'

'Poor Steven.' She stroked his hair.

He caught her hand. 'You're a patronising little devil, aren't you?'

She smiled. 'Yes. I'm beastly. I don't know why you want me round.'

'Neither do I. But it seems I do.'

'Well.'

'And you?'

'And me what?'

'You haven't told me yet. Do you want me round?'

'I don't know,' Ella said. 'We could have fun, I think. But what about Frances?' She spoke gravely, like a thoughtful child.

'Well . . .' He reached for cigarettes. 'I've been thinking. You know she's gone to see her mother today.' Ella nodded. 'Well, she's always wanted to have her living with us only I put my foot down. She could do that if I moved out.'

'You mean she'd rather?' Ella seemed surprised.

'I don't know.' It all felt so suddenly plausible that he was convincing himself. A whole new life sprang into existence. 'At the moment she hasn't got anything she wants. Her mother or children. We're just jogging along. I'm away a lot and when I'm here . . .'

'You fight?'

'Oh no. Nothing so dramatic.'

'You'd fight with me,' Ella said.

'Yes, I probably would.'

'And I'd certainly fight with you.'

'Okay,' he said, 'we'd both fight. With each other.'

'And is that what you want?'

'I don't know.' He looked at her. 'I think it probably is. How about you?'

She shrugged. 'It's better than being stuck in a room somewhere.'

'Well,' he said. 'You needn't be so enthusiastic.' But the more off-hand she was the more attractive he found her and the more urgent his plan became.

Ella sat back on her heels. 'You haven't really thought,' she said. 'I wouldn't be like Frances, you know, waiting patiently at home while you knock off other birds. You couldn't trust me. What you do I can do. And I would.'

'Yes, I know,' he said. 'We'd have to have a pact.'

'Oh no. Fat lot of use that'd be. But I could travel with you. We could go all over the place together. Would you like that?'

'Yes,' he said. 'I think I would.'

'We could go abroad. You could get a job anywhere.' She laughed. 'We could see the world. I've always wanted to see the world.'

'It's a big place,' he said soberly.

'You sound scared. What's the matter? Afraid of throwing up your nice safe job?'

'Why do you have such contempt for security?'

'I don't,' she said. 'Unless it makes people soft. Only it usually does. They get used to their cosy little rut and they stay. They pull the blankets over their heads and stay for ever.'

'Yes,' he said. 'You may be right.'

'Of course I'm right.' She sat back and clasped her arms round her knees.

'Oh, Ella. You're so sure of yourself.'

'Well. It's like marriage. You should stay because you want to, not because it's too much trouble to move. I'd never marry you, Steven.'

'That's all right,' he said. 'I didn't ask you.'

'That's right, you didn't. But I wouldn't marry anyone. I've seen it. Ugh.'

'Okay,' he said. 'If you feel like that we'll have a little bastard, that's all.'

She eyed him thoughtfully. 'D'you mean you would marry me if I wanted you to?'

'I don't know,' he said. 'I hadn't thought that far. I suppose so. A child ought to have a name.'

'Huh,' she said contemptuously. 'That's all it is. If I wasn't pregnant you'd let me rot, wouldn't you? There'd be none of this come away with me, Ella. You'd be too busy trying to save your shaky little marriage.'

'That's not true.'

'Isn't it? If I hadn't come here what would you have done? Gone on seeing me in Birmingham till you'd had enough. Found someone else. And someone else. Gone on living with Frances— if you call it living. Why d'you do it, Steven? Does it make you feel a hell of a chap?'

'No,' he said.

'Then why? What d'you get out of it?'

'You don't understand. You think life's so simple. But not everyone has a choice.'

'Well, you've got one now.'

'Yes. And I've made it.'

'Aren't you worried about hurting Frances?'

'I don't think it will. At least—not too much.'

'Do you think she loves you?'

'There you go again—using that word.'

'If I loved someone,' Ella said, 'I'd never let them go, never. But I'd see they didn't want to. And if they knocked hell out of me I wouldn't love them any more so it wouldn't matter. I'd be off.'

'I believe you would,' he said. 'But it's not always as simple as that.'

'Then it should be,' Ella said fiercely. 'If I were Frances and you'd treated me the way you've treated her, I'd be glad to see you go. In fact I'd kick you out.'

'Then that's all right,' he said, 'isn't it?' But he felt uneasy. The ferocity was something he hadn't seen before. 'She won't be hurt then, will she?'

Ella, instead of answering, held out her arms to him. 'Come on,' she said. 'Do we have time before she gets back?'

'You're insatiable.' But he joined her on the floor. 'Why do we choose these bloody uncomfortable positions?'

Her eyes looked up into his. 'You're a rat, Steven Howarth. D'you know that?'

'Steady now. Careful. Or I'll hurt you.'

'A genuine, grade one, yellow-bellied rat.'

He hurt her.

'So why are you going away with me?'

'Maybe I like rats.'

27

THEY HAD talked for half an hour about India and Dad and the
servant problem.

'You have to watch them, you know,' the old woman said.
'You have to watch them all the time. They're like children. Did
I ever tell you about Artif and the jam tarts?' She chuckled to
herself. 'I said, "Artif, you make me four dozen tarts and I want
half of them with jam and half with lemon curd." And he said,
"Yes, memsahib." And when I went into the kitchen there they
were. Half jam and half lemon curd.' She rocked with laughter.
'In each tart. Just like children. You couldn't be angry.'

'No,' Frances said.

'He was very loyal, Artif. When your brother died he came to
me and he said, "I'm sorry, memsahib." He was a baby and he
died, just like that. It was the climate, you know. When a child
gets fever in a climate like that. . . . But Artif came and said,
"I'm sorry, memsahib." And I couldn't say anything. I was crying,
you see. I let a servant see me cry.'

Frances said, 'I'm sure he understood.'

A sharp look. 'Oh, you had to be firm with them. Kind but
firm. Make them know who's boss. Otherwise they don't respect
you, you know. Your father was like that. Kind but firm. That's
the way. He never struck a servant, you know. Not like some I
could name. It doesn't do. Shows you can't control them and they
don't respect you. You remember that.'

'Yes,' Frances said. 'I will.'

'Must have respect. It's the only way. D'you have good serv-
ants?'

'No,' Frances said. 'Not really.'

The eagle eyes flashed, blurred with cataract. 'Get rid of them.
Never keep a bad servant. It doesn't do. They only take advantage.'

'I know.' Frances looked at the papery skin stretched tight over
the fragile old bones and her heart contracted with pity and love.

'It's not worth it,' the old woman said. 'Get rid of them.'

'All right,' Frances said. 'I will.'

'Get some good reliable boys. Treat them right and they'll stay with you. Kind but firm. It's the only way.' A sudden chuckle: such a harsh, dry sound. 'Never laugh at them. Oh, you'll want to. Now who was that boy? What was his name? You know, Artif's cousin.'

'Oh yes,' Frances said. 'I know.'

The thin fingers twitched. The rings hung loosely on them and the veins stood up, blue and knotted. 'What was his name? Oh, it's on the tip of my tongue. He was a good worker. But simple, like a child. Swallowed buttons, you know. Thought they were aspirins.'

Another chuckle, fading into a coughing fit. Frances held her till it was over. She felt so thin, so brittle. How could life be contained in something so brittle?

'So hot, you know. You had to get to the hills. All the women and children. Not healthy. I'm sure it shortened your father's life.' A heavy sigh. Her breathing filled the room, growing slow and regular. 'He was a good man, your father.'

'Yes, I know.'

'He always did his duty. When he was dying he said to me . . .' But the last words came slowly, dragging their way out, and the speech faded. Frances leaned forward.

'Mother.'

The eyes were closed, the breathing rhythmic and slow.

'Mother, are you asleep?'

No answer. Only one day, Frances thought, this will happen and there won't be any breathing. Will I be there? Oh God, how long can it last? Does she have to die here?

She leaned forward again and stroked the lace on her mother's sleeve. The clothes smelt of mothballs: their pattern was rich and dark. There was a dribble of saliva from one corner of the old woman's mouth. Frances took out her handkerchief and gently wiped it away. Her mother began to snore slightly.

'I'm frightened,' Frances said to her very softly. 'I don't know what to think. And I'm frightened to think at all. Do you know that feeling?' Through the window she could see other old people moving slowly and stiffly across the lawn. 'When he looks at her there's something strange. Oh, it's nothing you could put your finger on. But he looks at her without expression, that's the trouble. His face is too blank. He doesn't look cross or interested or bored or anything. And it's the same when he speaks to her. His voice is too careful.'

An old woman stumbled on the grass and an old man caught her arm. They walked on together and paused at the edge of the lawn.

'You see, I like her. I don't know why but I do. She's young and helpful and lively. I want to help her. But I keep thinking— no, that's not true. I keep not thinking, trying not to think. It couldn't be, could it? I mean I must be imagining things.'

The snores went on; grew a little louder. Don't wake up, Frances prayed. Stay asleep a little longer so I can talk to you.

'I can't ask him, you see. And I can't ask her either. Oh, I know there's no reason to suspect and I don't, not really. But—what am I going to do if it is?'

The old woman snorted and woke herself up. She looked round her, confused, and saw Frances.

'Hullo, my dear,' she said. 'Have you been here long? You should have woken me. It's not like me to drop off in the middle of the day.'

Frances stood up and kissed her cheek. It was soft and powdery.

'We had a long chat,' she said. 'And then you had a little sleep. Now there's nothing wrong with that, is there?'

The old woman frowned. 'Oh dear,' she said. 'I'm afraid my memory's not what it was.'

Frances lingered by her chair. 'I'll come again soon,' she said. It was useless to name a day; the days of the week meant nothing. 'And I'll bring you some more flowers.'

The old woman touched the bunch in the vase. 'Thank you. They're so pretty.'

Frances kissed her again. The grip on her hand was surprisingly strong. 'See you soon,' she said. 'Now you take care of yourself.'

At the door she shook her head sharply. It was unlike her to cry and it was a weakness she could well do without.

28

'How WAS SHE today?' Steve asked. He was putting up bookshelves in the living-room when Frances got back.

Ella called from the kitchen, 'Shall I make you some tea, Mrs Howarth?'

Frances sank into a chair without answering. She felt very tired. 'Oh, extremely colonial,' she said, watching Steve. 'Sometimes I doubt if the India she remembers ever really existed.'

Ella appeared in the doorway. 'I've put the kettle on, Mrs Howarth.'

Frances said, 'Thank you.'

Steve said, 'Don't you remember it too?' And Ella looked from one to the other.

'Am I interrupting?' she said. 'I can go away.'

'Oh no.' Frances shook her head. 'We're just talking about my mother.'

'Oh yes.' Ella seemed interested. 'How is she?'

'Lost in the past,' Frances said. 'I was just telling my husband. She talks about India all the time but I hardly remember it. I was only a child.'

Ella pulled up a stool and sat down. 'Is she happy?'

'I doubt it,' Frances said.

Steve started to say, 'Oh, come now,' but remembered the afternoon's conversation and stopped abruptly.

Ella said, 'Could I come with you the next time you go? I'd like to meet her.'

Frances was taken aback. 'Yes, I suppose so. She likes young people. Would you really like to come?'

'I'd love to. Is it a nice home? Are they kind to her?'

Frances sighed. 'Oh yes,' she said. 'I'm sure they are.'

Ella said, 'It's not the same though, is it? Being in an institution, I mean. We had my granny living with us for years till she died. It was fun. She used to tell me stories.'

'Yes,' Frances said. 'It can be fun.' She felt oddly disorientated:

removed from time and space. The day was warm, yet it was all she could do to stop herself shivering. She stared into space, listening to the kettle starting to boil, and her eye caught the marks at her feet. 'What's happened to the floor?' she said.

'Oh, that,' Ella said. 'We were trying to make it better but we only scratched it. I'm sorry.'

'We'll get someone in,' Steve said. His voice sounded too loud to Frances. 'Don't worry, love; it'll be all right.'

'Yes,' Frances said. 'I'm sure it will.' She got up and went into the kitchen. Ella followed her.

'Oh, don't,' she said, as Frances began to make the tea. 'I can do that.'

'Not at all,' Frances said. 'You've done enough already.'

*   *   *

In bed she willed herself to keep calm. The scent she had put on now struck her as cloying and made her feel slightly sick. But she clung to her plan like a child thinking, If so and so happens it's an omen. She forced herself to move closer to Steve, to put a hand on his body. The warm flesh seemed so alien that she nearly drew back in terror. But she persisted; even tried to move seductively. She did not trust herself to speak.

Steve put his arm round her. Her hand lay heavily on his stomach; he seemed to ignore it. Frances, with a great effort, forced it to explore further. She felt shaky, almost disgusted with herself. Suddenly Steve put his hand over hers and held it fast.

'No?' she said. It surprised her that her voice could sound so normal.

'I'm tired,' he said.

But why did he not show surprise? It was so unlike her to make the first move. And why was he tired?

'All right,' she said, and tried to take her hand away. But he went on holding it.

'Nice idea though,' he said, rather hearty and appreciative.

Frances turned over with a big movement and this time he let her hand go. She manufactured a yawn. 'I'm tired too,' she said. 'Really.' She lay on her side and thought to herself over and over again, It doesn't prove anything, it doesn't prove anything, until she fell asleep.

29

ELLA SAID across the table, 'What are we going to do today?'

She and Frances were having breakfast together after Steve had left for the office. They ate very little but drank endless cups of coffee and listened to records on the wireless. At nine-thirty washing up was still waiting to be done. It was years since Frances had led such a lazy existence and in the clear morning light the previous night's doubts seemed absurd and unreal.

'Carry on painting, I suppose,' she said.

Ella frowned. 'Can't we . . .' she began and stopped. Frances waited. 'Can't we go to the zoo?'

'The zoo,' Frances repeated, amazed. 'Good heavens. Do you really want to? I haven't been since I was a child.'

'Neither have I,' Ella said. 'Wouldn't it be fun?'

Frances thought about it. 'Well, yes,' she said slowly. 'It might be. But what about the painting?'

'Oh, that,' said Ella with fine disdain. 'It'll still be here when we get back. So will the washing up. Can't we just drop everything and go?'

'Well . . .' Frances hesitated. 'I suppose we can. If you'd really like to.'

'Oh, I would.' Ella sprang up. 'It's such a lovely day, it's a shame to waste it on painting. Don't you think?'

'All right.' Frances got up. 'I'll get ready.'

'Don't be long,' Ella called after her. She was clearing the table, humming to herself.

'You're very cheerful today,' Frances said to her through the bedroom door, trying to decide on her clothes. What did one wear to go to the zoo?

'I feel marvellous,' Ella said. 'Oh, I know I ought to be worried but I just can't be. D'you know, ever since I told you about the baby I've felt better. It was being all alone with it that was so awful.'

Frances, putting on lipstick, looked at her reflection. Impossible, she thought. And yet . . .

Ella was ready and waiting when she emerged. 'Aren't we lucky?' she said. 'Men have to work. But we can go out and enjoy ourselves.'

'Well,' Frances said, 'that's one way of looking at it.' She felt hustled along—taken out of herself, that was the phrase. Not for years, not since she and Steve were first married, had she made such a sudden, pointless expedition like this.

They drove in silence for a while, then Ella said, 'D'you think I'm awful?'

Frances said, 'Awful? No, why should I?'

'Oh, you know. I suppose I ought to be all worried about the baby. But I can't be. I mean I am really but I can't be *all* the time.'

'No,' Frances said. 'I suppose you can't.' Then, because that sounded a little chilly, she added, 'Of course you can't.'

Ella sighed contentedly. 'It's like a holiday,' she said, 'staying with you.'

'Hardly that,' Frances said. 'You've been working very hard. Cooking, painting. You've more than earned your keep.'

'But it's *fun*.' Ella flung the word as a child might toss a ball into the air and catch it again, out of sheer exuberance. 'It's not like work. I've enjoyed it.'

'Well,' Frances said, noting the past tense, 'it's not over yet.'

'No, but it soon will be. You've been so kind, Mrs Howarth, but I really will have to move on. I can't go on imposing on you.'

Frances kept her eyes on the road. 'Well, suppose you move on,' she said, 'when I throw you out.'

'I've been thinking,' Ella said. 'Do you think maybe I could get a job at the home where your mother is? They must want people to clean the rooms or cook or something. Maybe even just someone to wander round and talk. I could work for six months at least, I'm sure I could. D'you think they'd take me?'

The idea was unexpected, yet immediately Frances wondered why they had not thought of it before. 'We could ask them,' she said. 'If you come with me next time I go we could ask them then. I know they do have trouble finding staff—apart from the nurses, I mean.'

'Well, I could do anything,' Ella said. 'That's my trouble. I can do anything but nothing very well.'

'We'll see.' The irony of the position struck Frances very forcibly: that this girl might end up helping to look after her mother. 'D'you really think you'd like it?'

'Oh yes.' The casual answer was more convincing than passionate enthusiasm. 'I used to do everything for Granny when she was alive. It was fun.'

'You use that word a lot, don't you?' Frances said.

'Do I? I suppose I do. Well, it's the only thing really, isn't it? I mean, if you don't hurt anyone why shouldn't you have fun?'

'Quite. But sometimes having fun does hurt other people. It depends on what kind of fun it is.'

'Yes, I know. That's the trouble. I think that's why I wanted to have an abortion. It wasn't just for myself. I didn't think it would be much fun for the baby having just one parent or living in an orphanage.'

'You sound,' Frances said, 'as if you'd changed your mind about that. Have you?'

'I'm not sure. I've been thinking about what you said. If I really knew it was going to a good home . . .'

'Well, I think you could know that,' Frances said. 'Sometimes adoptions are arranged privately, you know.' Her heart was beating very fast.

'Mm. Well, I'm not sure yet but I'm going to think about it. When I have that test I'll decide.'

'On Friday,' Frances said.

'Yes, I suppose so.'

'Not long now.'

There was a pause. Ella said abruptly, 'D'you mean I can stay till then?'

'Well, of course,' Frances said. 'I thought that was understood.'

'Not really. Oh, you've made me very welcome but I feel awful about staying on and on.'

'It's hardly that. Only a week.' But she felt it was longer. Not in terms of annoyance though: something else, that she could not define. It had to have been longer because so much had happened. And yet, in a sense, nothing had. So why did she feel that her whole life was altered? It was even beginning to be hard to remember a time without Ella.

'You've no idea,' Ella said slowly, 'what it's meant to me to be in a real home again, not just a hotel or something. It makes . . . all the difference in the world.'

*   *   *

The zoo was crowded, mostly with parents and children having a day out. At one time Frances might have envied them but to-day she had other things on her mind. She was still trying not to think but occasionally a thought slipped through and joined the others. They all fitted.

'Look.' Ella stopped in front of the lions. She and Frances had not bought a guide-book and were wandering aimlessly round, sometimes retracing their steps by accident. 'Aren't they marvellous? Only I want to let them out. Do you think they hate us?'

Frances looked at the animals staring into the distance with immense dignity. 'I don't know,' she said. She thought of the poems about caged lions she had read with the junior forms, the debates on zoos and circuses. Animal discussions were always popular.

'It makes me feel ashamed,' Ella said, 'to see them like that. But I still want to come. I'd like them to know I'm on their side. I'd like to rescue them.'

'They're not in cages all the time, you know,' Frances said. 'They do have a fair amount of space to run round in. It's not a bad zoo.' But she knew what Ella meant.

'I feel so selfish,' Ella said. 'I like them being here because I love looking at them. But they ought to be free.'

'Yes,' Frances said. 'I suppose they ought.'

When they reached the monkeys' cage Ella said, 'Now they're all right. I mean they're doing what they would be doing anyway, swinging on trees and eating. And I'm sure they love the crowds.'

Frances looked at the monkeys, showing off shamelessly to an enraptured audience of children. They looked alarmingly human. How could anyone who had seen a monkey ever seriously have doubted Darwin?

'Our ancestors,' she said.

Ella said, 'Mm. We haven't progressed very far, have we?'

Frances was thinking: I don't want to know. I don't. And there's nothing to know. Just the facts as they are. That's quite enough. She said, still watching the monkeys, 'Ella, I haven't talked to my husband yet so I can't promise anything, but how would you feel if—if we adopted your baby?' She had not meant to say it yet, but it came out by itself, sounding perfectly natural.

There was a long pause. The monkeys swung and the children squealed and poked nuts through the bars. Ella said slowly, 'Are you serious?'

'Yes,' Frances said. She was keeping an almost physical grip upon her emotions.

Ella said, 'But . . . why? You don't know anything about me. And there's Jack. What about him?'

'You're not in love with him, are you?'

'Good heavens no. I only meant—well, you don't like him very much, do you?'

Frances said, 'Do you mean bad blood or something?'

Ella clasped the rail outside the cage with both hands. 'Something like that.'

'A baby is a baby,' Frances said. 'It's . . . more than its parents. And anyway, what's so wrong with you and Jack as parents?'

There was another long pause. Then Ella said, 'Would it be different if you didn't know who the father was?'

Frances took a deep breath. 'But I do,' she said. 'Don't I?'

Ella's knuckles were white on the iron rail. 'You've only my word for it.'

'Why shouldn't I believe you?' The noise round them was deafening: what was she doing having this intensely private conversation in such a public place? And yet, anywhere else, it would have been impossible.

'Well . . .' Ella hesitated. 'I told you there were others.'

'Yes, I know.'

'Well, it could be any of them. I might have lied to you.'

'Why should you?'

Ella said, 'I only meant—aren't you disgusted with me?'

'No,' Frances said. 'I don't approve, of course, but . . .' It suddenly came out and she knew it was true though she had not thought of it before. 'I think I rather envy you.'

Ella let go of the rail. '*Envy* me? But why?'

Suddenly the noise and the inactivity were too much for Frances. 'Come on,' she said. 'Let's walk.'

They walked and at first it was hard to pick up the threads. Frances found herself full of intense resentment. 'I know it sounds crazy,' she said, 'but I do envy you. For all kinds of reasons. For being nineteen. For having fun. For having the chance of a baby. Even for having had more than one lover.' She laughed, embarrassed. 'Even though I don't approve. Now isn't that absurd?'

Ella said in a small voice, 'I think it's very nice of you.'

Frances swung her handbag. There was something distinctly liberating about the atmosphere of the zoo, crowded as it was with hordes of people she did not know and the smell of the animals. It was a place she and Ella could get lost in, away from Steve, away from everything. Perhaps this was why people took holidays in unfamiliar places; maybe they really did escape from their problems.

Ella said, 'It's not that I was—promiscuous or anything like that. But I did have one or two boy friends before this and we did have affairs. It was fun; it didn't hurt anyone. Only I didn't expect you to understand.' She smiled. 'It's marvellous that you do.'

'Well,' Frances said, 'things are different now. When I was your age—oh dear, how ancient I sound—well, anyway, when I was a teenager I suppose virginity was more important. You know—you saved yourself for your husband, that kind of thing.' How silly it sounded, she thought.

'I know,' Ella said. 'Lots of people still do.'

'Well,' Frances said, surprised at her own ferocity, 'it's a moot point if it does them much good.'

'Oh dear,' Ella said. 'Do you mean you wish you hadn't?' And then, immediately: 'I'm sorry, am I being cheeky?'

'No,' Frances said. 'Or maybe you are. I don't mind anyway. Yes, sometimes I do wish I hadn't.' This had not occurred to her before but now it seemed very clear. 'After all,' she said, 'men don't do the same for their wives, do they? They never have.'

'No,' Ella said. 'That's true.'

'So it's all rather pointless.' Frances was still swinging her handbag without even noticing, until it struck a passer-by and she had to stop and apologise.

Ella said as they moved on, 'Did you know Jack was married?'

'Yes. But he's divorced, isn't he? Or is it only separated?'

'I don't know. He just mentioned his wife. I felt awful. You know, Mrs Howarth, I ought to have yelled and woken everyone up and got out. I keep thinking about it. But I couldn't. D'you know why?'

Frances said, 'No, you tell me.'

'I think it was because he reminded me of my father. Does that sound funny? The boy friends I had before were my own age, it was different, sort of equal. I'd never got involved with someone my father's age before and I just couldn't make a fuss. I knew I ought to but I couldn't. It would have seemed worse somehow, to show him up like that, than to go through with it. Sort of . . . undignified. Can you understand that?'

'Yes.'

'It's an awfully silly reason though, really. As things have turned out, I mean.'

'Not silly. Just unfortunate.'

'Yes. It is, isn't it? Poor baby. You know, I keep forgetting about that test. I'm so sure now. I wasn't at first but now I just have that feeling. You know?'

'Well no,' Frances said. 'Not exactly. But I can imagine.'

'Oh, I'm sorry.' Ella caught hold of her hand. 'I *am* stupid, I keep forgetting. It's not poor baby anyway, if you're going to adopt it; it's lucky baby. Will I be able to see it sometimes?'

'Yes, of course.'

'Oh, only if you think it's all right. I could pretend to be an old friend or something.'

'Well, you will be, won't you?' Frances said. 'By then.'

*   *   *

They lunched on sandwiches, ice cream and orange squash in a crowded café. They couldn't talk much there because they were surrounded by harassed mothers, crying babies and children whose noses needed wiping. Frances kept thinking, When I ask him what will he say? When I put it to him. Is this the solution? In fact need we ever face it?

After lunch they saw the animals and birds they had missed before and she waited outside the reptile house while Ella did a quick tour of the snakes she loved and Frances feared. She looked at the people strolling past and wondered what problems they had. Were they anything like hers? She told herself she could still be wrong, was very likely wrong, but her over-riding emotion was still a sort of ironic anger. What a fool I've been, she thought, and almost laughed.

'Well,' she said to Ella when she returned, 'are you ready to go now?'

Ella said, 'Yes,' but she did not sound ready. They walked towards the gate and presently she said, 'Oh, I'm ready to leave here, I mean we've seen everything and it's been marvellous, but I don't want to go back yet.'

Frances looked at her watch. 'It's half past two.'

'I know. I suppose we ought to go back but can't we make a day of it? Go to a film or something?' She sounded wistful.

A film would take two or three hours, Frances thought. They could not possibly be home by six; in fact it might be nearer seven if they got caught, as they probably would, in the rush hour. She was always home before Steve, with the meal half-cooked; today, so far, she had not even shopped. What was there at home? Soup. Eggs. Some rather old cheese. And Steve hated scratch meals.

'Why not?' she said to Ella. 'Let's do that. A film might be fun.'

30

To STEVE, arriving home promptly at six, the empty house was not so much an affront as a puzzle. Where could they both have gone—assuming they were together? It was not the day for the test and even if it had been that could all have been done by post and phone. But he gave up the problem in favour of relaxation. In a way it was almost a relief to have the house to himself; impossible to think clearly at the office with people milling round him and requiring decisions about work when all he wanted was peace, to be left alone, to plan. He poured himself a large Scotch and sat down.

He supposed that since his conversation with Ella yesterday the ball was back in his court. It was up to him to tell Frances and to choose an appropriate moment to do so—if such a thing could be found. Her behaviour last night had disturbed him profoundly; it had been all he could do not to let her see how disturbed he was. What the hell had got into her? She had not done such a thing in years; he could not even remember the last time. Ironic, really, that she should do it now, so much too late; and doubly ironic that she should pick yesterday of all days, when it was quite beyond him to raise a flicker of interest even if his life depended on it.

But it didn't. He had a whole new life just waiting for him, if he could only nerve himself to make the break. It would mean a scene, of course, maybe more than one, and he hated scenes. Yet was it not perhaps a scene they should have had years ago? What good, after all, had they done each other by staying together so long? Once the question of children was settled, for want of a better word, everything had run steadily downhill, with nagging and tears and rehashing of the mother issue. Damn it all, Frances had not behaved as if she wanted him round half the time. Until last night. Well, that was her bad luck. It was simply too late.

But it would not be simple to tell her. Would she cry? Would

she be shocked, outraged? Would she fly at him, maybe even attack Ella? He would have to get Ella out of the house first.

There were so many practical difficulties: the time and place to
be arranged and Ella's absence. They would have to come to a fair
financial arrangement, of course, with the house in both their
names as it was. But it was a small mortgage, as mortgages went,
with the deposit from their previous house, and anyway it was
not as if Frances could not earn her own living. She had often
pointed out her capacity to do that in the past; well, now she
would have her chance to prove it.

Still, it was one thing to plan, another to actually visualise the
scene. He did not know how much it would hurt her and he did
not want to hurt her. He did not want to hurt anyone, but someone, given the present situation, would have to be hurt sooner or
later: Frances, or Ella, or the child.

The child. He hardly dared let himself think about that and
yet it intruded, a warm, reassuring sensation, like a puppy pushing
its nose into his hand. He supposed that logically he should wait
until Ella had the test before talking to Frances; he would look
ridiculous if there was, after all, no child. But there must be; it
was nearly two weeks. And in any case, he found himself thinking
with surprised clarity, would it really make all that much difference anyway? Child or not, he wanted to live with Ella. It was
extraordinary how sure he was of that. The child only made him
more sure and provided a reason for action as well as a surge of
power and achievement. The child would prove that it had been
Frances' fault all along and there had been no need for her to
look at him with the contempt he had sometimes glimpsed in her
eyes (and tried not to see) as if he were only half a man. The
laugh would be on her.

Not that life with Ella would be such a laugh. She would cut
down his freedom no end; he would never know where he stood
with her. But that in itself was exciting, even the very knowledge
that he could not trust her an inch. Of course the idea of giving
up his job was ridiculous and as for travelling round the world,
well, she was crazy even to suggest that. You couldn't travel round
the world with a baby. But she had probably not realised how
much the baby would tie her down: that was a point. It would
cramp her style considerably. Perhaps he would be able to trust
her after all.

He drank his whisky and poured another. It took the edge off his hunger but all the same he found himself wondering rather irritably where Frances was. It was unlike her to be out when he got back. To give her her due, she had always been very efficient about the house and the meals, had always seen to his comfort in that way. He wouldn't expect the same of Ella. But he would gain something else. She did not even seem keen on going away with him, merely saw it as an alternative to abortion, but she had agreed. With her twisted mind she could easily be jumping at a chance to punish him for her pregnancy, to make his life hell by living with him: he accepted that. It would at least be living. In a way it was like—yes, it was like joining Turner's gang. Not that he had ever succeeded in joining it, though by God he had tried hard enough. It was not even a question of forgiving Turner for tormenting him: the worse Turner was, the more desirable became the prospect of joining him. Even gang members were persecuted at times but it was a different thing: a badge of acceptance, the persecution of an in-group that could also, and more often, join forces against the outsiders. And he wanted to belong, he had forgotten how desperately.

He heard a key in the lock and jumped up. Another long triangular evening to be faced: there were times when he felt like the hero of a French farce, living as he was in this *ménage à trois*. At those times he could even picture the situation continuing indefinitely: his remaining with his wife and mistress under the same roof and all bringing up the child together. It would make life a lot easier in many ways. But he knew that was pure fantasy.

He expected to hear voices but there were only footsteps in the hall, very slow. Eventually Frances came into the room. She was alone.

'Hullo,' he said, 'where's our guest?' He tried where possible to avoid referring to Ella by name; he did not know why.

'She's gone for a walk,' Frances said. 'Have you been back long?'

He glanced at his watch. 'Since six.'

'Yes, we're late, aren't we? We stopped for a snack on our way home.'

'Lucky you,' he said. 'I'm starving. On your way home from where?'

Frances put down her handbag. 'Oh, we went to the zoo,' she said, 'and then to the pictures. I thought you'd be hungry. But there's food in the fridge. There always is.' She sat down heavily.

'The zoo and the pictures.' He stared at her. 'Whatever for?'

'Fun.' She smiled at him. 'It was Ella's idea. We had a very good day.'

'I should think you must be exhausted,' he said; 'aren't you?'

She shook her head. 'Oh no. They say a change is as good as a rest. How about you, are you tired? I hope you're not because I want to talk to you. That's why I sent Ella for a walk. I want to talk to you alone.'

31

IT SEEMED to him now that this was all they had been doing for as long as he could remember: having talks. At the same time each one was a fresh ordeal.

'Oh yes?' he said pleasantly. 'What about? Do you want a drink?'

'Not really,' Frances said. 'I think we're both doing far too much drinking these days. And I want to keep a clear head.'

'Okay. Please yourself.' He leaned back in his chair, endeavouring to look more relaxed than he felt. 'Fire away.'

Frances sat very still. Watching her, he thought she looked different and he tried to pin it down. Older, tired, defeated? But it was none of these things entirely. She said, 'Well, I've talked her out of abortion, I think.'

'Oh, have you?' he said. 'That's good.' His heart began to beat rather fast.

'Yes. We had another long talk. At the zoo. It's funny, it's quite a good place to talk. You wouldn't think so but it is. Maybe you and I should have gone there.'

He smiled, uneasy. Frances stared past him.

'We saw a French film,' she said, 'after the zoo. It was called "Le Bonheur".' She pronounced it rapidly with her best accent and he felt instinctively that she wanted to baffle him, to take advantage of his lack of education. He raised his eyebrows enquiringly; he might as well let her get away with it.

'Happiness,' Frances said. 'Isn't that a coincidence?'

'Coincidence?' He felt uncomfortable, as if she had him on the end of a piece of string that she could pull in and let out at will. 'Why?'

'Oh, don't you remember?' She was smiling to herself. 'No, of course you don't. But the day after we moved in here, the night you got back from Birmingham actually, we talked about happiness.'

'Did we?' He tried to remember. Did she mean that idiotic

scene she had made in the middle of the night? And yet this conversation was important; he was sure of that.

'I asked you,' she said pointedly, 'what we could do to be happy.
And you were rather cross.'

'I'm sorry,' he said. 'I was probably tired.'

'Yes, I expect you were. You said was I asking you for some
kind of blueprint and you rushed off to have a drink.'

Her verbal memory, accurate always he thought in direct ratio
to the unpleasantness of the material, astounded him as usual.
Was it developed as part of her job or was it simply Frances herself? 'Oh yes?' he said. 'That sounds like me all right.'

'The man in the film had a blueprint,' she said. 'In a way.
Without being aware of it, I mean. He had a wife and two children and a mistress and he was terribly happy. So happy in fact
that he just had to tell his wife. You see, he wanted to share his
happiness with her. She took it very well. Only then, after he'd
told her—they were on a picnic at the time—she left him and the
children asleep and went off and drowned herself.'

His mouth was dry. He said with an effort, 'How very unpleasant.'

Frances said, 'Oh, but that wasn't the end.'

'No? Then what happened?'

Frances went on smiling gently. 'Oh, he was terribly upset, he
really was. And they had a funeral and everyone was very sad and
he went away for a while. Then he came back and married his
mistress.'

'Good heavens,' said Steve faintly.

'Yes. And they both went for a walk in the woods with the children. It was autumn by this time and everything was gold and
brown and they wore sweaters to match and it was terribly idyllic.
The children had a new mother and he had a new wife and there
they all were, a family again. So lots more *bonheur*, on and on.'

She had stopped. The silence was like a vast pool, filling the
room.

Steve said at last, 'Is that what you wanted to talk to me about?'

'Not entirely. I was just telling you about my day.'

'I see,' he said. 'Well, I'm glad you enjoyed yourself—did you?'

Frances said slowly, 'It was a very good film and I'm glad I saw
it. It was Ella's suggestion; she said she'd always wanted to see it
and there it was, at a Classic.'

'How very convenient.'

'Yes. Anyway, that's why I was so late home.'

'I see,' he said again.

'Do you?' Frances said. 'I hope so. It's an interesting idea, don't you think? I mean the only real mistake he made was telling his wife. If he hadn't, everything could have gone on just as before.'

'Yes,' he said. 'I suppose so.'

'Though of course from his point of view it very nearly did anyway.'

'Yes.'

'Anyway,' she said, 'I'm getting off the point.'

Steve said, 'What is the point?'

Frances sighed. She still had the same small and gentle smile. 'Oh, I meant to lead up to it really but I suppose I better come right out with it. I told you I talked Ella out of abortion. Well, this is how I did it. I told her I'd ask you if we could adopt the baby.'

There was another huge silence. His nerves tingled fiercely. 'Are you serious?' he said at last.

Frances said, 'Yes, I am. Don't say anything, just listen. Just listen and think. Ella wants to work with old people, to get a job at Greystones if possible. She'd like to see the baby occasionally, with our permission. But we could adopt it.'

Steve said, 'Look, Frances——'

She cut in savagely. 'I said don't say anything. Just listen and think. That's all I'm asking you to do.' Her voice became more steady and calm. 'Now I know we talked about adoption before and never made a decision. I don't know what your reasons were, and mine . . . well, that doesn't matter. I think it's all different now. It's more . . . immediate, don't you think, right here on our doorstep. It might'—she paused—'have almost been meant.'

His brain reeled. The sameness of the room and their surroundings seemed like a joke in bad taste.

'That's right,' Frances said softly. 'Don't say anything. I want you to think about this very carefully. Because it seems to me that this might be our last chance.'

'Our last chance,' he repeated. 'For what? What d'you mean?'

'For happiness.' He expected her to get up and pace about as before but she remained sitting in the chair, very still and quiet, with her hands in her lap. 'I suppose this is a funny time to have a talk. Or it's a funny thing to talk about at this time. I don't know. I wanted to talk to you that night, you remember, but it didn't work out. Still, it's rather more urgent now. We're not getting anywhere, are we? I mean we haven't been for ages. I nag you, I know I do, though I keep meaning not to. I worry about Mother and take it out on you. I feel pointless. We're not getting anywhere; we're not even making contact any more. There's nothing to look forward to any more, nothing to aim at. But now I think there might be.'

Her generosity overwhelmed him. He had had no idea that she could ever react and behave like this. He wanted to accept, if only because such a gift should be accepted, completely, in the same spirit. But it was too late. He knew it, physically as well as emotionally. He felt enormous friendship and gratitude towards her but the life she was describing rose up to choke him like a malignant growth. Having once glimpsed an alternative he could not give up and accept less. He felt reckless, perhaps for the first time in his life.

'I'm sorry,' he said very gently. 'It's wonderful of you but I've got to——'

'No,' she said. Her eyes were very bright. 'Oh, I know people shouldn't adopt to put a marriage right but that's not what I mean. We wouldn't be doing that. This is a special case: we both know that. Okay, I accept it. Now you accept it too and we can start from there.'

But no Ella? No mistrust and uncertainty and cruelty and misery and—happiness? No freedom and insecurity and joy? 'I'm sorry,' he said. 'I can't accept it. I've got to tell you——'

'I *know*.' Her intensity burned him. 'Just don't tell me, that's all. Just don't say it. For God's sake, Steve . . .'

'I can't,' he repeated. 'I—I want to go away, Fran. I'm sorry. Love, I *am* sorry, but I want to go away with her.'

The words were out. He looked up, heavy with guilt, and saw that she was crying.

32

He gave her a drink and stood over her while she drank it. He lit her cigarette. The house was very quiet: they might have been miles from anywhere. Only the sound of her tears intruded on the silence.

He said over and over again, 'I'm sorry, love. I *am* sorry. I really am.'

Frances said eventually, 'Have you got a handkerchief?'

He gave her one and she blew her nose on it and wiped her eyes. He wanted to pat her shoulder or make some sort of sympathetic contact but the very idea seemed impertinent.

'Well,' she said at last. 'Well, well.' And blew her nose again.

He said, 'It's not your fault, you must believe that. It's entirely my fault.'

'Oh no,' she said. 'It's never that.' She opened her bag and groped for a mirror. 'What a sight I must look,' she said vaguely.

He said, 'I can't explain. I don't know how it happened. It just . . . crept up on me, I suppose. I mean, it was only yesterday I really knew what I wanted to do. It's all been going on sort of . . . off stage.'

Frances said, 'I think I knew from the beginning.'

He was shaken. 'What? How could you?'

'Oh, I don't mean the very beginning. Just when she came to the house.' Then she smiled faintly. 'No, that's not true. I didn't. I just feel as if I did, now. I've been feeling so odd for days.'

'I'm truly sorry,' he said again.

She looked at him with a flash of anger. 'I do wish you'd stop apologising.'

He moved his hands helplessly. 'I don't know what else to say. That's all I can think of. I mean it, Fran.'

She shivered at the name. 'Yes,' she said, 'I expect you do. I wish I could hate you. But I just feel numb.' She put the mirror away in her handbag and clicked it shut. 'Oh well.'

He said again, 'I don't know what to say.'

Frances lay back in her chair. 'Oh, there are things.'

He stared at her.

'You can tell me about it.'

He was silent.

'Come on,' she said, 'I want to hear. Don't you owe me that?' Then, as he still didn't speak: 'No, that wasn't a nice way to put it. But I'd like to hear.'

He sat down heavily in the opposite chair. 'What can I tell you?'

'Well . . .' She appeared to consider. 'To begin with, was she the first?'

He shook his head.

'No,' she said. 'I thought not.'

He looked up.

'Oh, I don't mean I was suspicious,' she said. 'Don't worry, you never gave anything away. No, I just mean she's unlikely to have been the first. How many have there been, by the way?'

'I don't know.' He felt intensely embarrassed, and ashamed too, in a way he had not expected.

'Too many to count?' she said with a tiny, ironic smile.

'No, of course not.'

'Oh, it's not of course anything. Not any more. But all right.' She actually laughed and the sound chilled him profoundly. 'I'll let you off the hook. Quite a few, anyway.'

He nodded, not looking at her.

'Well,' she said again. 'When did it start?'

He lit a cigarette. 'I—oh, Fran, do we have to go into all this?'

'We don't have to,' she said with a certain strange dignity, 'but I'd like to know.'

'About five years ago.'

'I see. About the time we started having all those tests.'

'Yes.'

She sighed. 'Well, I suppose that's logical in a way. Only—I've been wasting my time, haven't I?'

He could not bear it. 'Fran, please don't.'

She frowned. 'Do you think you could stop calling me that? It may be a funny thing to ask but I think it would help.'

'I'll try,' he said humbly.

'Well now,' she said, as if gathering new strength, 'so there were all these . . . girls, were there, on trips presumably? Just casual, were they?'

'Yes, of course.'

'And this never happened before?'

He looked up.

'I mean the *baby*,' she said savagely.

He shook his head.

'No, of course not,' she said. 'Silly question. You'd have left me before, wouldn't you?'

He said vehemently, 'I never thought of it before.'

She was swaying to and fro in the chair, rocking herself.

'I mean that,' he said.

'Oh yes,' she said. 'I believe you.' There was a long pause. Then: 'So tell me about Ella.' She almost flung the name at him.

He said feebly, 'There's nothing to tell.'

Again the chilling laugh but harsher this time. 'Oh, come on. You meet the love of your life and you get her pregnant when you thought you'd never have a child. There must be something to tell.'

'That's all,' he said. 'Except that she's not the love of my life.'

'Oh, isn't she?' Frances said. 'What is she then? Just the mother of your child, is that it?'

He winced at the bitterness in her voice. 'Not even just that. She's . . . more like a disease.'

'How sweet.' Frances tapped her fingers on her knee. 'Well, I shouldn't tell her that if I were you. Not that I'm in any position to give you advice but if you want my advice that's it. I don't think any girl, however much in love, would appreciate being told she's like a disease.'

'I don't think she is in love with me.' It was partly that he wanted to be honest, partly that he felt it would help Frances if he could run down his relationship with Ella.

'Oh, I'm sure you're wrong,' Frances said sardonically. 'You really mustn't be so modest. Of course she's in love with you. Why else should she want to go away with you?'

Steve stubbed out his cigarette and lit another. As an afterthought he offered them to Frances who took one, saying, 'Yes, I think I will. Thanks. That's one of the funny things about marriage, don't you think? Whatever the crisis, you have to go on smoking each other's cigarettes.'

He couldn't answer that. He said instead, 'I think she just sees it as an alternative to abortion.'

'Oh yes?' said Frances. 'Well, we've both worked hard at providing alternatives, haven't we? How very nice for her. She's had a wide choice.'

'Look,' he said desperately. 'Do we have to go on with this?'

'Oh dear.' She looked at him through a haze of smoke. 'Does it upset you? Of course men are very squeamish. All right, I'll try to make it easy for you. You met her—when? The day I moved in here? Or before?'

'No, that day. Nearly three weeks ago.'

'Ah yes. Three weeks on Wednesday.' She smiled brightly. 'It's nearly your anniversary, isn't it? And you got her pregnant straight away.'

'I don't know. I suppose so. I never meant to.'

'No, well, it doesn't make any difference, does it? I mean, these things happen. Or not, of course. Tell me, Steve, how does it feel to be a prospective father after all these years?' She waited for his answer and he could not speak. 'Oh well, I shouldn't ask such personal questions. I do hope for your sake that test is positive, though. Or doesn't it matter now anyway?' She waited again. 'You're awfully quiet. You know, I feel quite self-conscious; I'm talking too much. So when did you see her again?'

He muttered, 'Last week.'

'Oh yes, of course. On your last trip. Did you stay the night?' He nodded. 'Yes, naturally. You must have had to get up very early. Still, I expect it was worth it.'

He said with a groan, 'For God's sake can't we stop this?' and she burst into such savage laughter that he thought she might spit at him or attack him with her nails.

'No, we bloody well can't,' she shouted when the fit was over. 'Why should we, just to suit you? You're getting everything you want and don't you forget it. This is all I'm getting and I want it, all of it. Is she good in bed, is that it? Is she all exciting and different? Does she tell you how marvellous you are and make you feel a new man, is that it?'

Steve put his head in his hands. Presently he heard Frances make a retching sound and turn it into a cough. 'Oh Christ,' she said in a thin, stranger's voice, 'I'm disgusting myself.' And stopped.

The silence was as powerful as a blow on the head. Steve took a deep breath and felt dizzy. He realised he must have been almost forgetting to breathe and was groggy from lack of oxygen. Frances too was breathing deeply, even panting, as if she had run a long race.

'Oh dear,' she said at last. 'Oh God.' She took another deep breath and let it out slowly. 'Well. It just goes to show. You never really know yourself.' She got up. 'Well, that's that. I'm not going on any more, you'll be glad to hear. No, I really mean that, it's not a crack. I think I owe you an apology actually. I went too far.' She sighed and added in a thoughtful, surprised voice, 'Much too far. You were right; I should have stopped before. Still, maybe it's therapeutic, as they say. I certainly hope so.' She moved towards the door but stumbled and fell against the wall for support. He jumped up automatically but she put out her hand to ward him off. 'No, please don't.' She sounded almost apologetic. 'Don't touch me please. I'm not quite steady yet. But I'm getting better all the time.' She went out of the door. 'Really.'

33

HE HEARD the bedroom door close and went on sitting where he was, waiting for Ella. He could not think what else to do. But presently he got up and went into the kitchen to make himself a sandwich. He felt guilty about eating at such a time (for although he had seen plenty of wakes he had never accepted the principle behind them) but to his surprise he was hungry and he could not go on drinking whisky on an empty stomach. He took his sandwich back into the living-room and poured himself another drink.

The house was still unnaturally quiet. He had paused outside the bedroom door but heard no sound from Frances of tears or anything else. He thought he knew her well enough to assume that she would not do anything silly, or he did not like to flatter himself that she might, yet still he wanted to go in and say something comforting to her. But he did not know what he could say that might be in any way comforting, and the closed door seemed to put as much distance between them as an ocean or a continent.

So he sat in the living-room alone and ate his sandwich and drank his Scotch. Then he lit a cigarette. He looked round the room and supposed that he would have to sleep on the couch. But it was only eight o'clock—far too early to sleep anywhere. And anyway, how could he sleep with so much on his mind? In that case, however, there was an awful lot of evening to be got through and he did not like to put on the television in case Frances heard it and assumed he was cold-blooded enough to be enjoying himself. But he badly needed something to do. Eventually, with a high sense of absurdity, he took a pack of cards from the bookcase and began playing patience.

It was after nine when Ella returned. He had been half-listening for her all the time and at the first tentative knock on the front door he was up and out in the hall to let her in.

The first thing he noticed was that she was soaking wet. Her shirt and jeans clung to her body and her hair was plastered to her head and shoulders. He pulled her inside.

'Good Lord,' he said stupidly, 'is it raining?' He had not even noticed.

She looked at him. 'Oh no,' she said. 'Actually I went for a swim with my clothes on. You look like death. What's happened?'

'Come on,' he said in a low voice as if there were something more to conceal. 'Come in here.' And he took her into the living-room and closed the door.

'Where's Frances?' she said. 'I stayed out as long as I could. Have you had your talk?'

'She knows everything,' he said dramatically. He felt dramatic.

'Does she?' said Ella. She was shivering. 'D'you think you could get me a towel?'

He went into the bathroom and came back with a towel and his own dressing-gown for her to put on. She undressed, dried off and changed in silence, and for the first time he found the sight of her body unexciting. But he had never needed her more.

'Ella,' he said urgently, 'it was awful. We had a terrible scene.'

Ella was tying the cord of his dressing-gown tightly round her waist. 'Could I have a drink,' she said, 'before I get pneumonia or something?' And sat down on the couch.

He poured a drink and gave it to her. 'Did you hear what I said?'

She drank slowly before answering. 'Yes, I heard. You must have made a balls of it. Why was it terrible?'

He lit a cigarette. 'She was upset,' he said. 'That's why. Why d'you think?'

'But you said she wouldn't be.' She looked up from her drink.

'Yes, I know. I was wrong. It was God-awful.'

'Poor Frances.' She sounded genuinely sorry. 'Does she still love you?'

'I don't know.' He cradled his half-empty glass. 'I think it was just the shock. Although she said—she said she knew already. Ella, she came in and she *knew* and she still offered to adopt the baby.'

'She did *that*?'

'Yes. She didn't want me to tell her. She knew but she just wanted to go on as if nothing had happened and adopt the baby.'

'That's fantastic,' Ella said slowly. 'Why didn't you say yes?'

He stared at her. 'But—we're going away. I had to tell her. That's what was so awful.'

Ella said, 'But when you told her, didn't she see that she'd be better off without you?'

'Well, thanks.'

'Didn't she though? Wasn't she pleased about her mother and that?'

'We didn't get that far.'

'Oh, my God,' said Ella, rising. 'You did make a balls of it. I thought that was the whole point.'

'It didn't work out,' he said, defeated.

'So now what? Does she hate me? Does she want me to clear out this minute?'

He shook his head. 'I don't know. We didn't discuss that.'

'I hope she doesn't hate me,' Ella said thoughtfully.

'Why? I should think she probably does. She's got every reason to, after all.'

'But I don't want her to. She's been marvellous to me. I don't want her to hate me.' She stamped her foot on the floor.

'Oh, Ella,' he said, depressed and amazed, 'for Christ's sake, what else can you expect?'

'Well,' Ella said, 'her to hate you instead. There's more reason after all. I wasn't married to her. I didn't let her down. You were the one who married her and made all those promises and then started picking up girls. You're the one she should hate.'

'Well, she doesn't,' he said with a certain smug triumph. 'She said so; she said she couldn't. And anyway, aren't you forgetting? You were one of the girls.'

'So what? There were others—lots of them, weren't there? Lots before me. Does she know about them too?'

'Yes,' he said. 'She knows everything. I told you.'

Ella sat down again and drank some more whisky. When she spoke again her voice was sad. 'Oh, Steven, why ever didn't you give me some money and kick me out?'

He stared at her, 'I couldn't,' he said. 'You know that.'

'But *why* not? Why didn't you get me an abortion like I asked you? Why didn't you choose her? She's your wife after all.'

'I wanted you,' he said simply. 'What's the matter with you? I don't understand your attitude. You must have known it would be like this.'

'I didn't,' she said. 'I really didn't. You said she wouldn't mind.'

'Not exactly. I just didn't think it would be as bad as this.'

'But it is. Isn't it?'

'Yes,' he said. 'It is.'

'She's too good for you,' Ella said. 'That's all there is to it. But I'm not. I'm just what you deserve. We're two of a kind and both rotten.'

'Charming,' he said. 'How romantic. But probably true,' he added after a pause.

Ella drained her glass. 'Well, I'm going to bed,' she said.

He wanted desperately not to be alone again but they obviously could not sleep together, however innocuously, under this roof. 'All right,' he said.

At the door she paused. 'Do you feel guilty?'

'Yes.'

'You should,' she said. And went out.

34

At six Steve got up and took his customary bath, though at what was far from his customary hour. He had not slept until four o'clock or thereabouts when he had finally given up hope of sleep and devoted himself to listening to the birds. Now the prospect of facing a day at the office on what amounted to virtually no sleep filled him with only slightly less horror than the prospect of facing Frances. This was the really difficult part, he thought. Bad enough to be put in an impossible position, to come to a decision, to endure a painful scene. But the real ordeal, perhaps because he had been unable to visualise it in advance, lay before him now: the aftermath. The appalling, messy, anti-climatic business of meals and polite conversation and arrangements. No wonder people simply walked out, sometimes without even packing a suitcase. He began to see what was meant by a clean break and why everyone always said it was best.

When he heard the bedroom door open he felt that the bath water had suddenly gone cold. He had not locked the door because he never did but surely Frances would not come in—not today. He knew that he must face her sometime, and they must exchange looks and words, but he would have done anything to postpone the moment and was still telling himself that it could not happen when it did.

'Hullo,' said Frances, coming in.

He said hullo. He felt very naked and vulnerable in the bath, an object of ridicule almost, and it was not a time (if there was ever one) when he could afford to look ridiculous.

'I've run out of toothpaste,' she said. 'Isn't that silly? Can I borrow yours?'

He said yes of course she could. He could not look at her and became very busy with the soap. She paused at the door with the tube of toothpaste in her hand.

'I'll make some coffee,' she said, 'as we're both awake.'

He wanted to thank her but could not get the words out. As

soon as she had gone he leapt out of the bath and locked the door before towelling himself dry. He was suddenly terrified of Frances seeing him naked. But he had to go into the bedroom for a clean shirt. Mercifully she was not there.

When he was dressed and feeling slightly better for the protection of clothes and the ice-breaking words they had exchanged, he went into the kitchen. Frances was sitting at the table with a cup of coffee in front of her. She had even poured one out for him. He sat down opposite her, lit a cigarette and began to drink.

'Me too,' Frances said, picking up the packet.

'Oh, sorry.' He saw at once that coffee and cigarettes were the only things that could get them through the day and had in fact paid a two o'clock visit to the machine across the way. It had been a dark, cloudy night after the rain of the evening and he had felt very much alone, not at all like a man about to start a new life. He said, 'Did you sleep?' and she said, 'Oh, eventually,' and he said, 'Me too. That couch is a bit hard.' He wanted her to know, for some reason, that he had not been crude enough to sleep with Ella, and she looked back at him ironically, as if the point was clear.

'Do you want me to go right away?' he said humbly. 'I mean now, today.'

She regarded him calmly, almost with friendship. 'I know what you mean; but why should you? We're not going to be dramatic about this, are we?'

He said, 'No, I suppose not. Thank you.'

Frances yawned. 'Well, what's the point? After all, we haven't been dramatic for years, have we, about anything?'

He said, 'I'll make arrangements for her, though,' and jerked his head in the direction of the spare room. Anything was better than saying Ella's name. 'She can come in the car when I go and I'll find her a hostel or something.'

But Frances said, 'Oh, why?'

He looked at her in amazement. 'I thought—well, I naturally assumed you'd want her out of the house straight away.'

'Yes,' Frances said, 'so did I. But really, what's the point? I mean as I didn't throw her out last night . . .'

'I thought about that.'

'Yes, well.' She sighed. 'What does it matter after all? She's probably asleep. If she can sleep, good luck to her. I mean I really don't see any point in waking her up.' She poured herself a second cup of coffee and pushed the percolator in his direction.

'That's very generous of you,' he said, refilling his cup.

'Oh well. Is it generous? It's not . . . anything really. I mean, what would I do? Rush into the spare room, drag her hair out by the roots, scream abuse, throw her into the street.' She smiled faintly. 'It sounds awfully energetic.'

He managed a weak return of the smile. 'Yes.'

'So,' Frances said. 'She may as well stay.'

'But . . . all day?' The prospect of the two of them alone in the house suddenly alarmed him.

'You needn't worry,' Frances said. 'I won't hit her or anything.'

'I didn't mean that. I just thought—well, what can you say to each other?'

'Oh, I don't know. We might find something. After all, we've got quite a lot in common.'

The alarm crystallised into a definite fear. 'You mean . . . you *want* to talk to her?'

'Well . . .' She crushed her cigarette into a saucer. 'Oh, I know it's a bizarre situation but still, what else can we do? I don't mean I'm trying to be civilised or anything brave like that but—oh, it's just impossible to be any different. I mean, you go on. You have to breathe and you try to sleep and you make coffee and smoke cigarettes and . . . all that. You know?'

'Yes,' he said. 'I felt that too.'

'Well, there you are,' she said. 'We've got something in common after all. And anyway, as I didn't kill myself last night, or murder you or murder her, well, I may as well make coffee and let her sleep. I mean I've missed my chance to be dramatic.'

'Fran,' he said, forgetting, 'are you all right?'

'Oh yes.' She smiled at him quite genuinely. 'As well as can be expected, as they say. Better, actually.'

Strangely, much as he hated scenes, this new calmness was even more distressing. He felt suddenly that he was being discounted, written off, with hardly a backward glance. It was unbearable to be dismissed like that.

He said, 'Tell me something. When you made that fantastic offer last night—for us to keep the child and go on together—why did you do it?' Surely this would inject a little emotion into the scene—not too much, but just enough to be decent and fitting.

'Oh dear,' said Frances. 'Do you really want to know about that?'

'Please.' It was important to him, quite suddenly, and not entirely for the reason he had thought when he said it. Looking at Frances, he wondered with considerable shock how he would feel if it just happened that Ella had died in the night.

'Well,' Frances said, and paused, stirring her coffee. 'I suppose I thought I owed it to you. I suppose I thought that if either of us had the chance to have a child, the other one ought to accept it. It seemed only fair really. Since that's what it's all about.'

'But it isn't,' he said. 'Is it?'

'No.' She drank some coffee. 'Not entirely. No, that's only part of it really. But last night it seemed the most important part.'

'And today?'

She put down her cup with a sigh. 'Oh, I don't know. It's still the most immediate part, of course, but—well, suppose it hadn't happened, what would we have done? Just gone on as before?'

'I'd never have thought of leaving,' he said, 'for any other reason.'

'Wouldn't you? No, I don't suppose you would. But—you didn't have much to stay for really, did you, anyway?'

'I don't know,' he said. 'What d'you mean?' But he knew what she meant. He wondered why it hurt to hear her say it.

'Well, it's been the same for both of us really, hasn't it? That's what I wanted to talk to you about that night.'

'I know,' he said. And he did, though he had not admitted it to himself until that moment.

'Only I handled it all wrong. Oh well.' She got up and began to wash her coffee cup very slowly. 'Do you want a divorce, by the way?'

He was startled. 'I don't know.'

'Oh. I thought you'd be sure to want one.'

He hesitated. 'Well, I suppose I do. Only . . . I don't know if Ella really wants to marry me.'

She looked round at him with a gentle expression, almost of sympathy. 'Poor Steve. You're not sure of her, are you?'

'No.' Somehow it did not seem disloyal to admit this to Frances, after all the years. 'No, I'm not.'

She said softly, 'Perhaps that's part of the attraction.'

'I don't know. I don't know what the hell it is, to tell you the truth. I wish I did. She was so funny last night when I told her what had happened—upset.' Frances' expression became ironic and he added, 'Really. I mean it. She was . . . almost angry. In a way it's as if—well, as if she's on both sides at once.'

'How strange. I'd have thought she'd be pleased to get what she wants.'

'I don't really know what she wants. Me or the baby or . . . what. I'm not sure she knows herself.'

'But you want her.'

'Yes. Yes, I do. It's funny. In a way I wish I didn't.'

'I hope she'll make you happy,' Frances said. 'No, really' (seeing his look), 'I mean that. I want you to be happy. After all, why not? Your being unhappy won't do me any good, will it?'

'Will you be happy?' he said urgently.

'Oh, me.' She smiled. 'I don't know about me. Not any more.'

'You—you could have your mother here now,' he said. 'That was something I forgot to say last night. You can please yourself now and have her if you want to. Wouldn't that help?'

'I suppose so. I hadn't thought. How funny—you're making plans for me already.'

'Well,' he said, 'I just thought it might help.'

'Yes. Like "exchange is no robbery". Oh, I'm sorry, I didn't mean that. It's a good idea; I'll have to think about it. It's not simple though, you know; I might have to work part-time and there's the question of money.'

'But I'd still be helping,' he said quickly. 'We'll have to come to some arrangement, of course, about the house and everything.'

Her nose wrinkled. 'How very sordid,' she said with distaste.

'I'm sorry,' he said, 'but we'll have to, won't we?'

'Oh yes. Of course. You're quite right. Don't be too generous though. Remember you'll have a new wife and baby to keep. Steve'—she suddenly turned round from the sink and faced him— 'just tell me one thing. Did you . . . laugh at me, you and her? About me, thinking it was Jack to begin with?'

'No,' he said, shocked. 'No, of course we didn't.'

'I'm sorry,' she said. 'I just thought you might have.'

'But I thought it was too, at first. I wouldn't believe her when she said . . .' And then he couldn't go on.

'When she said it was yours,' Frances finished for him. He

nodded. 'Poor Steve. I wonder why. Were you so sure it was your fault we couldn't? I always thought you'd blame me.'

'I suppose I did,' he muttered. 'In a way. But . . .'

'You still weren't sure. Well, that's natural, I suppose. I wasn't either, although I blamed you, for what it's worth. I may as well admit it now.'

'Yes,' he said. 'I thought—no, that's not true, I didn't think. It was just a feeling.'

'I'm sorry,' she said, 'that I made you feel that. It can't have been very pleasant for you. Well. It just goes to show how wrong I was. It's ironic, isn't it?'

'Yes.' And then: 'Oh, Fran, the whole damn thing's so ironic. Just look at us now. We're being so bloody polite and reasonable.'

'Yes,' she said. 'I know. We haven't talked like this for years.' She put out her hand for his cup and he gave it to her. 'Well,' she said. 'There we are.'

35

WHEN HE had finally left for work, much earlier than usual because they could find nothing more to say, she made more coffee and took it in to Ella. The girl was asleep and Frances looked down at the sleeping face and felt a surge of pure hatred, despite all she had said and believed she meant. It was all she could do not to empty the scalding coffee over her and she was shocked to realise what savage pleasure that would have been. But the temptation passed, as brief and intense as a sudden physical pain.

'Coffee,' she said loudly and put the cup down. Ella opened her eyes, saw Frances and actually blushed.

'Oh God,' she said. 'I don't know how to face you.'

'Snap,' Frances said. She felt suddenly that only a certain brisk flippancy would sustain her.

Ella struggled up and began to put on her clothes. Frances looked at the thin body with the thought: in there is Steve's child. She felt sick.

Ella said rapidly, 'Look, Mrs Howarth, I wish you'd hit me or something. Really. I deserve it. I wish you would. I'd feel better.'

Frances, who had expected to walk straight out of the room, sat down on a packing case and lit a cigarette. She had taken to carrying them everywhere with her. It seemed too risky to be without them for a second, like losing her grip on a life-line. So I die of lung cancer, she thought. So what? At this moment it hardly matters. And yet, to be honest with herself, she had to admit that it did. She did not want to die, though it would have seemed more fitting if she had. The realisation shocked her.

'I expect you would feel better if I hit you,' she said. 'So might I. But that is hardly the point. And anyway, who knows? If I started I might never stop.'

'Please don't throw me out,' Ella said. 'Not yet. I've got to talk to you.'

'Have you?' Frances said. 'Whatever for? What is there left to say?'

'I don't know, but there must be something. I feel so terrible.'

'Well, I don't feel my best so we're quits. Come on, drink your coffee.' Her head was aching from strain and lack of sleep.

'You've made me coffee,' Ella said in a strangled voice.

'Well.' Frances looked round the room. 'Oh well, why not? Why the hell not? Oh God.' She took a deep breath. 'You must excuse me. I have a sudden impulse to shout all the foul words I know. It wouldn't take very long but I'm not going to do it.'

'Please do,' Ella said humbly, 'if it would help.'

'No. I think I should just feel silly. I'd be acting out of character and I always feel silly when I do that. The only alternative is to behave normally and feel I'm going mad. But I'm getting used to that so I may as well go on doing it.'

Ella said, 'Look, Mrs Howarth, I didn't expect this to happen.'

'No?' Frances said. 'What did you expect?'

Ella said simply, 'I thought he'd choose you.'

'What do you mean?'

'What I say. Honestly, Mrs Howarth, I'm not a homewrecker. Oh, I know it must look like that but I'm not, really I'm not. I've never been involved with a married man before.'

Frances said, 'Why did you come here?'

Ella hesitated. She stood in the middle of the room and appeared to be actually shaking. She put one hand on the rail of the bed for support. 'It wasn't just one reason. I wanted an abortion, that was one reason, and I thought Steven—oh, it seems awful to call him that to you——'

'For heaven's sake,' Frances said.

'Well, I thought he wouldn't give me the money if I asked him in Birmingham. I thought he'd just . . . laugh or something.'

'Well,' Frances said. 'Go on.'

'I thought if I came to the house he'd be so shocked he'd give it to me, just to get rid of me. You know. I thought it would give him a shock and he'd give me the money and that would be that.'

'I see. And the other reason?'

'Oh, I don't know.' She clasped the bed-rail more tightly and trembled all over.

'Come on,' Frances said, 'you must know. You said you wanted to talk to me.'

'Well . . .' She fidgeted, shifting from one foot to the other.

'Oh, it all sounds so mad. It's been going round and round in my head till I hardly know what I thought.'

'Try,' Frances said. 'Try to tell me. Maybe I can sort it out.'

'Well—oh God—I wanted to see what his home was like—oh no, not being nasty and curious—I wanted to understand how a man could be married and . . . do what he did. How he could keep his wife and his . . . girls in separate compartments and just go on as if it didn't matter. You see'—her voice fell almost to a whisper —'my father was like that. I wanted to understand. I thought maybe if only the two were together he'd see. I mean if he couldn't keep them apart, if he was forced to look at them both together—well, like I say,' she finished lamely, 'I thought he'd choose you.'

'Well, he didn't, did he?' said Frances.

'No. But I never thought he meant it, to go away with me. And he said you wouldn't mind, you wouldn't be too upset. And I believed him in a way. But I never thought he'd do it. Not when you offered . . . to take the baby and everything. I thought he'd throw me out then. Or I thought . . . when you knew it was his you wouldn't want him any more.' She was speaking rapidly now, breathing fast. 'I thought you'd see what he's like and you'd turn against him and oh . . .' Quite suddenly, without warning, she dissolved into tears.

'Well,' Frances said, ignoring the tears, 'you seem to have thought quite a lot. Just about everything that could happen except what actually has.'

Ella went on sobbing. Presently she said between gulps, 'Oh, I wish I was dead.'

'Oh, come now,' Frances said drily. 'None of us wishes that.'

The girl's head jerked up. 'But I do. Really I do.'

'It's your age,' Frances said. 'It will pass.'

Ella sniffed and wiped her nose on the back of her hand. 'I deserved that,' she said. 'You're quite right.'

Frances said, 'Yes, I'm being catty. How very distressing. I haven't been catty for years; I thought I'd grown out of it.'

Ella put out a hand as if she were drowning. 'Mrs Howarth, oh, Mrs Howarth, please . . .' but Frances interrupted her.

'You can drop the formality,' she said, 'in the circumstances,' and felt a wild desire to laugh. She had never bestowed the use of her Christian name under such insane conditions. All the same, she did not expect Ella to be able to use it, at least not straight away: it was quite a shock when she said, 'Oh, Frances, do I have to go away with him? Please don't make me.'

Frances stared at the tear-stained face. 'You mean you don't want to?' she said slowly.

'No. At least sometimes I do, but I'm not sure if it's because I love him or because I want to make him miserable. And the rest of the time I don't want to go at all.'

'Dear me,' said Frances. 'What a mess.'

'I had to tell you. There's no one else I can talk to.'

'There's Steve.'

'Yes.'

They sat and looked at each other. It suddenly struck Frances that she too had no one (apart from Steve) to talk to, except Ella: perhaps the greatest irony of all. Not only had she shed many of her friends with children in the past few years but she had also shed the habit of unburdening herself. And there was no one left whom she trusted sufficiently to tell something that was at once so tragic and so farcial. The three of them might as well have been on a desert island for all the good that the outside world could do them now.

'This is crazy,' she said slowly. 'I can't believe it's happening. A week ago everything was normal and now . . .' She stopped, wondering if it would seem less unreal if she put it into words. 'Now you're pregnant and my husband wants to go away with you and you're not even sure you want to go. And you and I have to sit here talking as if we were friends.' I must be mad, she thought. Am I the only woman in England who could behave like this? But there were no precedents of behaviour; it was not a situation for which anything in her life had prepared her.

'I wish we could be friends,' Ella said.

'What?'

'I do. I really do.'

'But how can we?' And yet as she said it, it did not sound as impossible as it should. After all, the very situation forced a certain closeness on them that was almost incestuous.

'We nearly were,' Ella said wistfully, as if recalling a golden age. 'We were getting on so well.'

'That was before.'

'I know. But can't we—can't we just go on?'

'You have a funny idea of friendship,' Frances said.

'But I know where I am with you. I know how I feel about you. I admire you; I like you. Honestly. Oh, I know that sounds funny but I do. But with Steven I don't know at all. It's like being on a ship. I don't know if I feel sick or if I'm enjoying it. But with you I'm on firm ground.'

'Please don't get metaphorical,' said Frances. 'It only confuses me.'

'I'm sorry. I thought it made things clearer.'

'Well, it doesn't. I doubt if anything could.' She stood up, putting out her cigarette. 'Look, I don't know what to say to you. I haven't had much sleep and my head is splitting. I think you should try to sort out how you feel and talk to Steve tonight. I really don't know what else to suggest.' She turned away.

Ella said in a voice of panic, 'Where are you going?'

'Oh, to lie down. I don't know. Away. I just want to be by myself.' But she didn't exactly. There was nothing she wanted that she could have. She wanted peace, to have her mind emptied, wiped clean like a slate.

'All right,' Ella said. 'You lie down. I'll do some painting, shall I? I'll be very quiet. Shall I unpack some more things for you?'

'Oh, I don't know.' Frances paused with her hand on the door. 'What's the point?'

'But I'd like to. I like doing things for you.'

'For me or to me?'

'Oh, please.'

Immediately she regretted the words. A part of her that she did not understand still wanted to be nice to Ella. 'Look,' she said. 'Just let me have a rest. Then we'll see.' Whatever that meant, she thought. Nothing made sense any more. Some vital cog had slipped, unnoticed, and the machinery of her life was out of control.

36

SHE WENT to bed and surprised herself by sleeping. At two she got up and found Ella making soup and boiled eggs with a great deal of fuss, as though for an invalid.

'Are you feeling better?' she asked solicitously.

Frances did indeed feel better for having slept but the enquiry struck her as amusing. It was almost as if Ella was concerned about a cold or a headache, nothing to do with guilt or injury. 'I think so,' she said.

'Oh, *good*. Can you manage some lunch?' She looked bright and innocent.

Frances said, 'God, you're extraordinary,' and took the tray. As she began to eat she noticed that she was really quite hungry. Ella ate too but with an anxious eye on Frances, jumping up to fetch things she had forgotten, like the salt.

'If you're really feeling better,' she said presently, 'could we go out?'

Frances looked at her but almost without surprise. She was nearly past being surprised at anything. Her life, she thought, had turned into a kind of comic surrealist nightmare. 'Where to?' she said. 'Not the zoo again?'

'Oh no. I just thought . . . well, maybe we could go to see your mother. You said you'd take me.'

'But that was before.' She wished she did not have to keep saying that.

'I know.' She had the air of a puppy being punished for some offence it has forgotten. 'Does it make a difference?'

'Oh, I suppose not.' Her mother, she now remembered, was the other person she could talk to—if only when she was asleep. 'Oh, the whole thing's so mad—all right, we'll go. Why not?' And it seemed to her that she was saying why not a lot.

*   *   *

In the car she tried to explain to Ella something of her mother's background and why the home was really unsuitable for her. 'She doesn't mix very well, you see,' she said. 'She only likes people she knows. She said once, "I'm too old to make new friends," and I think she's probably right. So I don't know how she'll take to you, although I know she likes young people.'

Ella said, 'Why wouldn't Steven let her live with you?' and her use of his name made him sound to Frances like some perverse stranger with whom they were both acquainted.

'Oh,' she said, 'it's a long story. He used to say she'd come between us, that we wouldn't have a life of our own any more if she moved in.' She paused. 'That's rather funny now, isn't it? Anyway, apart from that, I don't think he really likes old people.'

'I know,' Ella said. 'My father didn't like Granny living with us either. He said she ruined everything. But she didn't; she was fun.'

'Oh well,' Frances said. 'It seems you just can't win.'

*   *   *

The nurse on duty was surprised to see them. 'Why, Mrs Howarth,' she said, 'you were only here on Sunday.'

'Yes, I know,' Frances said. 'But this time I've brought a . . . friend.' She managed the word with only a slight hesitation. What was one further irony, after all, on top of all the rest?

Ella gave the nurse a stony glance and said to Frances as if they were alone, 'Are there rules about visiting this *place?*' She put a world of scorn into the word, as if Greystones was the worst kind of institution.

The nurse compressed her lips. Frances said hastily, 'No, of course not, Ella, nothing like that,' and the nurse said simultaneously, 'There are no restrictions on visitors here,' in a highly offended tone. Then they both looked embarrassed at speaking together.

'Well,' Frances said pleasantly, 'we'll go along then, shall we?'

She led Ella upstairs and they walked down the long corridors. 'Starchy old crow,' Ella said savagely.

'Oh, I don't know,' Frances said. 'I don't think she meant any harm.'

The house was clean and shiny, smelling of polish and flowers. Ella said, 'It's such a nice day, why isn't your mother in the garden?' They had passed many old people in deck chairs as they came up the drive.

'I don't think it's hot enough for her,' Frances said. 'She got so used to the climate in India.'

'Then it's lucky you've got central heating at home,' Ella said, as if the future was settled.

Frances stopped outside a door. 'And anyway,' she said, 'she doesn't really like mixing with the others.' She knocked and went in.

The old woman was in her usual chair by the window, her head sunk on her chest.

'Oh, she's asleep,' Ella said in a low voice. 'Do you think we should wake her? Maybe we should go away.' She sounded very disappointed.

'Oh no,' Frances said. 'She has little sleeps all the time.' She went over to her mother and touched her on the shoulder. 'Mother. Mother, it's Frances. I've brought someone to see you.'

The old woman opened her eyes. She slept lightly and could be instantly awake, a facility Frances found somehow comforting. 'Frances. How nice,' she said. 'Did you bring me the flowers? I've still got the others. They're so pretty.'

But Frances, in the stress of the past days' events, had forgotten. 'No, I'm sorry, I didn't.'

'Oh dear.' It was like the disappointment of a child.

'I brought you something else instead,' she said brightly. 'Well, somebody. Somebody who wants to meet you.' She beckoned to Ella who was hovering by the door. 'This is Ella Patterson. She's . . .' And she stopped, trying to think of an easy explanation of Ella's identity.

But it was not needed. As Ella put out her hand the old woman's eyes flashed with recognition. 'Angela Patson,' she said. 'Why, of course I remember you. How are you, my dear? How nice of you to come.'

Ella did not, to Frances' relief, appear at all taken aback. (Steve in the past, when he could be persuaded to visit, had been so confused and embarrassed by his various identities that Frances had given up trying to drag him along.) She shook the bony hand and said, 'Hullo. It's lovely to see you again.'

Frances was grappling with a dual problem: who was Angela

Patson and how could she inform Ella of her mother's surname which Angela Patson would presumably know. But her mother surprisingly answered both questions in one delighted statement: 'So you've come to see your Aunt Ruth at last. I thought you'd forgotten me.'

Immediately something clicked in Frances' brain. The Patsons had been out in India too, though she had not known them well, and Angela she did not remember at all, presumably because of the age difference. But how would Ella react at having this role sprung on her? She did not know whether to be glad or sorry that it had happened.

Ella, outwardly quite calm, drew up a chair and sat in front of the old woman, close to her. She was still, Frances noticed, holding her hand in both her own, almost lovingly.

'Aunt Ruth,' she said, 'of course I hadn't forgotten you. I wanted to come before but I've been away at school.'

'Yes, of course.' The old woman nodded. 'And how are your dear parents?'

Ella's face clouded. 'Oh dear,' she said, 'I'm afraid they've passed away. My father died ten years ago and my mother . . . well, it was only last week.'

Frances sprang to her assistance, impressed at this piece of quick thinking. 'Yes,' she said, 'that's why . . . er . . . Angela's staying with us for a while, to get over the shock.'

Her mother tightened her grip on Ella's hands. 'My poor child,' she said. 'How very distressing for you. Of course you must stay with my daughter as long as you like.' She turned to Frances almost indignantly. 'Why ever didn't you tell me? I'd have sent a wreath. I'd have liked to do that. Such old friends,' she added mournfully.

Frances said hesitantly, 'I didn't want to upset you.'

Her mother sighed. 'No. Well, perhaps you were right. But they're all going. It's that wretched climate, you know. It takes its toll.' She turned her attention back to Ella. 'My poor child, so you're all alone in the world. You must stay with Frances, she'll look after you.'

'Yes,' Ella said. 'She's being marvellous. I'm beginning to feel better already.'

'That's right,' the old woman said approvingly, patting her hand. 'It doesn't do to brood. No good can come of it. And you're young, you've got your whole life ahead of you. Now you tell me all about yourself.'

Frances took a deep breath, ready to plunge in with anecdotes, distractions, anything to ease what seemed an impossible situation. But she let it out again unused. Ella, with surprising invention on her own account and remarkable skill at picking up hints from the old woman's interruptions and reminiscences, produced a flawless account of her imaginary self. Frances listened with amazed admiration and relief. She almost began to believe that it *was* Angela Patson sitting there and talking about herself. And she thought suddenly that it was, after all, appropriate. In the world of lies and madness and unreality in which she now moved, this was the ultimate deceit and the first to do positive good.

Eventually, when she thought the visit had lasted long enough and Ella's invention must surely be strained to its limit, she made excuses to leave. The old woman let Ella go reluctantly.

'You must come again, my dear,' she said. 'You'll bring her again, Frances, won't you? It does me good to see a young face.'

Frances promised, though without knowing how she could possibly keep her word. It was strange, she reflected, but it really had done her mother good. She had not dropped off to sleep once, or become vague or even repeated herself unduly.

As they walked down the corridor together she felt bound to say to Ella, 'You were marvellous. I was very impressed.'

Ella seemed unconcerned. 'It was easy. I've got a vivid imagination.'

'Well, it's lucky you have. I'd no idea that would happen. It could have been terribly awkward.'

'But it wasn't,' Ella said. 'And she was so pleased. Wasn't that nice? Much better than trying to explain who I really am.'

'Yes. Well, I'm afraid that would have been impossible. I would have had to say you were an old pupil of mine. Would you have minded?'

'Not a bit,' Ella said. 'In fact I feel rather like one anyway.'

Frances let that go. They passed through the hall, ignoring the nurse at the reception desk, and walked out of the splendid front door.

'I liked the old lady,' Ella said, pausing on the gravel to look back at the house. 'I really did.'

'Yes,' Frances said, 'I could see that.'

Ella giggled suddenly. 'Wouldn't it be funny,' she said, 'if she didn't think I was Angela Patson at all? If she was just pretending, to see what I'd do, and I played along. Suppose we were both pretending all the time?'

Frances smiled; it was an odd idea. 'Not very likely.'

'No, I suppose not. But it would have been fun. And I wouldn't have blamed her.' As they walked to the car she added thoughtfully, 'I think she'd have been right. Sometimes it's better to pretend. You can have too much of reality.'

37

SHE HAD NOT thought that there was anything left to happen. It was as if she believed, without really considering the matter, that events must have a natural limit and that this had already been reached. In the car on the way home Ella was silent, shifting occasionally in her seat, and Frances too was quiet, busy with her own thoughts. The visit had been in its way therapeutic; she felt calmer already, as if seeing Ella behaving so competently with her mother and the old woman's obvious delight had begun to compensate her for something. When they got back to the house she said, 'I'll put the kettle on,' and went into the kitchen without waiting for an answer. Ella disappeared into the bathroom. Frances filled the kettle and was just about to plug it in when she heard Ella call. It was an urgent sound. She ran into the hall; a groan came from behind the bathroom door. 'What is it?' she asked, disturbed and suddenly alert to drama where she had thought no more could exist.

'Frances,' Ella said. Then there was a long pause. 'Oh, Frances, I'm bleeding.'

38

To STEVE, arriving home at six as usual, the world looked bright again. Though still desperately tired from two hours' sleep and a day's work, he felt in control of events. It had really all passed off very well. Frances had displayed all the sterling qualities he most admired in her: the worst must surely be over. His own future, however perilous, lay before him; it only remained to make plans, as briskly and unemotionally as possible, before he and Ella could leave. Or perhaps that could all be arranged by solicitors: that might be the most comfortable method for all of them. He did not know what people did in these circumstances. His thoughts turned away from the unknown practicalities and slid again and again, with delighted apprehension, to Ella and the child. He felt warm and powerful and almost reborn. It was like acquiring a new face or a new identity, almost as if he had not really existed before. If only Frances could feel the same way. He was immensely grateful to her for behaving so well. He promised himself he would be as generous as possible over the settlement to show his appreciation. There must be no bitterness. Perhaps —who could say?—perhaps years later they might all be friends.

He let himself into the house, slamming the door to show he was back. There would be the embarrassment of seeing them both together, of course, but that was all he was dreading. He braced himself for it. But Frances came alone to meet him, out of the spare room. There was an odd look on her face. She closed the door quietly and stood in front of him.

'Steve, I'm sorry,' she said. 'I've got some bad news for you.'

He stared at her, not hearing her words.

'She's having—well, she's either having a miscarriage or a period.'

'What?' he said stupidly.

'Yes. I'm sorry. But there's no doubt about it.'

He could not move. The words penetrated his mind but made no sense. 'What d'you mean?'

'There's no baby,' Frances said. 'Either there never was or she's lost it. I don't know. She wouldn't let me call a doctor. She's been in the lavatory for hours and now she's lying down.'

He said, 'No baby?' He was suddenly very conscious of his extremities: his legs and feet seemed leaden and his hands much too big and heavy on the ends of his arms.

Frances made a small, helpless gesture. 'No.'

'But . . .' He stopped.

She looked at him almost with sympathy. 'I've got to go to the shop,' she said. 'They're open till seven. You go in and see her. But be kind. Whichever it is, she's had a bad time.'

The door closed behind her. Like a man in a trance, or a sleep-walker, Steve went into the spare room.

Ella's face was whiter than the pillow it lay on and there were dark circles under her eyes. He advanced and stood over her. 'You've lost it?' he said. And it was only then, when he heard his own voice say the words, that the meaning became real for him. 'You've lost it? What have you done?' For immediately the idea sprang into his mind that she had gone back to her original plan and got rid of it. 'What have you done to my child?' And he took hold of her shoulder and shook it.

Ella wrenched herself free with surprising strength. Her hair swung across her face as she violently sat up in bed. Words poured from her suddenly as if some overworked dam had finally burst.

'Your child!' she said. 'Your child!' Her lips curled back, reminding him of a snarling animal: he could see her teeth. 'What child? There never was a child. You bloody fool, d'you think I'd let *you* make me pregnant? Even if you could? But you can't. You never will. D'you hear me? All you're good for is leaving your wife and picking up tarts and having it off and all for what? That's all you are. *Nothing.*'

He hit her across the face.

'Yes,' she shouted triumphantly. 'And you're good at that too. I nearly forgot. You're good at hitting people who don't do what you want—provided they're smaller than you, of course. You're a coward and a bully and a . . .'

He watched the red marks of his fingers come up on her pale face like invisible ink under heat.

'Oh, you make me *sick.*' She literally spat the word: a thin trickle of saliva ran down her chin. 'You disgust me. Did you really think you could do what you liked and get away with it? Well, you've run out of luck. This is *it*. You're finished. With your hole in the corner girls and your big fist and your big cock . . .'

He hit her again. She nearly fell out of the bed.

'Well, it's useless,' she shouted. There were tears in her eyes. 'It's nothing. You've lost. We don't need you. We can manage without you.' With a great heaving sob she turned her bruised face away from him and hung over the edge of the bed.

The sound of her vomiting brought him to his senses. He felt icy cold and strange in his own skin. The retching went on. He leaned across and tried to hold her head but she pushed him away. The sour smell rose up and he tried to ignore it.

Presently she was silent. She lay on the edge of the bed, exhausted and quiet.

'Ella,' he said. 'That wasn't true, was it?'

'Yes it was.'

He could not bear it. 'But there was a child. Whether you hate me or not, there *was*. Wasn't there?'

She turned round to face him, green eyes bloodshot and swimming. 'No,' she said. 'Never. There never was. And if there had been it would have been Jack's.'

He advanced towards her.

'That's right,' she said. 'Go on, hit me again. Why not? If it makes you feel better.'

He stood over her, clenching his fists by his sides. There were tears in his eyes. 'You bitch,' he said. And he hardly knew if it was a cry of hatred or love.

Frances came into the room. He had not heard her return. 'What the hell is going on?'

He turned on her. 'She's nothing but a tramp,' he shouted. 'Just a bloody little tramp. And you believed her. We both believed her. She's taken us both for a ride. Well, I'll show you.'

Frances was looking from one to the other. 'For God's sake——'

The rucksack was lying on the floor. Steve grabbed it. 'I'll show you,' he said again. 'I'll show you what she's like. She's got a notebook with all the names in creation, every man she's ever had, God help them.' He rooted in the bag, spilling make-up and underwear, groping for the little black book. But he found only a pink nylon rabbit, its fur rather grubby and its waistcoat creased.

He tore it out and flung it at Ella. She didn't move and it hit her with a soft thud.

'You're mad,' Frances said. 'You're crazy. What's got into you?' She put herself between him and the girl.

'She has.' The words were torn out of him. 'Damn her. Get out of my way, Fran, I——'

But Frances stood her ground. 'You're overwrought,' she said. 'You've got to calm down.' Behind her Ella began to cry noisily into the pillow.

All the violence ebbed out of Steve, leaving him drained and weary. He dropped the rucksack and stood helpless and quiet, unmoving. Frances looked at him. Ella went on crying. For a while no one spoke.

'Come on,' Frances said gently. 'You're not doing any good here.'

39

THEY HAD whisky in the living-room. Frances lit cigarettes and fussed round him. Eventually she said, 'What on earth was all that about?'

Steve found it enormously difficult to speak. His mouth was dry and he took a great gulp of whisky.

'It was all a game,' he said. 'An obscene joke. That's all it was.'

'I don't understand,' Frances said. 'What happened? What did she say? I've never seen you in such a state.'

Steve shook his head. 'She hates me,' he said. 'I don't know why. She says . . . she was never pregnant. It was all a trick and we believed her.' He leaned forward urgently. 'We believed her, Frances. Why did we? Did we want to so much?'

'But she doesn't know,' Frances said. 'She told me. She's had a lot of pain and bleeding but she can't tell what that means and neither can we. We'll never know now, Steve. That's the truth. I'm sorry.'

'But it isn't,' he said desperately, wanting to believe her. 'She says there wasn't ever a baby. She . . . flew at me. And I hit her. Oh, Fran, I hit her twice.'

'Oh God,' Frances said.

'She got me so angry I didn't know what I was doing. I think she wanted me to be like that.' He fell back in the chair. 'Oh, I don't understand.'

Frances was frowning. 'But she was so upset. When it started to happen she just cried and cried. Really. Look, I think you must have got it all wrong.'

'No.' He groaned. 'Oh God, I should have seen it coming. Christ, I've been such a fool.'

Frances said, 'Steve, what was all that about a notebook?'

He put his head in his hands. 'Oh God. Well, when I first met her she had this book of names. All the men she'd met and sort of . . . ratings, I suppose. She kind of graded their performances.' The tragedy suddenly spilled over into farce. 'She's—oh God,

Fran—she's a sort of Maggie May of the M.I.' He began to laugh.

'Steady,' Frances said. 'You're getting hysterical.'

'But it's funny.' He went on laughing. 'It really is.' Between gasps of laughter that shook him like coughing he said, 'Why don't you hit me? Go on, I'm hysterical, hit me. Hit me like I hit her. Go on. Let's all hit each other. Let's make it a party. Oh, Christ.'

At last it was over. Frances stood up. 'That's right,' she said. 'You calm down. I'm going to talk to her.'

40

She sat by the bed.

'Where's the notebook, Ella?'

Ella was silent.

'Come on. I know there was a notebook. Where is it?'

Ella's eyes were closed. Tears were still on her cheeks and splodges of damp on the pillow. 'I threw it away,' she said, her teeth clenched.

Frances said, 'Why?'

'Because I didn't want it any more. It was all lies anyway. I got bored with it.'

'And what else was lies?'

'Nothing.'

'Why not tell me? It can't matter now. I want to know, Ella. Steve said you had a lot of other men. Did you?'

Ella let out a long sigh. 'I made them all up.'

'But why?'

'It made me feel better.'

Frances felt helplessly out of her depth. 'And was there a baby?'

Ella started to cry again. 'I don't know.'

'Then why did you tell Steve there wasn't?'

Ella shook her head from side to side on the pillow. 'I wanted to hurt him.'

'Well, I think you've succeeded. But why did you want to?'

The weeping increased. 'I don't know. Because he's so rotten to you.' A sudden howl of misery. 'Because I love him.'

Frances said, 'What?'

Ella said, 'No. No, I don't mean that.' She pounded the pillow with her fist.

Frances said, 'Look at me. Open your eyes and look at me.' She shook Ella's shoulders but Ella only screwed up her eyes tight shut as if Frances might try to open them by force. Frances stopped shaking her. 'Look,' she said. 'All right, listen. Are you listening? Now calm down. I only want the truth. If I call Steve back in here will you tell him the truth?'

'I don't want to see him.'

'But I want you to.'

'No.'

'Ella, listen. I want you to see him and tell him the truth. You owe him that much. I'm going to fetch him.'

She began to move but Ella, suddenly opening her eyes, reached out and grabbed her. 'Don't go,' she said. 'Don't leave me. We don't need him. We can manage without him.' Her fingers dug into Frances. 'Please.'

41

'She doesn't want to see you.'

'That's all right. I don't want to see her. Hell, I can do without a repetition of all that.'

'But I don't think it would be. That's just it. She's terribly mixed up, Steve.'

'*She* is?'

'Yes. She—she said she loves you.'

He laughed.

'No, really. I think she meant it. Though she took it back immediately.'

'There you are.'

'No, that's all part of the same thing. Steve, there's something awfully funny here. It's all mixed up with her parents.'

'That hardly helps me, does it?'

She stared at him. 'Don't you *want* to know?' He shrugged, looking helpless, defeated, even, of all things, bored. She got a sudden vision of how he would look when he was old because his life had not worked out as he wanted it. She said, 'Steve, I really think . . .' But the phone rang. She wanted to ignore it but the ringing was more intrusive than any conversation could be. She picked it up to silence it.

'Oh, Claire. Hullo, love, how are you? Good. Oh, I'm fine. Yes, quite well. Did you? Oh, never mind. Yes, I was actually. Mm. Oh, how nice of you. Only I don't think we can. I—we've got a girl staying with us, someone I used to teach, and she's not very well. No, nothing serious. Could I ring you? Say maybe next week? Oh, good. Only things are a bit hectic here right now. Oh, he's fine. How's Jimmy? Good. And the kids? Oh, good. Yes. I will. I'm sorry, love. Bless you. Bye.'

She put down the phone and said shakily, 'That was a bit creepy.'

'Why did you say that?'

'Well, it was. Her ringing up just now. I've been dreading that——'

'No, what you said about Ella.' His expression was hostile.

'Well . . . I had to say something. She asked us to dinner.'

'But why say *that*?'

'Oh, I don't know. What else could I say? I had to think quickly.'

Steve stood up. He looked a bit hunched to Frances. 'Fran, will you do something for me?'

'Well, what?'

'I want you to get rid of her.'

'What?'

'Get rid of her. Throw her out if necessary. Now.'

'But Steve . . . I can't.'

He straightened up, hovering above her threateningly. 'Why not?'

'Well, she's ill.'

'Huh!'

'No, really. Even if it's just a period I can't turn her out. She's had a bad time.'

His shoulders slumped. 'You don't believe there was a baby, do you?'

'I don't know. How can I know?'

He took hold of her arm in an almost savage grip. 'You don't believe it. And you're glad, aren't you?'

'Let go of me.'

He let go.

'I didn't know you were so violent.'

'I told you I hit her.'

'Yes. Are you proud of it?'

'Oh, for God's sake, Fran.'

'Well, I don't know. I don't know you any more.'

He walked about the room, clasping his hands as if to prevent them from doing further violence.

42

THEY VISITED Ella together but she refused to speak to them. They tried to question her in turn but she would not answer. Eventually they gave up and went away.

Steve followed Frances into the garden. She had thought some fresh air might help, in a vague way, like aspirin. They walked about looking at the mown grass and the half-weeded flower beds. It was all very nearly presentable. Suddenly Mrs Messenger's grey, cropped head popped up over the fence.

'Quite a transformation,' she said, looking round approvingly.

'Yes,' Frances said.

'It makes such a difference. Do you have green fingers, Mr Howarth?'

'I don't think so,' Steve said.

'My husband has green fingers. He can make anything grow.' She launched into a long horticultural account of all the unlikely plants that Mr Messenger had succeeded in growing in their garden. Frances looked for a pause in which to say, 'How nice,' and stem the flow. But before she could find one Steve turned violently away and went into the house. Mrs Messenger stopped talking and looked surprised.

'You must excuse him,' Frances said. 'He's not feeling very well.'

*   *   *

'That was very rude,' she said when she rejoined him.

'So?' He was drinking a large glass of whisky.

'Well, it was.'

'Does it matter?'

'You forget,' she said. 'I have to live here.'

He stared at her. 'Yes,' he said, 'that about sums it up.'

'Whatever do you mean?'

But he was rushing out of the room, crossing the hall; the bedroom door slammed. After a moment's hesitation she followed him. She found him throwing things into a suitcase, wildly, not folding them, like someone in a film. It looked melodramatic and absurd. Did people really pack like that? She said, 'Here. Let me,' and tried to take the garments out of his hands. He pushed her away, roughly, and she stumbled.

'Yes,' he said. 'You have to live here. You. Not me.'

She said, 'Don't be so dramatic. Where on earth are you going?'

'Does it matter? You're staying here, aren't you? So is she. Oh, it'll be very cosy. You can have your crazy old mother too and make it a party.'

She tried to suppress her resentment at that. 'But why rush off now? What's the point?'

He paused for a moment with a shirt in his hand. 'D'you mean you want me to stay?'

She hesitated. 'Well, I . . .'

He stuffed the shirt in the suitcase. The jumble of clothes that she had so recently washed and ironed appalled her. 'No, of course you don't. You've made that perfectly clear.'

She said, 'But you wanted to go. You were—surely you remember—you were going away with Ella.'

He swallowed. 'Yes I must have been mad.'

She said, 'Look, it's just your pride that's hurt.' But what she meant was he had been stripped of his dignity. She felt the stirrings of pity, surprising herself. 'Look, at least stay the night.'

He stood still. 'Do you mean that?'

'Well, of course.'

He said rapidly, 'Fran, if she goes we can start again, can't we? Tell me we can. It's . . . been like a nightmare. But it's over now, isn't it?'

The pity was awful. It swelled up and choked her. But that was all she could feel. 'It's all over,' she said. 'I think.'

He looked at her with a flash of hope. 'You mean . . . we can start again?' Then she saw the hope falter as he translated the expression in her eyes more accurately.

'I'm sorry,' she said. 'I mean us. The whole thing. I'm sorry.'

He began packing again, very fast. 'That's what I thought,' he said. 'That's why I was packing. Only you confused me just now.'

'I'm sorry,' she said again. She sat down on the bed. 'But how could you think I meant anything else?'

'No, of course not,' he said. 'You want her here, for some extraordinary reason. Well, that's fine. You've got what you want.'

'But it's not that at all.'

He slammed down the lid of the case and pressed it shut. 'Isn't it? You won't turn her out so you must want her here.'

'But I told you before. I can't turn out anyone who's ill. How can I?'

'You could,' he said, 'if you wanted me to stay. But you don't. Oh, I don't blame you at all, don't think that. Why should you want me here? But what I can't understand is why you want her.'

She said, trying to understand, 'But why do you want me to be alone?'

'Is that why you're keeping her? For company? My God, I don't understand you.'

Frances said, 'Look. Do you mean if I got rid of Ella you'd stay?'

He fiddled with the lock of the case. 'If you wanted me to.'

'But . . .'

'But you don't. Of course you don't. Well, that's perfectly reasonable.'

Frances said, 'But how do you think it would be? Do you really think we could just . . . go on, as if nothing had happened? How *could* we? I mean, it was pretty shaky before but now . . .'

'No, of course we couldn't.' He spoke briskly.

'I'm sorry, Steve.'

'Please don't apologise. I should apologise to you. It's my fault, all this, after all, isn't it?'

'Well not entirely.'

'Oh, you don't have to be generous. But for me it would never have happened. Well, the laugh's on me, isn't it? Serves me right. Why don't you laugh? Go on, it's funny.'

Frances said gently, 'I don't think it's funny and I don't think the laugh's on anyone. But I equally don't think we have a future together any more. I'm just hoping we may possibly have one apart.'

He laughed. 'What an elegant paragraph. How well you express yourself.'

This still had the power to annoy. 'I'm sorry you're so bitter.'

'Bitter! Yes, and I'm not entitled to be, am I? You are, only of course you're being sweet and saintly as usual and so bloody reasonable.'

Frances said, 'Is that what you think of me?'

He picked up the case. 'No, of course I don't. I'm sorry. I'm not thinking straight.'

Frances got up. 'Well, we're both upset.'

But he looked at her with fresh accusation. 'No, I don't think you are.'

'What, because I'm not making a scene? Steve, I can't. I don't know . . . I'm just numb, I suppose. But that doesn't mean I'm not upset. It's—been a long time.'

'Yes,' he said soberly. 'I never thought it would end like this.'

The clichés of real emotion oppressed her intolerably. 'Neither did I.'

He went to the door, still holding the case. He paused. 'I still wish you'd tell me. Otherwise I'll never know. How can you possibly want her here? How can you bear to look at her?'

Frances shrugged helplessly. 'But there doesn't seem any point,' she said, 'in throwing her out. Not now. What good would it do? We didn't do it before and now it's too late.'

His face darkened. 'I see. Well, if that's your reason. . . . Look, I'm going. I'll get a solicitor or someone to write to you.'

'All right. There's no hurry.'

'No. Okay.'

They looked at each other.

'I feel so silly,' she said. 'I feel we should kiss or shake hands or something. I don't know how you just . . . end a marriage.'

'No,' he said, 'neither do I.'

But neither of them moved.

'Well,' she said, 'I hope things improve. For both of us.'

'Yes,' he said. 'Thank you. So do I.'

Still he hesitated by the door. The intensity of anticlimax, unbearably prolonged, seemed to drain her of strength. She felt limp and remote, a sudden, bemused onlooker.

'Phone me sometime,' she said.

*   *   *

She sat alone in the empty bedroom and listened to the car drive away. She felt she should have given the moment more import: there should have been a ritual ceremony to go through. But her wedding too had had more impact both before and after than at the actual time it occurred.

Presently she got up and went into the bathroom. Everything of his had gone except his shaving brush: he would have to buy another one. She stared at it for a moment, wanting to touch it, and then it began to blur before her eyes. She was glad. It would have been wrong not to cry.

43

ELLA SAID she would move to the study so that Frances' mother could have the spare room. It was bigger and she was used to space. They were both very subdued in the days following Steve's departure, treating each other gently at a certain distance, as if both bore scars that might be bruised afresh by too close contact. When Steve sent for the remainder of his things Ella volunteered to pack them up for Frances. ('I'll do it. You needn't touch a thing.') 'It's all right,' Frances assured her. 'He's not dead.' So they did it together. Sitting next to Ella and sorting Steve's clothes into piles gave Frances a strange feeling. They made frequent stops for tea and cigarettes. Frances did not realise how great an ordeal it had been till it ended and relief flooded through her. Ella said urgently once, 'Oh, it will get better, it will. Won't it?' and Frances said, 'Yes, of course it will.'

She studied *The Times* Ed. for a good local school within easy driving distance. Financially they would be comfortable. 'If you work full-time,' Ella said, 'I can work in the evenings. I can be with your mother all day. And he'll send us something, I suppose.' She had never referred to Steve by name since he left and Frances, without meaning to, had found herself following suit. It all helped.

The old woman was delighted by the prospect of her imminent transfer, which was scheduled for September. Frances simply told her that she and Steve had separated; she saw no point in a complicated network of lies about jobs abroad and long absences from home. Friends and neighbours could be told the same truth in its simplest form, for why should she involve herself in deceit? And in any case the drama (or tragedy?) of separation would silence enquiry more effectively than any tale she could tell.

She took sleeping pills at first, scared of the big double bed and the staring room, till she frightened herself by taking too many and waking heavily to find Ella shaking her shoulder, her face anxious and pale. 'Oh, you didn't,' she said, 'did you?' and Frances said, 'No, I didn't.' Ella sat on the bed. 'You don't want him back, do you?' she said fearfully, tremulously, and Frances said, 'No. No, I don't think I do.' The very words tested her reactions: she might have been putting a broken leg to the floor for the first time and gingerly resting her weight on it. Afterwards she found when she tried that she could sleep without pills and with only the occasional dream.

They decided the hall was too white after all and painted one wall orange. They chose together a deep blue-green carpet for the floor and congratulated each other on their taste. For Frances' mother they prepared a flowery room, as Edwardian as they could make it, and in the living-room Ella had a minor triumph when she found a little man round the corner (he was actually wizened, bent double, as well as handy) who with much loving labour returned the floor to something quite near to its former beauty. This proved expensive but when it was done Frances felt that something important had been accomplished.

They began to read books that they recommended to each other and to discuss them. Sometimes when the subject matter gave a lead, Frances was tempted to venture a question about the past, about Ella's parents. Part of her wanted confirmation that what she suspected was true, but she doubted if Ella was entirely sure of her own motivation or willing to admit it, and at the same time another part of her shrank from exposing something that could, after all, have no actual effect on their current position. So she kept the discussions general, wondering if the relief she thought she detected in Ella was real or imagined, and discovered that the girl really had a good mind. 'You should never have left school at eighteen,' she said, 'and just drifted. You should have gone to university.' Ella smiled. 'Perhaps I can make up for it now,' she said. 'I can learn at home, can't I? You can teach me.' She had begun to refer to the house as home.

Steve phoned only once (unless he phoned Ella when she was alone and she did not mention it). The conversation was stilted and Frances, who had nerved herself constantly for the ordeal, found it something of an anti-climax, like talking to an old friend she had not seen for a long time and who now lived abroad. There seemed boundless goodwill but nowhere to direct it. They talked trivialities with a great show of interest. He had been living in an hotel, he said, near the office, but hoped to move soon to a flat. A service flat, he said, and they both laughed a lot. He was glad that Frances was well. She was glad that he was well. He was glad about her mother; she would probably be much happier. She supposed he was working hard. Yes, he was about to leave on another trip. He would enjoy that. She would be hearing from the solicitor again. There was no rush. But everything was all right, wasn't it? Yes, everything was all right.

They did not mention Ella, either of them, though Frances felt herself about to at every moment and was certain that he was avoiding her name on purpose and with difficulty. In the end they rang off, wishing each other good luck and promising to keep in touch.

On the last day of August the room was ready (having taken exactly as long as they had to prepare it) and the house in good order to impress Frances' mother. They were tired with their last-minute efforts and sat in the living-room, silent, in a warm glow of achievement. Ella wore a new dress which Frances had bought her, and her face was made up again, dark eyes and pale lips. Frances too was wearing more make-up than usual: Ella had begun encouraging her to make the best of herself, though for what purpose she hardly knew. 'She can come tomorrow,' Ella said. 'Let's go and fetch her in the car, first thing in the morning. Can I drive?' She had started a course of lessons and was already handling the Mini with signs of future expertise. Frances said, 'Mm.' She was reading and Ella had been watching television with the sound fairly low so as not to be a distraction. Frances concentrated on the print deliberately: it was too soon to let thoughts filter through. Thoughts about jobs, about the new life they would have, all three of them, about new people, new hope, new prospects. It would all have to come; she was aware of that. But not yet. For the moment she wanted her mind to lie fallow and blank.

'Oh,' said Ella with sudden passion. 'We *have* done well. She'll be here tomorrow. It's going to be absolutely alpha plus.'

Frances, aware of the voice not the words, looked up indulgently. 'What did you say?'

'Oh,' Ella said, 'nothing much.' She smiled at Frances. 'Just that we're going to have fun.'

'Yes,' Frances agreed. 'I expect we will.'

44

THE ROAD STRETCHED out endlessly. He was heading for Glasgow, on a special assignment to overlook a new man about whom the firm had doubts. The September weather was mild but overcast. Earlier in the day it had rained and the hitch-hikers he passed *en route* for the motorway were bedraggled. The car, newly serviced, was going like a bird and in top with his foot down and no lorries weaving in and out of his path, it was as good as an automatic. The new chap might be all right but reports were disturbing; he would have to look into it all very thoroughly.

He stopped for a snack at the Fortes place. It was crowded and at first he did not notice the girl staring at him as he ate alone. Presently she came over to his table and asked for a light. He gave her one but did not encourage her further. It was not, he told himself, that he had learned his lesson, for what lesson, after all, was there to be learned? He was free. Nor was it that she was unattractive: though her skin was a shade coarse and overlaid with make-up, her figure was good and she had long blonde hair. But he finished his tea and walked out. It was too soon; he was not interested. Who could say? Perhaps in Glasgow. Either way, it would not matter a damn. Nothing would any more.

He filled up the tank and filtered out of the station, waiting. At last his lane was clear. He drove on.